# perfect distraction

# perfect distraction

# ALLISON ASHLEY

This book is a work of fiction. Names, characters, places, and incidents are the product of the author's imagination or are used fictitiously. Any resemblance to actual events, locales, or persons, living or dead, is coincidental.

Copyright © 2020 by Allison Ashley. All rights reserved, including the right to reproduce, distribute, or transmit in any form or by any means. For information regarding subsidiary rights, please contact the Publisher.

Entangled Publishing, LLC
10940 S Parker Rd
Suite 327
Parker, CO 80134
rights@entangledpublishing.com

Amara is an imprint of Entangled Publishing, LLC.

Edited by Erin Molta
Cover design by Elizabeth Turner Stokes
Cover photography by Photographee.eu and mevoo/Shutterstock

Manufactured in the United States of America

First Edition March 2020

**AMARA**
an imprint of Entangled Publishing LLC

*For the patients I've known, for the ones I will meet, and for the health care providers always fighting to save.*

# Chapter One

It all started with boobs in the coffee line.

Lauren Taylor stared at the image populating the screen on her phone, and her eyebrows shot up to her hairline. With the image came a question.

Emma: *Is this OK to wear to work?*

Lauren typed her response. *No.*

A second image appeared almost immediately. A close-up of her friend's chest, barely contained within the black fabric of whatever shirt she'd changed into.

Emma: *What about this one?*

Lauren glanced up to make sure no one had come to stand behind her. The photo looked like something from the cover of *Maxim* and wasn't something she wanted another customer to see her looking at. She held her phone close to her own chest as she replied, *Definitely no.*

A minute passed with no response, and Lauren dropped

her hand to her side. She leaned to the left and counted... three people ahead of her. Glancing at her watch, she tapped her foot, a rapid staccato on the tile floor. The door to her right opened with a gust of crisp autumn wind and several people filed in.

She considered leaving, but she *really* wanted coffee. She closed her eyes and rehearsed the introduction in her head.

*Good morning. Today I'll be discussing the management of toxicities associated with immunotherapy...*

Her phone dinged.

She slid her thumb across the screen, and a new image materialized.

So.

Much.

Cleavage.

*OMG Emma. No. Just...no.*

A deep chuckle sounded behind her. Lauren pressed her phone to her stomach, jerked her head around, and forgot all about Emma's boobs.

Standing behind her was quite possibly the most attractive man in Kansas City. No, the most attractive man in the United States. Maybe even the entire universe.

He was tall, with thick brown hair tousled in that perfectly mussed way. High, defined cheekbones, full lips pressed together like he was trying not to smile, and the cutest little dimple right in the middle of his chin. Warm brown eyes darted from the phone in Lauren's hand to her face for the briefest second, and then to the menu on the wall. He tucked his hands into the front pockets of his jeans and cleared his throat, his eyes now fixed above her head.

Lauren turned to face forward again, her cheeks warming. Her heart fluttered in her chest like a bird taking flight, and the nape of her neck tingled. Taking care to shield the screen with her upper body, she furiously tapped out another text.

Lauren: *I'm going to kill you. There's a hot guy behind me at The Grind House and he saw me looking at your boobs on my phone. He probably thinks I'm some sex fanatic or exhibitionist.*

Emma: *Hot guy, you say? Did he like what he saw? Tell him I'll show him the real thing if he follows you to work.*

Lauren: *Stop. You stop now.*

Finally, it was her turn, and she stepped up to find Tyler's cheerful face behind the counter. His familiar presence soothed her frayed nerves.

"Hey, Lauren! Quad Americano?"

"Actually, just a regular coffee. Please."

Tyler frowned. "You're not going soft on me, are you?"

"It's just for today, I promise. I've got a big presentation this morning and I'm plenty wired as it is."

"Okay, I'll let it slide this once."

"Thanks, Ty."

As he took her credit card, Tyler leaned across the counter. Ducking his chin to his chest, he widened his eyes and whispered, "Did you know the guy standing behind you is exceptionally good-looking?"

Lauren let out a nervous laugh and mirrored Tyler's position. "I'm aware. And I'm sure he is, too."

Tyler swiped her card with a sigh, appearing unhappy that she wasn't matching his level of excitement. The thing was, Lauren made a wide berth around guys like the one behind her. She learned a long time ago to stay away from extremely attractive men. Instead, she preferred cute ones. Adorable. Good-looking (regular variety, not the exceptional type). The kind who might be considered average to start with, but whose appeal grew as she got to know their personalities.

The hot ones were heartbreakers.

This, she knew from experience.

She tucked her card back into her purse and picked up the empty cup Tyler set before her. "See you tomorrow."

"Good luck on your presentation," Tyler called out as she walked away.

She checked her watch again as she stepped up to the coffee bar. *Son of a biscuit.* She needed to hurry. Shoving her cup underneath the spout of the large silver dispenser labeled MEDIUM ROAST, she filled it to the brim, nearly spilling it in her haste to step sideways and grab a lid. She swiveled on her heel, but instead of dashing to the exit as planned, crashed face first into a hard, broad chest.

The loose-fitting lid popped right off, and coffee splashed out of the cup, all over her hand and onto the shirt of the person she'd run in to. Instinctively she jumped back, as did the stranger, and she set the dripping cup onto the counter.

"William Shatner," she hissed in the same way a normal person might say dammit, and swiped several napkins to clean her hand. Thank God it didn't feel like she'd been badly burned, though her hand would no doubt be red for several hours. "I'm sorry—" she started, and looked up into a set of chocolate-brown eyes.

Of course. It had to be the hot guy. His lips pressed into a tight line, but he didn't seem angry. He leaned in to take a few napkins, and his chest passed in front of her face, along with a wonderful scent of cedar and soap.

"I'm so sorry," she said again.

"It's fine." He pressed the napkins to his heather-gray T-shirt, but at this point there really wasn't much to be done.

Lauren wondered how firm the stomach underneath his ministrations was.

Shrugging, he gave up and tossed the squares of paper in the trash. He pulled the sides of his navy hoodie to the front of his body and zipped it up to cover the wet portion of his shirt. "It's the perfect start to this day."

An odd thing to say, but Lauren didn't have time to ask what he meant by it.

"And did you just curse with Captain Kirk?" he asked.

She also didn't have time to explain that right now. She resisted the urge to look up at him again and pretended not to hear, wrapping a napkin around her half-empty cup. "I hope your day gets better. I have to go, but again, I'm sorry."

She ignored the ding of an incoming text message and rushed out of the shop.

• • •

Two hours later, Lauren exited the elevator on the fourth floor of the Coleman Cancer Center. The sixth-floor conference room had been packed with physicians and residents, and now that the stressful part of her day was over, she could relax.

And think about other things…like the guy from the coffee shop.

It was a good thing muscle memory took her to the leukemia and lymphoma clinic, because her mind was definitely elsewhere when she entered the room where she'd spent the last several weeks.

"How'd it go?"

Lauren looked up to find Kiara looking at her expectantly. Kiara wore her usual dark blue scrubs, which made the white name badge stating she was the Nurse Team Lead even more distinct.

Lauren blinked. "It went great." She dropped into her usual chair and leaned back with a sigh. "Dr. Hawthorne stopped me afterward and told me how well he thought I did."

Kiara swiveled in her chair, her braided black hair

swinging with the movement. "I knew you'd rock it."

Lauren smiled at the young woman who had become a close friend. "Emma here yet?"

As if on cue, the physician assistant waltzed through the door. "I am now."

Lauren directed her attention to the barely five-foot tall beauty, who sat down beside her with a grace Lauren herself would never possess. "Well, let's see what you went with. Coat off."

Emma raised an eyebrow and shrugged out of her white coat, her silky black hair sliding across her shoulders. "I don't know why it matters, I'll be wearing my coat when I go into patient rooms," she grumbled.

Lauren was pleased to find Emma had chosen a modest blouse that covered her newly enhanced chest. For the most part. "See? That's lovely and perfectly appropriate for work."

"What's happening here?" Kiara asked.

"Lauren's a prude," Emma said.

Kiara's expression went flat. "What else is new?"

"Excuse me," Lauren protested. "You can put those things on display all you want, on your own time. But at work? Gotta keep it professional. You don't want Mr. Jones to have a stroke when you examine him today, do you? I'm only thinking of your patients."

"I know. You're right. I just got excited. Today's the first day I didn't have to wear that restrictive support bra. It's been weeks since I had my surgery, and I haven't been able to enjoy them."

"They look great. You definitely made the breast choice," Lauren said, careful to keep a straight face.

Kiara burst into laughter, and Emma dropped her forehead to the desk with a groan.

Lauren cracked a tiny grin. "Come on, I've been dying to bust out the boob jokes."

Emma's shoulders shook. "Holy shit. Stop it."

"Eh? Bust? That was a good one, wasn't tit?"

The three of them dissolved into giggles.

"Why don't we go to happy hour after work?" Kiara suggested after she'd caught her breath. "We'll celebrate Emma's boobs and Lauren killing her presentation today, bringing her one step closer to being our permanent clinical pharmacist."

"I'm in," Emma said, wiping a tear from her cheek.

"Me too," Lauren said.

"Excellent." Kiara turned back to her computer and straightened her back—her cue that social time was over. "Okay, time to work. Lauren, Dr. Patel's already in the room with a new lymphoma patient. You're still on that rotation, right?"

"Yep, today's the last day." As a resident, Lauren was required to rotate through the various clinics to gain experience in all areas. She'd become close with Kiara, Emma, and Dr. Patel over the past two months, and part of her hated to move on. Luckily, her next clinical rotation shared the same office space, and she'd still see them most days. "Tomorrow I start multiple myeloma."

"Dr. Patel will want you to do a chemo education for the new guy," Kiara said. "We're going to use you every second we can. I guarantee tomorrow morning when Dr. Patel realizes she doesn't have a pharmacist anymore, she's gonna march to Dr. Hawthorne's office and demand he hire one."

Lauren shook her head. "Not yet! You have to wait until I'm done. You handled the clinic without a pharmacist before I came along, you can do it again. It's only until next summer."

"You want us to suffer for eight months just so you can have a job waiting?"

"Yes."

Kiara pursed her lips. "Fine. Emma, Mr. Jones is waiting

in room twelve."

"Got it." Emma looked around. "Where's my stethoscope?"

Lauren pointed to the apparatus, resting on the counter beside Emma's computer.

"Thanks."

Lauren logged into the computer system and pulled up the chart of the nine o'clock patient, Andrew Bishop. Her heart sank when she saw his age. Twenty-six. It was sad for anyone to get cancer, but it was particularly hard to see the young ones. This guy was a year younger than her.

*Newly diagnosed Hodgkin lymphoma, stage IIB.* Her frown lightened. *High cure rate.* She knew right away what chemotherapy regimen he would need and printed out patient education leaflets for each of the medications.

A few minutes later Dr. Patel entered the room. "Can you get me the images from the PET-CT done at St. John's? I have the report, but I want to look at it myself. I want blood work today, return in two weeks," she said to Kiara, then turned to Lauren. "Mr. Bishop needs ABVD, start with four cycles and then a repeat scan. Could you talk to him?"

Lauren stood. "Of course."

"Just to warn you, it's crowded in there."

"No problem." Lauren scanned the appointment board for the room assignment, grabbed her papers, and went to number eleven. She knocked twice and entered.

Dr. Patel was right. It was crowded. Lauren counted five people, four women and one man, who must be the patient. The exam rooms weren't large, containing an exam table, a sink, three chairs, and a stool on wheels. Two women were on their feet in the corner, and the other two sat along with—

The guy from the coffee shop.

The impossibly sexy, brown-haired, tall one who had seen her ogling a photo of Emma's breasts and then had coffee spilled all over his shirt. He still wore said shirt, with his navy hoodie zipped up over the stain.

Lauren blinked.

"Hi."

The sound of his deep, rich voice jolted Lauren out of her trance. She cleared her throat, thankful that she'd said these words dozens of times before. "Um, hi, I'm Lauren. The pharmacy resident who works with Dr. Patel. I'm here to tell you more about the chemotherapy you'll be receiving. You must be Andrew?" She held out her hand, like she always did. Her fingers trembled slightly, which they always did not.

He gripped her hand in his large warm one. "That's me." Thankfully, he didn't bring up their early morning encounter. He released her and patted the arm of the woman sitting next to him. "This is my mom, Susan." He gestured to the younger women gathered nearby. "My sister Jeni. And my other sisters, Rhonda and Valerie. They insisted it was necessary they all be here. All four of them." His tone was irritated, but the soft expression on his face as he eyed the women showed a fondness for each of them.

"That's great." Lauren sat on the stool and centered herself between the half circle of people looking at her. "It's important to have a strong support system."

Andrew's mom sniffled. "And support him we will," she said in a shaky voice.

"Mom."

"Don't 'mom' me, Andrew Nathan Bishop. I'll be here every step of the way whether you like it or not."

"I can guarantee you I will not."

"Son, may I remind you that—"

The sister sitting down, Jeni, leaned forward and said loudly, "You should probably get started. Once they get going, they can carry on for hours." She grinned wryly and pushed thick-framed tortoise-shell glasses up her nose.

Appearing the youngest of the sisters, she had a smattering of freckles across her cheeks and bore a strong resemblance to her brother.

Andrew and his mother went silent and directed identical glares in the girl's direction.

"Jeni's right," one of the standing women said. This one sported a short bob of blond hair and her T-shirt announced she was a proud member of the George Washington PTA. "Let the lady talk."

Lauren wasn't sure how to react. She gauged her level of enthusiasm based on the demeanor of the family...some liked to joke and even laugh during their visit, while others were somber and kept it strictly down to business. The people in this room exuded the full spectrum. Andrew and Jeni seemed the least concerned and the most relaxed, and Andrew's mother and the sister wearing the PTA shirt looked on the verge of a breakdown.

This might be a challenge.

*Just stick to the routine.*

"Let me start by saying I'll give you a lot of information today, and it can be overwhelming. I like to go over things in person, but everything is in these papers I'm giving you." Lauren noted a pad of paper and a pen on Jeni's lap. "You're welcome to take notes, but don't worry if you just want to listen and ask questions. It's all here for you to look through after you get home and have time to process everything."

Lauren looked at every member of the family as she spoke, and they watched her in rapt attention. Each time her eyes met Andrew's, she felt her face heat. It embarrassed her, but she kept going, trying her best to ignore his perfectly sculpted bone structure and long legs stretched out in front of him, his left foot a mere three inches from the tip of her peep-toe heel.

She was a professional.

She didn't even know him.

He was a patient.

She began by telling him the logistics of receiving chemotherapy, including where the infusion center was and why he needed to have a port placed in his chest for intravenous access. "Dr. Patel has prescribed a chemotherapy regimen called ABVD, which is just an acronym for each chemotherapy agent. You'll hear all of us—myself, Dr. Patel, the infusion nurses—refer to it by this shorthand name. ABVD has four chemotherapy drugs—"

"*Four?*" His mom stuttered. She started to cry, and Lauren handed her the box of tissues sitting next to the sink.

"Mom, calm down," Jeni said, rubbing the older woman's hand with her own.

"Why does he need four? Is it that bad?" she sobbed.

Lauren leaned forward and rested her forearms on her knees, clasping her hands. "I know it sounds like a lot, but most patients get multiple chemotherapy drugs at once. Cancer is sneaky, and a drug that works on some cancer cells may not work on others."

"Wily bastards," Andrew put in.

Lauren flicked her gaze to him and grinned for a second. "That's one way to put it. That's why we mix several drugs together that work in different ways, to make sure we hit them all." She moved to squeeze Mrs. Bishop's hand at the same time she looked at Andrew. "Dr. Patel is the one to speak about response rates, but I can say in your type of cancer, ABVD typically works well."

There was a beat of silence.

"It will work, Mom." Jeni's tone was resolute.

"You're right." Mrs. Bishop sniffed and took a deep breath. She moved her hands in a repeated motion near her face, as if to waft fresh air toward her. "We have to keep a positive outlook about this."

"We?" Andrew raised an eyebrow. "You're the only one crying."

This brought on a fresh wave of tears. "You're my s-son! And you have c-c-cancer."

"I'm aware." His tone was deadpan, but he put his arm around her shoulders.

"Andrew," Jeni admonished. She pulled another tissue out and handed it to her mother. "Stop making Mom cry."

"Seriously? Don't get mad at me." He turned to Lauren. "Don't I get a free pass? A card to put in my wallet or something? An 'I have cancer, so give me a break' card?"

"Uh…" Lauren shifted on her stool. He was joking, right?

"For heaven's sake. Can we let her tell us about the chemo?" The dark-haired woman standing against the wall spoke up for the first time.

The blond sister wiped a tear from her cheek.

"Yes, let's get back on track," Lauren said with a nod. Heat rushed through her when she turned her attention to Andrew, but she pressed on. "You'll come in every two weeks for chemo and get all four drugs each time. Two rounds of chemo make up one cycle."

Once she got in the groove, she relaxed and regained the confidence she usually felt when talking about the drugs she knew so well, spending the next half hour reviewing side effects he could experience. She mentioned which ones were common—fatigue, increased risk of infection, nausea, and vomiting. And a few that were rare but serious enough to mention—lung toxicity, heart damage, neuropathy.

She also told him about the nausea medications she'd send in for him to use at home in between cycles.

Lauren's eyes met Andrew's brown ones. "Everyone has a different experience. Dr. Patel or her PA, Emma, will see you after your first chemo to find out how you did after you got home." And just because he was a guy, a young guy, and they were sometimes hesitant to be honest about their symptoms, she added, "They can't fix something they don't know about. You have to speak up if you have any issues. Okay?"

Andrew nodded at the same time his mother said, "We will." Andrew shook his head the tiniest bit, and Lauren bit her lip to contain her smile.

"Will we see you, too? When we come back?" his mother asked.

"Actually, this is my last day in this clinic. Starting tomorrow I'm moving to a different one. But there are several clinical pharmacists in the building available to Dr. Patel and her staff if any medication questions come up," Lauren said, burying the disappointment she felt that she wouldn't be following Andrew's care. "What other questions do you have? About the chemo?"

"Will he lose his hair?" Jeni asked.

Lauren couldn't help but glance at the thick, brown, soft-looking hair covering Andrew's head. Her fingers twitched, and she gripped her thigh as she brought her eyes down a few inches to meet his. "Yes, I expect you to lose all of it. It starts to thin right after chemo begins, but it usually isn't noticeable until after the second or third treatment. There comes a point where people get tired of hair everywhere, and that's when they get it cut short or shaved off."

Andrew nodded slowly. He swallowed hard, his Adam's apple bobbing in his throat. "When do I start?"

"I'll write the chemo orders as soon as we're done. It takes some time to obtain insurance approval, and we have to get your port placed first. Our nurse, Kiara, is probably getting that appointment set up as we speak. Best guess, I'd say in a week."

"Does he need to wear a mask when he's in public?" This from the short-haired, blond sister.

"That's usually unnecessary with this chemo. We'll get

lab work done often, and if we ever feel something indicates special precautions, we'll tell you."

"I have two young kids. Can he be around them?" the same sister continued. That explained the PTA shirt.

"You can't keep them from me." Andrew said to his sister, then frowned at Lauren, like she actually had control over who he saw and who he didn't. "I'm not going months without seeing my niece and nephew."

"Of course, that's fine. Just not if one of them is sick, okay? Otherwise, there are no restrictions. Doing the things and seeing the people that make you happy are important."

There was a brief silence, and Lauren waited for additional questions.

"I have one," Mrs. Bishop said. "Can Andrew…um, that is…is it safe for him to, you know," she lowered her voice. "*Be* with a woman? Intimately?"

The sudden eruption in the room was startling.

"Oh my *gosh*, Mom."

"Did you really just ask that?"

The only sound from Jeni was the slap of her hand across her mouth.

"Mom!" Andrew was the loudest. His face flushed beet red.

Lauren told herself to stay calm, despite the fact that thinking about Andrew and sex sent her heart into a dangerous rhythm. She was a professional, and she'd been here before. "It's common to ask about sex during chemotherapy—"

Andrew cut her off. "Do *not* answer that question. Please."

"Andrew, I wasn't born yesterday," his mother protested. "You've been with Caroline for months now, and you need to kno—"

"No, I don't."

"Andrew…"

"Stop."

"It's completely natural—"

"Caroline and I broke up, okay?"

Four sharp gasps told Lauren this was something Andrew hadn't yet told them.

"You did?"

"When?"

"What happened?"

"If she dumped you because of this, I'm gonna punch her in the ovaries." Jeni's jaw was clenched, her eyes positively murderous.

"Can we talk about this later?" Andrew bit out. "All that matters right now is that we don't need to talk about sex while I'm on chemo. Okay?" He turned pleading eyes on Lauren. "Can we move on?"

"Sure, um…I'm all done, if there are no other questions."

Mrs. Bishop crossed her arms.

The two sisters standing against the wall watched Andrew.

Jeni stared straight ahead, not looking at anything in particular, hands fisted tightly in her lap.

Andrew was the only one looking at Lauren. His eyes scanned her face and stopped at her mouth for a second before returning to her eyes. "I'm good. Thank you, this was helpful. It's nice to know what to expect." He smiled then, a wide, beautiful smile that exposed straight white teeth and transformed his face into something even more glorious than before. Which was really saying something.

Lauren couldn't look away. Without conscious thought, she felt her own lips widening to return the smile, like a flower might stretch its petals open to the sunlight.

"Yes, thank you, Lauren," Mrs. Bishop's voice broke in.

Lauren shifted her gaze. "You're very welcome." She stood, careful to look anywhere but at a smiling Andrew. "I'll send Kiara in, and she'll walk you out."

She stepped into the hallway and closed the door behind her. She closed her eyes and leaned her head against the wood. Her heart pounded and the tremble in her hands returned. Taking in a deep breath, she returned to the workroom.

"All done?" Kiara asked.

"Yep. They're ready to go."

Kiara stood, paperwork in hand, and walked out.

Lauren unlocked her computer screen and opened Andrew's chart. His name on the screen seemed different somehow, now that she knew who he was. They'd barely spoken this morning at the coffee shop, but it still felt like they were keeping a secret, from his family and from Dr. Patel. Like their prior involvement was more than a few glances and an accidental crashing of their bodies. When it had happened, she'd been mortified and unbalanced, and could think only of getting to the presentation she didn't want to be late for. But in the half hour between when she'd finished her lecture and met Andrew in the clinic, she'd replayed the moment in her head over and over. How firm and strong his body had been, and how good he'd smelled.

Was this some kind of cruel joke the universe was playing on her? For the first time in years, she felt that magical, toe-curling attraction to a man. Yes, he was miles out of her league and way too good-looking not to be a jerk. It seemed she was destined to forever be attracted to men guaranteed to break her heart.

But the thing that bothered her the most?

Now he was completely off-limits.

# Chapter Two

"First chemo tomorrow, huh?"

"Yeah."

"Nervous?" Logan stuffed several fries into his mouth.

Andrew shrugged and glanced around the restaurant. Servers wove through the room like ants, taking orders and delivering food and drinks to crowded tables. The smoky-sweet aroma of barbeque mixed with fried food wafted from the kitchen, and a burst of laughter sounded from the table behind them. "I just want to get it over with."

"Didn't seem all that bad when my mom went through it," Logan said. "I went with her a few times, and she just hung out and watched TV the whole time."

"I'm not worried about the chemo part. It's the days that come after that are supposed to suck. I don't want to be so tired that all I can do is lie around my house, you know? I don't want to miss class, and I can't take time off from my internship. I want to go to the gym. Go out with you and the guys. I don't want my mom and sisters to hang around here… they need to go back to Nebraska if I'm gonna stay sane. But if I get sick after this first round, they'll never leave me alone."

"What about your dad?"

"He's not here." Andrew kept his eyes on his food.

Logan paused like he wanted to ask more but seemed to decide against it. "It's not enough that Jeni lives here in Kansas City? She can keep an eye on you."

"Have you met my mother?"

"Yeah, you're right." Logan took a drink of beer. "If it gets too crowded at your apartment, just send Jeni over to my place. She can take care of me instead."

Andrew straightened and looked Logan hard in the eye. "Watch it."

Logan grinned, unconcerned. "You've got a hot twin, man."

"The fact that she and I look alike doesn't bother you?"

"She doesn't look at all like your ugly ass. She's a hot piece of—"

"If you want your balls to stay attached to your body, I wouldn't finish that sentence."

Logan snorted. "Fine."

Their waitress sauntered up to the table and tossed her long, white-blond hair behind her shoulder. "How we doing, guys?" She flashed a coy smile, and her blue eyes passed back and forth between the two. She focused on Andrew and gave him a blatant once-over, just like she had when they'd first sat down. Another time, he might have encouraged her and asked for her number at the end of the meal. He knew she'd be happy to provide it.

Wasn't happening, though. Not today.

"We're good, thanks," Andrew said.

"Let me know if I can get you anything." She brushed her fingers across Andrew's shoulder as she turned. "Anything at all."

Logan leaned halfway out of his chair to watch her walk

away. "You'd better do something about that, Andrew."

"Nah."

"Why the hell not? She's cute, and aren't tall blondes your type? She actually kind of looks like—"

"Caroline. I noticed. Not interested."

Logan was right. Andrew was usually attracted to blond women. But over the last week-and-a-half, no matter how many times he tried not to, he'd had a certain redheaded pharmacist on his mind.

He'd been in a terrible mood the day he met Lauren. Part of it had stemmed from his desire to avoid going to the appointment with the entire female side of his family. He wished he could have just told them no, that he wanted to go by himself. Or allowed only Jeni to come with him. As twins, they were the closest siblings of the group, and she was the one he felt most comfortable sharing this with. But it would have hurt their feelings, especially his mom's, and it wasn't worth the weeks of grief they'd aim in his direction.

The other reason he'd started the day pissed off wasn't something he'd ever say out loud.

It was hard to even admit to himself.

He was scared.

Scared of what the doctor would say, scared of getting chemo, of losing his internship with the best attorney in town.

If he was really honest, scared of dying.

Then he'd walked into that coffee shop and caught sight of a curvy redhead standing in line. Her hair wasn't the typical orange he'd associate with the description; it was a deep auburn, like a glass of red wine. He hadn't meant to, but he'd looked at the lit-up phone in her hands and saw that she was looking at a very nice set of breasts. The laugh that escaped him in that moment had been such an unexpected delight that morning that he'd watched the back of her head the remaining time he'd stood there.

She'd known the cashier's name, and Andrew made a mental note she probably went there often. She'd also laughed at something the employee said, and the sound alone had lifted Andrew's spirits.

He'd had every intention of saying something incredibly clever and impressive when he'd walked up behind her at the coffee bar.

"Hi," or maybe even, "Good morning."

But then she'd turned around so quickly and slammed into his chest, and it had been like she doused him with cold water instead of hot coffee.

He remembered his diagnosis and who he had an appointment with later that morning. His life was suddenly extremely complicated, and no woman would want to get involved in that.

Caroline sure as hell hadn't.

Lauren, though he hadn't known her name at the time, had looked up at him with those big green eyes, the freckles across her cheeks fading as a pink flush slowly encompassed them. And Andrew had grown angry. He felt constrained by his disease—which meant he would never get to know this unconventionally beautiful woman standing before him.

She was the last person he'd have expected to walk into his exam room. For forty-five minutes she talked about things he knew were important, but he'd had a hell of a time paying attention. It took everything in him to keep his eyes high, away from her mouth and the collarbone on display with the blue button-up shirt she'd been wearing.

Then his mom had asked about sex.

Embarrassment flooded him even now, just thinking about it. He loved his family. Really, he did. But sometimes he just wanted to be left the hell alone.

"Got it. No more blondes for a while." Logan's voice jolted Andrew out of his thoughts.

"It's not that." Andrew put the last bite of his burger into his mouth and chewed. "There's just no point in getting involved with someone right now."

"Dude. Come on. Girls don't care about that kind of stuff."

"Caroline did."

"Caroline was a bitch."

"No argument there." Andrew just wished he'd seen it sooner.

Logan tried again. "Women have that caretaking instinct. They'd line up to take care of you, if you'd let them."

"I've got four nagging women at my door as it is. I don't need another one."

"Fine." Logan pushed his empty plate to the side and held up his hands in surrender. "Do you want me to come with you tomorrow?"

"Hell no. It's gonna be embarrassing enough to have my female entourage."

"Okay. Let me know how it goes, though. Yeah?"

Andrew offered his friend a tight-lipped smile. "I will."


"Andrew Bishop?"

Andrew's mom and sisters were on their feet before he'd even registered his own name.

"That's us," Valerie walked toward the woman in scrubs who'd called out into the waiting room.

"Us? Funny, I only heard *my* name," Andrew grumbled.

Jeni's small fist connected with his left bicep when he stood. "Cut it with the attitude. That won't help anything. Take this first round like a champ and they'll go back to Nebraska and leave us be."

"You're right," he agreed.

"To be clear," Jeni said in a low tone. "I'm asking for my sake. I'm the one they're staying with." She bugged her eyes out at him meaningfully.

Andrew laughed. "How's that been going?"

"I've been eating well." She paused. "It's not worth it."

"I bet not." Andrew smiled and shook his head, and he and his family followed the woman through the door.

"I'm Karen, one of the medical assistants. Is this your first time here?" Her smile was kind but not pitying, something Andrew appreciated.

"Yes."

"I'll point out the important things as we go, then. The infusion center is U-shaped and separated into five nursing pods. Your chemo nurse is Mandi, and she's wonderful."

They passed rows of large leather recliners. Each chair had its own small flat-screen television in front of it, and curtains that could be pulled around for privacy. Few people had their curtains closed, and Andrew's eyes passed over the other patients receiving treatment. The wide range of ages and health conditions was surprising. Before his own diagnosis, he thought cancer was something that only old people got. He hadn't known anyone his age who'd had it, with the exception of a high school buddy whose little sister had had leukemia. They'd had a big fundraiser at school to raise money for a bone marrow transplant she needed, and as far as Andrew knew, she was okay now. Most of the patients he saw appeared to be older than fifty, but there were also a few who looked to be his age, or maybe in their thirties.

"There are two bathrooms in each pod. You can get up and walk around if you want...just stay on this floor and take your IV pole with you."

Finally, they arrived at an empty recliner with two wooden chairs nearby. Karen glanced at the women who flanked him, two on each side. "Here we are. Have a seat, I'll go grab two more chairs, then I'll take your vitals."

Karen left and Rhonda followed behind to help. Andrew hesitated before he sat down.

His mom sat down beside him and immediately started to cry.

Andrew took a deep breath. *Patience*, he told himself. "You okay, Mom?"

"I'm sorry," she sniffled. "I'm f-f-fine."

Jeni gave her a small shove from behind. "Move over. Andrew doesn't need that right now."

This was why Jeni was his favorite. Without argument, his mom moved to the second chair over, and Jeni replaced her in the one nearest to Andrew.

Karen and Rhonda returned, and while his sisters settled themselves around him, the medical assistant strapped a blood pressure cuff around his arm. She chatted with him as she worked, reading off his blood pressure and pulse aloud when she wrote it down. "Perfect numbers."

"Look at that, healthy as a horse," he said. "You know, except for the cancer."

Karen averted her eyes, and Jeni glared at him. A fresh wave of tears came from his mother.

Andrew shrugged. "Not ready to joke about it yet? Okay."

Karen gathered up her equipment and offered him an unsure smile before she left.

A tall blond nurse in blue scrubs soon approached, pushing a rolling cabinet with several drawers and a kit of supplies on the top.

"Hi there, I'm Mandi," she said in a southern drawl. "You must be Andrew."

"That's me."

"Looks like you've got a nice cheering section started over here," she said as she took in the overcrowded space.

"That's a nice way to put it," Andrew remarked.

"He's right. We're more like squawking hens than a cheering section," Jeni said.

"I resent that," Valerie said. "I'd prefer to be called a mother hen."

"If anyone's the mother hen, it's me," his mom said, wiping her nose.

"One's enough, thanks." Andrew leaned his head back against the cushion. He felt a headache coming on.

Mandi widened her eyes in Andrew's direction, almost as if she were commiserating with him.

"First thing I'm going to do is access your port, okay?" Mandi frowned. "Unless you want to stretch out the neck of your T-shirt, you'll need to lift it up for me. Next time try to wear something with buttons for easier access."

Andrew hadn't even thought of that. The device had been surgically implanted into the right side of his chest just three days ago, and it was still sore. He'd chosen the softest shirt he owned, hoping to avoid irritating it any further.

Mandi put on bright pink gloves and bent over the tray, getting the equipment ready. She held up a little plastic stick with a round pad on the end. "This is for cleaning the skin around the port before I use the needle."

Andrew lifted his shirt up to his neck, baring the entire right side of his abdomen and chest. Mandi leaned forward and eyed the circular lump underneath his skin, and lightly touched around it with her glove-tipped fingers. The light pressure was painful, and Andrew held as still as possible.

"Sorry, it's probably still tender. That's normal. The incision is healing well, and it looks good." She scrubbed the moist pad all around the area, and an antiseptic stench rose to Andrew's nostrils. She turned back to the tray and faced him once again with a large, thick needle.

"Holy shit, that's a big needle," Jeni said loudly.

"Jeni!" his mother admonished.

"It's quick," Mandi said.

"Do you want to hold my hand?" Valerie asked.

Andrew resisted the urge to roll his eyes and remind his family he was a six-foot-three, two-hundred-plus-pound man who'd been through worse. "I'm good."

"Take a deep breath in and hold it, and you'll feel a big stick."

He did as asked, and Mandi pierced his skin.

*Fuck*, that hurt. He clenched his teeth and caught a grunt of pain that rose in his throat just in time.

"All done."

An odd, slightly cold sensation tickled at the area. He looked down at the plastic apparatus now attached to him, and saw clear fluid move through the tubing.

"That's just saline for now. I'll get the premedications ready and bring them back in a few minutes." Mandi pushed the cabinet on wheels against the wall and left.

"Are you okay?"

"Did it hurt?"

"Can we get you anything?"

His sisters all spoke at once, but Andrew didn't hear a word they said, because as he watched Mandi walk away, his eye caught on someone else.

Lauren stood at the nursing station directly in front of his chair, several yards away. Her alluring red hair was loosely pulled back in a braid, a style that had always fascinated Andrew. He'd watched Caroline weave her hair into braids and had joked about her ninja skills as she'd worked her fingers behind her head, not even looking at her progress as she went.

Lauren's hair was longer than Caroline's—but why was he comparing them, anyway? They'd broken up only a month ago and had dated for six, so he'd probably compare women to Caroline for a while. But Lauren wasn't a romantic interest, and her involvement in his life had nothing in common with Caroline's.

He needed to remember that.

She was talking to a man in scrubs. A nurse, maybe? Whoever he was, he was into Lauren, that much was clear. He stood close to her with a lazy smile on his face, and his eyes drifted down her body more than once as they conversed.

At least when Andrew had talked to her he'd *tried* to keep his attention up top. This guy didn't even attempt to show her respect.

*Dick.*

Not that it made a difference to Andrew one way or another, but Lauren didn't seem to enjoy the guy's attentions. Her posture was stiff, and she kept looking around while the guy went on and on, obviously not getting the hint that she needed (or wanted) to be somewhere else. Another woman in scrubs joined them, and Lauren backed away, turning to leave.

Her green eyes landed on Andrew, and she froze. A smile lit up her face, and Andrew grinned in return, raising his hand in a wave. As he hoped she would, she made her way over. Her eyes dropped to his still-bare midsection, and Andrew gingerly tugged his shirt back down over his chest and stomach, arranging the tubing at the bottom so it didn't pull on the needle.

"Look, it's that pharmacist from Dr. Patel's office," Jeni said. "What was her name?"

"Lauren," Andrew murmured.

"That's right," Jeni said as she approached. "Hi, Lauren!"

"Hey, everyone. How's it going so far?" Lauren asked.

She smiled and her demeanor was friendly, but there was an edge to her voice Andrew hadn't detected when they'd met previously. Had it been her conversation with that guy? He suddenly wanted to know what had been said, and if it had upset her. It was none of his business, but that didn't lessen his curiosity.

Lauren locked eyes with him, and her cheeks flushed, but she didn't look away. He liked that. "So far so good," he said.

"Lauren, did you know how big those port needles are? I thought I was going to pass out when I saw it," his mom said.

"It's really big," Lauren agreed.

"That's what she said," Jeni muttered under her breath.

Andrew coughed and kicked her.

"Couldn't they start a regular IV in his arm?" His mom continued, oblivious to her two youngest children's immaturity.

"Chemotherapy can irritate the small vessels in the arm, and if a patient is dehydrated or doesn't have good veins, it's hard to get a line that way. It's safest to do it like this." Her eyes brightened, and she grinned. "I'd even say...im-*port*-ant to do it like this." She paused with her mouth slightly ajar and her eyebrows raised.

Jeni giggled and a laugh burst forth from Andrew's chest.

Lauren looked so proud of her little joke. *Dammit, she's cute.*

"That was terrible," he teased.

"Then why are you laughing?" she retorted.

"People laugh at bad jokes all the time."

She tilted her head to the left and put one hand on her waist. "What's the end goal of a joke, Andrew?"

Strike that. Standing there with her hip out to the side, her braid across her shoulder, trailing down the swell of her chest, and her green eyes daring him to argue—she wasn't cute. She was sexy as hell.

"To make people laugh."

"And what was that, just now? That sound you made?"

Andrew narrowed his eyes even as he smiled. "A laugh." He drew the words out slowly.

"Well then. Mission accomplished."

"I like her," Jeni announced. She turned to face Lauren. "I like you."

Andrew thought maybe he liked her, too—a little too much.

"Oh." Lauren sounded surprised, and she smiled at Jeni. "Well, I like you, too."

"What about me?" The words were out of his mouth before he could stop them.

The smile faded from Lauren's face, and suddenly she looked like he always felt in math class when called on to answer a question.

Completely at a loss for how to answer.

Andrew could feel his mother's stare. Out of the corner of his eye he noticed Jeni's wide grin.

Thankfully, Valerie spoke up from the other side of his chair. "Of course she doesn't like you. Few women do."

Andrew snorted. Those toddlers of hers were fogging his sister's brain.

"Sure, you're nice to look at," Valerie went on. "But then you open your mouth." She shook her head sadly, and next to her Rhonda nodded in solemn agreement.

"I've been told I'm exceptionally charming," Andrew argued.

"By whom?"

He paused. "Mom." He swiveled around to look at the woman in question.

She smiled at him lovingly. "Of course you are, honey."

Andrew shot Valerie a triumphant look and crossed his arms in front of his chest. "See? Charming."

Jeni rolled her eyes in a manner that would put any thirteen-year-old girl to shame. "That doesn't count. Not only does she have to say you're charming because you're her only son, but you have cancer and are about to get your first chemo treatment. She'd tell you you're next in line as the King of England if you asked her to."

His mother leaned forward to meet his eye. "Don't listen to them. You could be a king if you wanted to. You can be anything you want to be."

"That's completely untrue," Jeni said. "Unless you marry a princess, you'll never be king. Does anyone know a princess who's single we could introduce Andrew to? No?" She arched an eyebrow at him. "You'll be a mediocre attorney. But that's what you want to be, right? So, it works out."

Andrew stiffened. "Why will I be mediocre?"

"The great ones are workaholics, who leave time for nothing else. You care too much about your family to be one of those guys."

His posture relaxed. Even though it was an odd kind of compliment, he'd take it, because it was true.

"Or maybe it's because you were never good at winning arguments," Valerie countered. "You usually just give up and walk away."

"Arguing with you isn't worth it," he muttered, and rubbed a hand across his face.

Lauren stood two feet away with both hands tucked into the pockets of her white coat, her expression bewildered and amused.

"Is there a limit to how many family members can be back here with me?" he asked, pleading with his eyes. "Tell me someone forgot to mention it and I need to ask at least two to leave."

Her eyes twinkled, and the corner of her mouth twitched. "Sorry. The only rule is no visitors under twelve."

Andrew turned his attention to Jeni. "Sorry, little one. You gotta go."

Jeni put her hand up to her face and rubbed the side of her nose with her middle finger, turning in such a way their mom couldn't see the gesture.

"Worth a shot," he said under his breath.

"Well, I'd better get going." Lauren cleared her throat as her eyes traveled up the IV pole. "Any questions or issues before things get started? Did you get the pills I sent to your pharmacy?"

"We have them," Valerie said before Andrew could. She patted her purse.

"Great. I hope you won't need them, but I want you to have them just in case." Lauren brought her eyes back to his. "You'll call Dr. Patel's office if they don't work, right?"

"You act like I'm not good at following orders," Andrew said, feigning offense. "Why is that? You don't even know me."

"She's a smart woman," Jeni said.

Lauren grinned at Jeni, then darted her gaze back to him. "I know male patients, and generally, as a group, you don't like taking medication."

"We also don't like to kneel at the porcelain throne."

"Sounds like we're on the same page, then. Give me a call if you need anything." Twin spots of color formed on her cheeks, and she quickly added, "I mean the clinic. Call the clinic if you need anything."

Andrew kept his eyes on Lauren as she walked down the hallway. She raised one hand to smooth her hair and slid it down the back of her head, gripping her neck for a moment as she walked. Just as she turned the corner she dropped her arm to her side and looked back, meeting his eyes for the briefest second before she was out of view.

"Andrew?" Valerie's voice sounded in his ear. "Are you listening?"

"What?" Andrew found five women staring at him. Four, he was used to. But Mandi had apparently rejoined them and was eyeing him as well. "Sorry."

"No problem. I just wanted to let you know what I'm about to give you," Mandi said. "All three of these are medications to prevent nausea. I'll run them separately, one right after another. Should take about forty-five minutes."

Andrew nodded understanding. *Here we go.* Nerves unfurled deep in his gut, and he suddenly felt antsy. He had a strong urge to get up and leave, but that wouldn't do him any good. Inhaling deeply, he pulled his phone out of his pocket, hoping to distract himself with Instagram.

Mandi manipulated the tubing and pressed a few buttons on the computerized pump attached to the IV pole. His mother asked Mandi where she was from and how long she'd been an oncology nurse.

Jeni jumped in at the first break in conversation. "Do you know Lauren well, Mandi?"

His phone was suddenly much less interesting.

"The pharmacist? Sure. She's our oncology resident this year. The best one we've ever had, if you ask me. I really hope they find a job for her here when she's done. I know she wants to stay, but from what she's told me, persuading the hospital administration to fund another position isn't easy."

Andrew had no idea pharmacists even did residencies. He wondered how long it was. Would she finish and move on while he was still getting treatment? Had she said anything about that before? He thought back to his first office visit, trying to remember.

"Is she single?" Jeni asked.

Andrew shifted in the chair, the movement creaking across the leather material. He glared at Jeni, and she shot him a deceptively innocent expression.

Mandi paused. "Yes, I think she is." Her eyes went to Andrew as she answered, like he'd been the one to ask the question.

He looked at her blankly, not sure how to respond.

Mandi offered a small smile. "You're all ready to go. I'll be back when it's time to switch them out."

"Thank you," Rhonda said, and Andrew realized he'd almost forgotten she was there. She'd always been the quiet one.

Maybe she should be his new favorite sister.

Mandi walked away and Andrew immediately whisper-yelled at Jeni, "I'm going to kill you."

The smug expression on her face grated on his nerves.

"We'll see about that."

# Chapter Three

Lauren exited the infusion center with mixed emotions.

Gavin had cornered her as soon as she'd arrived, which had put her on edge. He was one of only two male nurses employed on the third floor—the other a graying, fifty-something who was happily married and showed off photos of his grandkids at every opportunity. Gavin was young, single, and clearly ready to mingle, chasing after anything with breasts. He'd dated his way through half of the female nursing staff and a few weeks ago had set his sights on Lauren. At first it had been harmless flirting, but then he'd asked her out.

Too bad for him, she'd been warned.

Even if she hadn't, his arrogant approach wouldn't have gotten him far. She'd politely declined each invitation for dinner or drinks, but he didn't seem deterred. It was almost as if her disinterest was a challenge Gavin was determined to overcome, which only deepened her dislike for him. A guy who didn't know the meaning of the word *no* was one she wanted nothing to do with.

And then, not ten seconds after she extracted herself from Gavin's wandering eyes and condescending chatter, her gaze had landed on Andrew. And her heart had leapt so high, it'd nearly lodged in her throat.

Not the appropriate response a health care provider should have for a patient. Even one that wasn't under her direct care. It still felt...wrong, somehow.

But she couldn't help but smile when she saw him...and good Lord, his shirt had been pulled up slightly by the IV tubing, and the ridged muscles she glimpsed were enough to make her knees go weak.

The image flashed through her mind now, as she rode the elevator to the sixth floor.

*Stop. He's a patient going through a serious illness. Plus, looking like he does, he's probably just as much a womanizer as Gavin. If not more so.*

Her phone buzzed in her pocket, and she glanced at the screen.

*Dad.*

She quickly silenced the call and put her phone away. He knew she didn't like to answer her phone while she was at work.

Which was probably exactly why he chose now to call. He wasn't much for texting, so he'd taken to calling her during work hours and leaving voicemails outlining his requests when he wanted something.

Lauren reached the office she shared with two other clinical pharmacists, finding the small room empty. One of them was on service at the hospital this month and was never around, and the other was probably still in clinic. As a resident, rather than a full-time employee, Lauren's desk was the smallest and shoved between a bookcase and the back wall with no room to spare.

Lauren approached her desk and opened the bottom

drawer, pulling out her purse and sliding it over her shoulder in one fluid motion. She didn't spend more time in here than she had to…preferring to either remain in Dr. Patel's clinic after hours or leave the cancer center altogether when she'd finished with her patient responsibilities.

It was just after three o'clock, and there were no patients left to see. But she had a review article for the *American Journal of Pharmacy* due on Monday, so she stopped at The Grind House before going home.

She'd discovered the nearby coffee shop during her first week at the cancer center. It was close enough that if they called her in, she could be there within minutes, and offered a less sterile backdrop when studying or working on a research project. The warm, comforting scent of coffee and low hum of conversation were just enough to distract her when she needed a break.

Ten minutes after she'd settled into her usual table, Tyler plopped down across from her.

He slid a chocolate chip cookie across the table with wide eyes, one finger against his lips. He would forever be her favorite barista.

"You're so good to me," Lauren said. "On your break?"

"Yep."

"How's your day going?"

"No small talk. I need to go make a call, but I *had* to stop over and tell you."

Tyler's charisma never ceased to make Lauren smile. "Tell me what?"

"The hot guy came back."

Lauren played dumb, despite the fact that every time she walked through the door she thought of Andrew.

*Pre*-patient Andrew.

She'd also gone back to her routine beverage and hadn't ordered a self-serve coffee since that morning, lest she repeat her clumsiness with some other hotter-than-sin man who might be in the vicinity.

"Hot guy?" she asked.

Tyler lifted his eyebrow like it was his job. "Don't pull that with me. You know exactly who I'm talking about, and he was in here yesterday."

"I don't know why you're telling me," Lauren said. Patient privacy laws prevented her from telling Tyler about Andrew showing up at the cancer center, so she had no out other than pretending to be uninterested.

"Damn, you're infuriating." Tyler stood. "Fine, I'll act like I didn't notice you checking him out the other day, before *and* after you spilled coffee on him. And I'll pretend I didn't notice him doing the same thing."

*That* got her attention.

"He did?"

A smug grin settled across Tyler's features as he nodded.

Lauren filed that tidbit away to think about later. For now, she said, "Well, be that as it may, I don't know the guy, and I'm sure he's not interested in me. No matchmaking, okay?"

Tyler snorted and turned away.

Lauren jolted up and grabbed his arm. "Tyler, I mean it. Promise me."

Tyler held up three fingers before he left, and Lauren giggled at the image of him as a pre-teen in a Boy Scout uniform.

She stayed for another hour before starting her commute home.

When she'd first started pharmacy school at UMKC College of Pharmacy, she'd lived in an apartment nearby and could have walked home from here. But halfway through the four-year program she'd decided to rent a house farther south in Waldo. Living near downtown had been fun at first, but she preferred something quieter. Now, her drive was twenty or thirty minutes, depending on traffic, but the charming ranch-style home she'd found, built in the 1940s, was worth it. With a soft gray-blue exterior, white shutters, and a yard full of mature trees, the twelve-hundred-square-foot home was the first place she'd ever called her own.

She realized as she checked her mailbox—empty, as usual—and pulled into the partially shaded driveway that she'd lived in this house nearly four years now, with almost nine between the states of Missouri and Kansas, if she counted undergrad at KU.

By this point, she rarely thought of her prior life in Oklahoma. Other than a few good friends who kept in touch, there wasn't much left for Lauren in the state where she was born. Her only contact with her mother was a call on her birthday. She spoke to her dad more frequently, but she certainly wouldn't consider them close.

Lauren fished her phone from her purse and pulled up the voicemail as she walked through the dappled sunlight to the front door.

Might as well get it over with.

*"Lauren, it's Dad. I was just calling to ask if you were planning to come home for Thanksgiving or Christmas. Several of my staff asked for the holidays off, and I was hoping you might be around to cover some shifts at the store. It's a good idea to keep up your familiarity with the system, you know, if you decide to—"*

Lauren cut the message off, silencing her father's nasally voice and the guilt-ridden thoughts that arose in her own head. She'd deal with that later.

She stepped into her house. Enough sunlight streamed through the sheer curtains in the entry and living room that she didn't even flip on a light switch. Ever practical, she'd chosen furnishings that were neutral-colored and cozy, and she felt a sense of calm each time she walked through the door.

She changed clothes, warmed up leftover pizza, and ate in front of the television. Just after seven, her phone buzzed with an incoming message.

Emma: *Let's go out tonight.*

Lauren: *Meh.*

Emma: *Come on. I know you're just sitting on your couch watching some weird ass documentary.*

Lauren: *Am not.*

She was sitting in the oversized armchair.

Emma: *What are you doing, then?*

Lauren: *I don't wanna say.*

Emma: *I knew it.*

Emma: *We're young, hot twenty-something's who work hard and deserve a night on the town.*

Lauren: *But I'm already in my Netflix pants.*

Emma: *Please? I'll bring you a Danish from Annie's on Monday.*

Lauren: *Damn you.*

Emma: *McNellie's at eight?*

Lauren: *Fine.*

She remained in her chair for a few minutes before dragging herself from the living room to her bedroom and stood in front of the open closet. She was a natural homebody, but she needed to put herself out there if she ever wanted to meet new people in this town. She'd made several friends in pharmacy school, but most had moved away after graduation. The first year of residency had been grueling, and she'd barely had time for a social life, but the second year felt more relaxed.

She had been lucky to be assigned the lymphoma clinic early on, because she'd immediately hit it off with Emma and Kiara. If it weren't for Emma, she doubted she'd ever leave her house other than for work. Even though it sometimes took convincing to get her out, she usually enjoyed herself.

Lauren chose a black top that went with jeans, finishing the look with a pair of heels. She grabbed a dark gray cardigan and stuffed it into her oversized handbag, anticipating that the October evening would turn chilly as the night wore on.

The low-key pub was in the River Market district, an up-and-coming area popular with young professionals. McNellie's was one of Lauren's favorite places to go, because it felt more like a place to hang out with friends than a place to see and be seen. The décor was eclectic, the servers were friendly, and televisions were mounted throughout, playing whatever game was on that night.

Unsurprisingly, Lauren arrived before Emma. Punctuality was a habit Lauren couldn't seem to break, despite knowing that Emma would be ten minutes late to her own wedding.

Lauren found a two-person high-top table near the bar and ordered a beer while she waited. She took a sip and her gaze roamed around the low-lit room. Several yards away, a man wearing a fitted long-sleeved navy shirt and jeans leaned casually on the bar. His shoulders were broad and his brown hair was just barely visible underneath a worn baseball cap on his head.

From the back, he looked an awful lot like Andrew.

Without conscious thought, Lauren straightened, a vibration of excitement zipping through her. Just as quickly, she pursed her lips and scolded herself for her reaction. She forced herself to look away, focusing on the basketball game playing overhead. Yet her eyes kept drifting down, hoping he'd turn so she could really see him. Was it...?

"Sorry I'm late."

Lauren jumped at the sound of Emma's voice and twisted around just as her friend hopped onto the stool beside her.

"I'm used to it by now," Lauren said.

Emma laughed and reached over to rotate the bottle of beer. She regarded the label and made a face. "I don't know how you drink that stuff. I need a cocktail."

As Emma opened the drink menu, Lauren glanced at the bar once more.

The guy was gone.

She looked around but didn't see anyone wearing a navy shirt and a hat.

A server approached, and Emma placed her drink order.

"Thanks for coming out," Emma said. "I really need to let off some steam. This week was rough."

"It was," Lauren agreed. Clinic had been packed full with new patient visits, and they'd received the sad news that two of their patients had passed away. "I must have written twenty chemo orders this week."

"Before you came along I was the one writing them." Emma's eyes went wide. "I don't want that job back, okay? Finish your rotations and come back. Don't leave us for good."

"I'm trying not to."

"Any updates on a job opening?"

Lauren shook her head. "Dr. Hawthorne said there's a budget meeting in late November, and he'll propose adding a third full-time clinical pharmacist. If they approve the position, I can apply for it."

Emma frowned. "Can't they just grandfather you in?"

"I guess not. But there aren't that many oncology specialists running around, so hopefully I won't have much competition."

"You'd better be right. Intelligence aside, I doubt we'd find another pharmacist who'll drop bad puns all day to keep us laughing. It's gotta be you."

Lauren laughed and took a drink of her beer. "Laughter is the best medicine."

When the server returned with Emma's drink, Emma made a show of scoping out the room. "Any cute guys here tonight?"

It was on the tip of Lauren's tongue to say she'd seen one before Emma arrived. "I'm not sure."

Emma rotated on her seat, tapping her chin as she went. "What am I looking for? What's your type?"

"I don't really have one."

"That's not helpful." Emma paused. "Actually, maybe it is. *Any* guy is fair game?"

"Emma, what are you doing? I don't want you to find me a guy."

"Too bad."

Lauren shook her head. "What about you? Has one even seen your newest additions, yet?"

"I got them for me, not for men." Emma shimmied her shoulders, and Lauren couldn't stop her eyes from dropping to the ample cleavage on display.

"So you say. But you sure were eager for me to bring my coffee shop guy to work a few weeks ago."

What would Emma think if she knew that guy was Andrew? The "hot patient" who all the women in the clinic now fawned over? Anyone who had a hand in his care would remember him.

Emma waved a hand in the air and made a sound of dismissal. "I was kidding. Besides, I'm not the one who hasn't gone on a date in *two years*. Gotta prioritize, here."

Lauren grimaced. "You make me sound like such a loser. I'm focused on my career."

"And now that you're this close"—Emma held up her thumb and forefinger a centimeter apart—"to locking down a job here, it's time to get back out there."

"I haven't gotten an offer yet," Lauren reminded her. She went back to the original point. "Besides, I'm perfectly content with my life right now. I'm doing just fine on my own. What do I need a man for?"

"Do you really want me to answer that?" Emma said with a quirk of her brow. "There are several things I like to use a man for—"

"I get the idea," Lauren interjected with a laugh. She wrapped one hand around her beer bottle. "I guess I just want to meet a nice guy, for once. I seem to be a magnet for jerks... guys who get by on charm and always get what they want. My first serious boyfriend cheated on me in college, and then in pharmacy school I dated a third-year medical student. Just when I thought things were going well he ghosted me out of nowhere. Found out later he started dating the daughter of the Chief of General Surgery, which happened to be the residency program he wanted to get into. Just once, I'd like to date a guy who's honest, dependable, and kind. One who likes me for me, not for what he can get from me. You know?"

"Yeah. If only we could all be so lucky," Emma said. "Until then, I'm gonna have my fun, and use guys for what *they* can give to *me*." She waggled her eyebrows up and down.

Emma resumed her perusal of the room, and Lauren regarded her friend with envy. Lauren hadn't had good luck in love, and as a result kept her guard up pretty high. *Why can't I be more like Emma?* More carefree with men and the dating scene?

The truth was, she'd always taken relationships pretty seriously, even from the start. She didn't understand Tinder or Bumble, had found that sex wasn't something she could treat casually, and wanted a guy who supported her career aspirations. She'd spent a lot of time on her own growing up, feeling like an outsider even within her own family. Independence was a trait learned early, and except for her father's willingness to pay her way through pharmacy school—she wasn't an idiot to say no and rack up student loans if she didn't have to—she'd put in the hard work to get where she was. She wasn't the kind of woman who wanted to rely on a man to support her.

Or vice versa. She wanted a partnership.

It wasn't that she thought there wasn't someone out there for her...she just hadn't had the time or energy to find him.

Some days it felt like an insurmountable task. Couldn't fate intervene on her behalf—just this once—and drop the perfect guy into her life?

Was that really too much to ask?

# Chapter Four

"How'd it go?"

"Not as bad as I thought it would be."

"Told you." Logan tapped the barstool next to him. "You gonna sit? Dan's coming, too."

"I'm not sure." Andrew wavered, leaning forward on the bar. Was that a twinge of nausea he felt? Just the thought of vomiting in the middle of his favorite bar, in front of his friends and the bartenders he knew, was enough to make him want to turn around and walk out.

"You okay?" Logan asked.

"I don't know. I think so. I feel okay, but I'm not sure how long that will last. I almost didn't come, but I had to get away from my mom and sisters."

His friend regarded him for a moment. He tapped the bar and called out to the bartender. "Can I get a water for Andrew? He's driving tonight." None of the employees knew about his diagnosis, and Andrew was grateful to Logan for keeping it that way.

"Let's sit over there." Logan nodded to a cluster of

couches and chairs near the back of the room, and near the restrooms. "You can head out whenever you want."

Andrew nodded. "Okay. Thanks."

Dan, a friend Andrew had met during his first year of law school, soon joined them. Andrew's brief anxiety over getting sick passed as they fell into their usual conversation about work and sports. They were in a fantasy football league with several other guys, and Dan's team had smoked them all the past weekend.

"Didn't your star wide receiver go out with an injury on Monday night?" Dan asked Logan.

"I don't want to talk about it," Logan grumbled.

"My team isn't doing any better," Andrew said. "I'm just glad this league was only fifty bucks. I joined a high-stakes game with my brother-in-law and his buddies last year, and the winner got five grand. I was pissed off the entire season, knowing how much money I was missing out on with my shitty team."

"Didn't your sister play in that one, too?" Dan asked.

"Yeah, both Valerie and Jeni. It's impressive how much they know about football."

Logan perked up. "There's a lot that's impressive about Jeni."

"Don't you need another beer?" Andrew asked.

Logan stood, a shit-eating grin on his face. "As a matter of fact, I do."

As Logan walked toward the bar across the room, Dan shook his head. "That guy's just asking for an ass kicking, isn't he?"

Andrew frowned. "I don't know what's gotten into him. I introduced the two of them a few months ago when Jeni moved to town, and they didn't seem to like each other at first. They've sort of become friends, and lately he's made several comments like that. I try not to let it get to me because

I know he's all talk and that he's a good guy. It's never really bothered me when he said things like that about other women, but when it's my sister…"

"I don't have a sister, but if I did, I wouldn't want Logan to even look in her direction."

Andrew didn't respond and took a long drink of water.

"How's it going at the DA's office?" Dan asked, taking the hint and changing the subject.

"It's great. They've assigned me to a new domestic violence case, and right now I'm helping with the preliminary legal research and paperwork. I'm hoping it moves through the court proceedings before we graduate, so I can experience the entire process and see how it all plays out."

"I can't believe you landed that internship. It's competitive."

"I can't either," Andrew said. Though he had worked his ass off on his application and, luckily, had really hit it off with the attorney he'd interviewed with. He hoped to secure a position at the District Attorney's office after he graduated, but even if they didn't have an open spot, the networking opportunities the internship created would no doubt get him a nice offer elsewhere.

It was a bittersweet feeling, to be succeeding in his chosen career path. On one hand, there was nothing he'd rather be doing, and it felt good to know he'd spend his last year of law school training under some of the best prosecutors in the state. But with every good thing that happened, his mind conjured up an image of his father and the look of disappointment on his face when Andrew had told him he wouldn't follow in his footsteps to manage the family farm.

His dad had put up a good fight, to be sure. Andrew had actually thought that his dad would have made a good attorney, but he didn't dare say that. His dad had offered strong arguments about family values and carrying on the farming legacy that was three generations strong, but Andrew wasn't swayed.

Things had never been the same.

"Didn't you shadow a criminal defense attorney last year?" Dan asked, bringing Andrew back from his musings.

"Yeah, I wanted to see both sides of the coin."

"Isn't that sort of frowned upon?"

Andrew shrugged. "It was on my resume, and they asked about it during my interview. I explained that I thought the entire criminal justice system was worth learning about, and that I thought I'd be a better attorney if I knew how both sides worked. I also wanted to make sure I was making the right decision, pursuing a career down the path of prosecution. I think they appreciated my honesty."

"Probably so," Dan said. "Most people just spout shit they think the boss wants to hear."

"I can do that, too," Andrew said with a grin. "Gotta know when to do which."

"Nah, that's why I'm doing patent law," Dan said. "Cut-and-dry, no ass-kissing necessary."

"Sure. Good luck with that." Andrew clapped him on the shoulder good-naturedly. "While you're focused on intellectual property, I'll be getting criminals off the streets."

Dan took a swig of beer and leaned back on the couch, used to Andrew's digs on his choice of specialty by now. "I'll be helping people protect their dreams."

Andrew tipped his glass in Dan's direction. "I'll give you that. It might be boring as shit, but that's the one thing that would make it worthwhile."

"Speaking of boring, I can't believe I let you talk me into taking Oil and Gas Law this semester. Professor Shaw talks so slowly, I swear I could listen to him at triple speed and still understand him."

Andrew groaned. "I haven't forgiven myself, if that helps.

I figured in this part of the country it would be a good thing to know."

Logan returned with an even bigger smile on his face than when he'd left. He set a full glass of amber liquid on the table and slammed his other palm down. "Gentleman, I just got myself a date with a ginger." He sat back and lifted his hand to reveal a square napkin displaying flowy, feminine handwriting: *Lauren—555-1122*.

Andrew frowned and leaned closer. "A ginger? You mean a redhead?"

"Yup."

"Her name is Lauren?"

Logan took a drink. "That's what she said."

"Point her out to me," Andrew demanded.

Logan picked up on his tone, and his eyes narrowed. He didn't argue, though, and nodded his head to a few high-top tables on the right side of the bar. "There, with the cute Asian girl. She's the one I went over for, but somehow I ended up with the redhead's number." He shrugged. "I'm not complaining. They're both hot. Friendly, too."

Andrew's eyes found her immediately. From this far across the room she almost appeared to be a brunette, but if he was closer he would see shades of red. "That's my pharmacist."

"Nice. I like smart women. Does she work at the drugstore by your apartment?"

"No." Andrew snatched the white scrap of paper from the table. "You can't call her."

Dan raised his eyebrows in surprise.

Logan sat up straight. "Why the hell not?"

"Because it would be weird."

Logan's forehead wrinkled. "How would it be weird? She know about your STD's, or something?"

Andrew ignored that. It seemed Logan really was looking

to get his ass kicked. "She's some sort of oncology specialist. She works with Dr. Patel." Wait, had she said she wouldn't be with Dr. Patel anymore? Andrew shook the thought away. *Irrelevant.*

Logan fell silent, and Dan looked away.

"But—"

"I just don't like it, okay? I could see her when I go in for chemo, and I don't want to be wondering if you took her out the night before, or if you've kissed her."

Logan appeared dumbfounded.

"There are fifty other women in here who would be happy to let you buy them dinner. Pick any of them. Just...not that one. Okay?" Andrew stared at his friend, determined not to back down.

Something passed between them, and Logan's jaw tightened in frustration, but he sighed in surrender.

"Fine. But you owe me."

Andrew nodded. "I owe you."

He had a feeling she'd be worth whatever he had to pay.

...

Three days later, Andrew found himself in Professor Shaw's class, completely unable to focus. The aging professor never took a single step out from behind the podium and was every inch the stereotypical law professor in his pleated khakis and tweed jacket. His bushy white eyebrows even appeared to be trying to escape, pointing in several directions. Today he lectured on mineral rights, and the dry subject combined with his sluggish, monotone voice was too much to bear. Andrew would buy Dan's drinks the next time they hung out. He wanted to kick his own ass for choosing this elective.

He surreptitiously reached for his phone. Without really thinking about it, he pulled up the contact he'd created with

Lauren's phone number. He shouldn't have saved the napkin at all, much less programmed her number in.

But what if he had some medical emergency and couldn't get through to Dr. Patel's office? It might come in handy to have it.

In case of emergency.

The number had an unfamiliar area code. Where was she from? How long had she lived here? Andrew had his number changed from Nebraska to Kansas City within weeks of moving. It had probably been a petty way to send a message to his father, who, at the time, was still trying to convince Andrew he had a responsibility to the family farm.

Andrew sort of thought he had a responsibility to society at large and didn't see why doing that meant he didn't love his family. After all, it had been the injustice done to Jeni all those years ago that had sparked his interest in law in the first place.

Why couldn't Rhonda take over the farm? Why did Andrew have to be the one, just because he was the only son? Rhonda already did the accounting work for their dad—she might as well learn the ropes of everything else while she was at it.

His phone vibrated, and for a second his heart stuttered at Lauren's name on the screen. But then he realized she didn't have his number, and he'd just been looking at her contact. A banner announcing a new message was on display at the top of the screen.

Dan: *I'm dying a slow death.*

Andrew tried to stifle his snicker and peered behind him at the back row. Dan had snuck in late, and apparently hadn't wanted to join Andrew in their usual spot in the third row. Andrew was a good student and tried hard to attend every class, sit close to the front, and participate when appropriate.

For this class, though, he might need to move to the back for the rest of the semester.

"Something funny, Mr. Bishop?"

Andrew straightened and dropped the smile, tucking his phone underneath his thigh. "No, sir."

Professor Shaw's lips thinned in a disapproving manner, but he moved on. Andrew studied the clock on the wall and tried his best to stay awake.

Only forty-five minutes to go.

...

The following week, freedom was finally within reach.

"I think that's everything." Andrew reached above his head to shut the back hatch of his mom's Suburban. "I can't believe you're still driving this beast."

His mom and sisters stood in the grass beside the driveway. Rhonda approached him first.

"You'll call if you need something, right?"

"Sure," he said with a wink.

She pursed her lips but didn't argue, and turned around to say goodbye to Jeni.

Valerie came up next, wrapping her arms around him. "I'm sorry we can't stay longer," she said, her brow furrowed in concern.

"Val, you've got two kids who have been missing you these last few weeks. Even with his parents helping, I'm sure David's ready for you to come home."

"David's fine," Valerie said. "My children are angels."

Andrew snorted. "I love my niece and nephew, but angel is not the word I'd use to describe Alva. She's a terror."

"I'm telling her you said that."

"Don't you dare. I'm her favorite uncle."

"You're her only uncle."

"Doesn't matter. I won't have her knowing that she scares the living daylights out of me. I have to keep up the appearance I'm the one in control."

Valerie cocked her head to the side. "I'll think about it."

"I have cancer," he said.

Valerie narrowed her eyes. "Fine. But that's the last time you get to use that on me. I love you, little brother."

"Love you, too."

The sound of sniffling alerted Andrew of his mom's approach. Valerie gave him a look that said *good luck* and stepped aside.

"Mom..." he began, pulling her close. Her head came to his collarbone.

"Do you"—she sniffed—"want me to stay? I can send Valerie and Rhonda back with the car and rent another one to drive home when you don't need me anymore."

He winced above her head. "No, Mom. I'm fine. Really. You've seen for yourself, it's not that bad."

"But the doctor said it gets worse as you go."

"I've got a good support system going here. Jeni, Logan, and Dan...and Dr. Patel is the best there is. I live close to the cancer center. It's been great having you here, but you're not putting your whole life on hold for months while I get chemo. Dad needs you back at home. You know he can't cook worth a damn."

She nodded into his shirt. "That's the truth." She pulled back a little and looked up. "I've kept him in the loop while we've been here. He loves you, you know."

Andrew blinked. "I know that." His voice was a little sharper than he intended.

She noticed. "He's just...having a hard time with this."

"*He's* having a hard time with this?" *What about me?*

His mom gave him that look, the one where her eyes went all soft and her lips turned down at the corners. It was the same look she'd given him as a kid, when he hurt himself playing too hard and needed tending to. "Be patient with him. He's not good with emotions, and he's even worse when he's scared. I'm afraid he's dealing with both, and his default response is to shut down."

"He's kept me at arm's length for the past eight years. We really gonna pretend it's about the cancer?"

"Andrew," Jeni chided from nearby.

"I'm not getting into that right now," his mother said with a sigh. "I just want you to know that he's thinking about you, and he cares about what you're going through."

*He has a funny way of showing it.* His dad hadn't called him once since the diagnosis.

"Okay, Mom," he said. His mother had enough to worry about, and he hugged her once more. "Thanks for being here. Have a safe drive back."

He and Jeni stood by and watched the women climb into the car and drive away. When the SUV was out of sight, Andrew turned to his twin. "How does it feel to have your house back?"

"I was just thinking I'd open a beer to celebrate. Want one?"

"Nah, I think I'll head home. Let you enjoy the peace and quiet."

"Feeling okay?"

"Yeah, I have an exam tomorrow and I should study. See you Friday for chemo?"

"I'll be there."

He walked toward his car parked on the street, and Jeni called out after him. "You realize that if anything goes even the tiniest bit wrong, they'll be back?"

"I know."

"Just take care of yourself, okay? And let me help when you need it. Do us both a favor, get through your chemo without any problems, and we'll be home free."

Realistically, he knew there were many parts of this journey that were out of his control. Still, he gave Jeni a firm salute and got into his truck.

*Get through chemo without any problems.*

That was exactly what he intended to do.

# Chapter Five

"Has anyone seen my stethoscope?"

Lauren kept her eyes on her computer screen. "It's wrapped around the arm of your chair."

"How the—" Emma twisted around and the metal head of the device clinked against her seat as she unwound it. "Thanks. Hey, did that guy ever call you?"

"Nope."

Emma huffed out a breath. "I can't believe that."

"I can. He was clearly more interested in you, but you kept forcing me on him. Poor guy didn't know what to do."

Emma blinked. "Maybe he's been busy."

"It's been two weeks, Em. Let it go."

"Not a chance. We're gonna find you a guy."

"We?"

"Yes, we," came Kiara's voice. "Just because you two ditched me that night doesn't mean I'm not part of this."

"We didn't ditch you," Emma said in an exasperated tone. "You had plans with your boyfriend."

"Fiancé," Kiara corrected with a smile. She'd had special

plans that night, indeed.

"Don't rub it in," Emma grumbled.

"If you want your own fiancé that bad, you can't keep avoiding guys who want to talk to you," Lauren said, leaning back in her chair. "I guarantee if you'd offered your number instead of mine, that guy from the bar would've been blowing up *your* phone."

"Whatever."

Lauren feigned a stern expression. "Stop distracting me. Just because Dr. Stanford left and my morning clinic is over doesn't mean you can heckle me about my love life. Go see your patients and let me finish my notes."

Their conversation paused when Dr. Patel entered the room and set a paper chart next to Kiara's keyboard. She rambled off instructions and Kiara rose to discharge the patient.

"I keep trying to convince Dr. Stanford he doesn't need you for myeloma," Dr. Patel said to Lauren as she sat in front of her computer. "But he's not falling for it."

Lauren just smiled. She'd loved being in the leukemia and lymphoma clinic, but she needed a well-rounded residency education.

Emma swiveled in her chair to face Dr. Patel. "Would you like me to see one of the next ones, Dr. Patel?"

"Please." Dr. Patel unlocked her screen and pulled up the schedule. "Could you see Mr. Bishop? Zeke Young is here, and that will be a difficult conversation."

Lauren perked up. Her first thought was *Andrew's here?* followed by *What happened with Zeke?* Zeke was a forty-year-old man with non-Hodgkin lymphoma, and was the first patient she'd seen when she'd started in Dr. Patel's clinic. He'd completed his chemo regimen and gone into remission, and without the need for medication, Lauren hadn't been involved in his follow-up visits. But she thought about him often. He was a farmer and had always been accompanied by his parents, and all of them had been such kind, soft-spoken people.

She technically shouldn't ask what was going on, since she wasn't part of Zeke's care team anymore, but it was hard not to care. She'd followed him for months. Thankfully, Emma seemed as surprised as Lauren was and voiced the question in her mind.

"Why?" Emma asked.

"His surveillance bone marrow biopsy came back. His disease relapsed."

Lauren felt the word *relapse* like a punch in the gut. "Oh no."

Emma's face was stricken. "He was doing so well, I really hoped…"

Dr. Patel nodded solemnly. "Me too." She took a deep breath. "We've still got options for him, that's the important thing. But I'm worried about how today will go. I called him with the results yesterday, and he was very upset. He refused to speak to me, but his mother called back. I asked if she thought he'd come talk about his options in person, and she said she'd try to get him here."

The room was quiet for a few seconds, and Dr. Patel looked at Emma. "All that to say, I'll take that one and you see Mr. Bishop. He's here to follow up after his first chemo two weeks ago and will get day fifteen today as long as there are no issues."

"Of course." Emma turned back to her computer. "Did he get labs done?" she asked no one in particular.

"Yes," Kiara said as she reentered the room. "They're good. Want me to print a copy to take in there with you?"

"Sure."

Dr. Patel stood up and left as Kiara went to the printer to retrieve the papers. She handed them to Emma, while Lauren did her best to focus on her own screen.

Suddenly there was a loud bang in the hallway, like a door had swung open and slammed into the wall.

"I don't believe you," a deep voice bellowed.

Lauren and Emma looked at each other with wide eyes. They both went to the doorway. Lauren stepped into the hallway to find Zeke a few doors down, standing with his fists balled at his sides. His dark hair was in disarray, and even from several yards away Lauren could see his eyes were bloodshot.

His parents came out of the exam room, but he moved away from them. "Don't touch me," he yelled.

Dr. Patel remained in the exam room doorway, speaking in soothing tones. "Zeke, please calm down. I don't want to call security, but I will if I need to. Come sit down and let me talk about your options, okay?"

"I'm sorry, doctor," Zeke's father began. His voice trembled. "I think he's been drinking. He seemed subdued when we picked him up, but I didn't think…"

"Shut up, Dad!"

Zeke's mother flinched and gripped her husband's arm.

"What should we do?" Lauren jumped at Emma's whispered voice in her ear.

"I don't know. I've never seen him like this," Lauren said.

A door opened between where Lauren stood and Zeke's family congregated. Andrew's head poked out into the hallway. He surveyed the area, his eyes finding Lauren, and then turned in the opposite direction to the other occupants. Lauren heard Jeni's voice and Andrew replied to her quietly in a firm tone. He stepped fully out of his exam room, closed the door behind him, and stopped in the middle of the linoleum floor.

He stood three feet in front of Lauren, his back to her and his body slightly in front of hers, facing the distraught family. "Is everything okay?"

"Who the fuck are you?" Zeke asked.

"I'm Andrew." He held out his hand and took a step

forward. "I'm just a patient."

Zeke just looked at him, then swayed to the left, and slumped his shoulder against the wall.

"Zeke, honey..." his mother began.

At the sound of her voice, Zeke's face crumpled, and in an instant he transformed from a defensive, angry man to a fearful, forlorn son.

The hallway was silent, and it suddenly felt intrusive to be there. Zeke's father approached him and put an arm around his shoulders. For a moment they looked like a father and child about to head out to the back porch for a long talk about life. "Let's go, son."

Zeke allowed his father to lead him toward the waiting room as his mother trailed behind them, sniffing and dabbing at her eyes. She turned and mouthed, *I'm sorry* before she went through the doorway.

It seemed like everyone in the hallway exhaled at once, like they'd all been holding their breath.

"I apologize for the disturbance, Mr. Bishop," Dr. Patel said. "My PA will be right in to see you."

"No problem," Andrew said. He turned and passed a glance at Lauren before he went back into his room and closed the door.

Emma poked Lauren in the ribs, startling her again. "That's the hot patient everyone's been talking about, huh?"

Lauren gaped at her. "After what just happened, that's what you're thinking about?"

"Zeke's not the first patient to show up drunk." Emma shrugged.

He was the first one Lauren had ever encountered, but she didn't comment, noticing Emma's dress for the first time. It was perfectly professional, but accentuated Emma's tiny waist and petite, curvy body in all the right places. Emma started toward Andrew's room and Lauren frowned, darting into the workroom and back out again, a knee-length white garment in her hand.

"Emma? You forgot your coat."

Lauren found herself in the infusion center after lunch. She liked to walk through occasionally and check on the patients she knew, and chat with the nurses she'd become friends with.

Her eyes definitely weren't searching the chairs for a specific patient.

And if she was, it was purely out of professional interest. Per Emma's report to Dr. Patel, Andrew had done well after his first treatment and didn't need any changes to his regimen. Lauren wasn't convinced, though. ABVD was a nasty chemo combination.

He was young and healthy, sure. Strong and...virile, even. But you never knew with chemo, and the common phrase "everyone's different" was 100 percent true. They could give the same chemo to an eighty-year-old woman and a nineteen-year-old man, and the former could waltz through it while the latter landed himself in the hospital with fever and dehydration.

There was no way to know. He might have a medication question that he forgot to ask Emma, and maybe Lauren could help.

So. As she said...professional interest.

As she passed through a nursing station, her phone buzzed, and she fished the device from the pocket of her white coat. She'd received a text from a number she didn't recognize.

*Hi, do you remember me from McNellie's the other night?*

Lauren frowned at the screen. She considered not responding, because it had been two weeks since Emma had given Lauren's number to that guy at the bar. Either he was too busy to be dating, or he was playing games. Both were equally unappealing.

Lauren: *Kind of...it's been a while. Logan, was it?*

Logan: *Yeah. Sorry it's taken me so long to send you a message.*

He offered no additional explanation. Lauren locked her phone to put it away, but it vibrated against her hand.

Logan: *I'm not an asshole, I promise. I had a family emergency I had to deal with.*

Logan: *Forgive me?*

Lauren: *It's fine.*

Logan: *What are you up to?*

Lauren: *I'm at work, so I can't really talk right now. Can I text you later?*

Logan: *Sure.*

"Hey, Lauren."

She cringed internally when she heard the voice behind her. She turned around.

"Hey, Gavin."

He wore black scrubs today, the top way too small for his bulky frame. Either he was clueless when it came to shopping, or he was attempting to show off the muscles he seemed so proud of.

"Heard you had a crazy patient in the clinic this morning.

You okay?" His ice-blue eyes barely connected with hers as he spoke, which drove her crazy. Did he think she wouldn't notice the way he watched her mouth or looked at her chest? He leered at her when he spoke, but then when she responded he often glanced around aimlessly, like what she had to say was less important. And yet, he had repeatedly heaped useless flattery upon her and had asked her out on multiple occasions.

She assumed it was an ego thing, because she always turned him down.

He didn't know a thing about her, and his current display of concern for her well-being was almost laughable.

Instead of laughing, Lauren stiffened, feeling protective of Zeke. "He's not crazy. He'd just received terrible news and didn't handle it well. He's not a bad guy."

"Coming here wasted off his ass is pretty crazy, if you ask me. But okay." He ran a hand through his wavy blond hair. "A bunch of us are going on the Plaza this Saturday. You should come."

"No, thanks."

"Got a date?"

*None of your business.* "I need to study."

"For what? You're already a pharmacist."

She'd explained this to him no less than three times. "My oncology board exam."

"Oh."

The familiar beep of a pump indicating a finished infusion sliced through the air, and Lauren prayed it was one of Gavin's patients. Thankfully, he muttered something about catching up with her later and walked off.

Lauren resisted the urge to roll her eyes at his back and continued her circuit of the infusion center. She saw two of her other patients and stopped to check on them before moving on. Mandi's section was the last she came upon, and Mandi looked up from her computer when Lauren approached.

"Hey girl."

"Hey," Lauren said. "Busy day?"

"Always." Mandi returned her attention to the computer. "I saw Gavin talking to you a minute ago...still trying to get with you, huh?"

Lauren shrugged. "I think it has less to do with me and more to do with him thinking he's God's gift to women."

"Based on his success rate with dating the nursing staff, most of them agree with him."

Lauren was well aware of the rounds he'd made through the employees throughout the cancer center. "I don't get it. He's not bad looking or anything, but he seems like such..."

"An asshole?"

"I was going to say son of a motherless goat, but we can use yours."

Mandi snickered. "You and your fake cussing. I'll never forget the first time I met you, you hit your shoulder on the doorjamb and instead of *shit* or *dammit*, the words out of your mouth were *Bob Saget!*"

"I'm nothing, if not original," Lauren said with a grin. "But really, it's because of the kids."

Mandi nodded. "I figured," she said, and continued to type at the keyboard.

Lauren put her hands in her coat pockets and shifted on her feet. She glanced down the row of chairs in Mandi's section.

"He's not here."

"What?" Lauren forced her expression to remain calm. She'd always been a terrible liar.

Mandi's face remained expressionless, but her eyes were sharper than a twenty-seven-gauge needle. "Andrew Bishop. He just left."

"Oh. I um, I wasn't..."

The older woman's face softened, and she shrugged. "I

know he's a patient of Dr. Patel's, so I thought maybe you came to check on him. That's all."

Lauren nodded, probably too emphatically. She searched for something else relevant to say, but came up empty-handed. So she went with, "I'll see you later, then."

"Sure." Mandi winked and waved her off. "See you in two weeks."

...

Logan: *Did you forget about me?*

*Jiminy Cricket.* She totally had. She'd planned to text him when she got home from work, but now it was almost eight o'clock, and she'd holed up at The Grind House, studying.

Lauren: *I had a family emergency I had to deal with.*

Logan: *Ouch. Sounds like someone didn't forgive me after all.*

Lauren: *\*shrug\**

Logan: *Can I make it up to you? What are you doing?*

Lauren: *I'm studying, probably won't be home until late.*

Logan: *Studying for what?*

Lauren: *If you're going to ask me out, shouldn't we save that for date conversation?*

Logan: *Planning ahead. I like it. Dinner on Saturday?*

Lauren: *I can do Saturday. I'll meet you, just tell me when and where.*

Logan: *There's a new grill called Republic on the Plaza. 7:00?*

Lauren: *See you then.*

Logan: *Have fun studying.*

Lauren released a sigh and set her phone facedown on the table. She attempted to focus on her work for several minutes but had trouble concentrating.

She was trying to put herself out there because Emma was right. It had been two years since she'd been on a date. But she didn't particularly want to go out with Logan. He'd been smooth and charming at the bar that night and was attractive in a boy-next-door kind of way, with curly blond hair and blue eyes framed by laugh lines. His approach had been confident and flattering, and he'd clearly been interested in Emma at the start. But Emma had claimed that she had a boyfriend—she didn't—and to his credit, Logan hadn't seemed disappointed to shift his attention to Lauren. He said he was in marketing, which was a perfectly respectable career.

So why wasn't she more excited? Why did she feel indifferent toward him, and the prospect of getting to know him better? Was it ridiculous for her to think she'd one day feel that spark…that sudden, unexplainable attraction, to someone? Like she'd felt when she'd run into Andrew, in this very room?

Lauren closed her eyes and laid her forehead in her palm, her elbow propped on the table. She couldn't stop thinking about him, and it was becoming a problem.

Andrew's eyes.

Andrew's smile.

Andrew's hands.

She ground her teeth together in frustration. This was

bad. Very bad.

He was a patient. He was off-limits. *Right?* Even if she wasn't directly over his care anymore, she was a provider at the cancer center where he was receiving treatment.

Plus, as previously discussed, he was too attractive. Even if he hadn't ended up in her clinic that day, she still wouldn't have been interested.

Shouldn't have been, anyway. She couldn't even convince herself—no wonder Mandi had given her the side-eye.

*Stop it. Focus. You're here to study, and you're going on a date with someone else. Everything is F-I-N-E.*

Pep talk complete, Lauren lifted her head and opened her eyes, to find herself looking right at a smiling Andrew.

"Hi."

Lauren blinked.

He was still there. Still smiling.

"Andrew? What are you doing here?"

"I'm here to study." He held a laptop and notebook in one hand. "What are you doing here?"

"Same." Lauren's pulse sped up and she pulled at her ponytail, a nervous gesture she'd picked up in her teenage years.

She took him in, standing tall before her, wearing fitted jeans and the same blue hoodie as the first time they'd met. Square shoulders and rounded biceps filled out his upper body, and his pushed-up sleeves revealed muscled forearms. A light, scruffy layer of facial hair covered a perfectly symmetrical jaw and his thick, chestnut hair was still very much present, the chemotherapy not having ravaged that part of his body yet.

His brown eyes scanned the tables that surrounded them. Lauren knew they were all full, as she'd hovered for ten minutes for a couple to leave before she'd snagged the one she currently sat at.

"You can sit here," she offered. She was alone at a four-top table. "There's plenty of room. It gets packed here on Friday nights."

"You sure?" At her nod, Andrew set his stuff down diagonally across from her. "Thanks."

Lauren had spread out all over the table and pulled her materials closer to her corner. "If I remember right, your sister said you're soon to be a mediocre attorney...that must mean you're in law school?"

"Yep. I'm in my third year."

"What kind of law do you want to practice?"

"Criminal justice." He opened his laptop and leaned back in his chair. "What are you studying for?"

"The oncology pharmacy board exam. It's an optional certification, but if I get a permanent job at the cancer center after my residency, they'll expect me to take it."

A slight frown formed between his eyebrows. "What is a pharmacy residency, exactly?"

"After I finished pharmacy school, I could have gotten a job at a retail pharmacy, like the chain drugstores, right away. Or gone back home to work for my dad—he owns an independent drugstore in Oklahoma." A wave of guilt rose up at the thought of her dad, but she forced it down. "But during my second year of pharmacy school I got a job at Children's Hospital for some extra money.

"There's a clinical oncology pharmacist who helps manage their medications, and before that I'd never seen that side of pharmacy. Kind of like physicians, we have to do extra training if we want to specialize. After I got my degree, I applied for residencies in oncology. There aren't many of them, but they're becoming more common. It's two years for oncology, and I'll finish next spring."

"That's cool," Andrew said. "I didn't know pharmacists did that sort of thing. My sisters couldn't stop talking about how great you were, telling us about the chemo."

Lauren smiled at the compliment. "I really want to stay. I love it here." Kansas City had become home to her, and the girls from the cancer center were like her family. It had been a long time since she'd felt like she belonged somewhere.

She wasn't eager to go back to being nothing but an afterthought (by her mother) or simply a solution to a business crisis (by her father). But if this job didn't pan out, she wasn't sure she'd have another option.

"You're from Oklahoma, you said?"

She nodded. "Cedar Creek. It's a suburb of Oklahoma City. What about you?"

"A tiny town in Nebraska. I moved here for law school."

"Your whole family moved with you?" The involvement Andrew's family had in his care warmed Lauren's heart. His family seemed nothing like hers, and though she found it overwhelming, she was envious of the obvious love between them.

"Hell, no. Thank God," Andrew said with a laugh. "Just my twin sister, Jeni, lives here. She moved here for a job a few months ago. The others still live up north. They all came down for the first oncologist visit and chemo treatment. We have a farm, so my dad had to stay behind to keep an eye on things, and I guarantee he enjoyed having peace and quiet for once. Those women are suffocating."

"They seem wonderful."

"Wonderfully annoying."

"They obviously adore you."

"Who wouldn't? I'm adorable." He grinned at her, his white teeth flashing.

Returning his smile, because she couldn't possibly respond in any other way, Lauren searched for something witty to say.

Her buzzing phone saved her, but as she retrieved it her elbow pushed several papers off the table.

"Peter Parker," she said under her breath, as the pages fluttered to the floor like snowflakes.

Andrew immediately joined her on the floor to gather them together. Papers in hand, Lauren straightened and slammed her head on the underside of the table. The grunt that came out of her mouth was exceedingly unladylike, and her cheeks flushed scarlet.

"You okay?" Andrew's hand brushed the top of her head as they both stood up. Her breath caught at the contact.

She stepped back and sat down. "I'm fine."

"Peter Parker?" He resumed his seat. "What is it with you and superheroes?"

Lauren recalled what she'd said the day she spilled coffee on him. "I wouldn't consider Captain Kirk a superhero."

Andrew raised an eyebrow. "I respectfully disagree."

Lauren waited a moment. "That's all you've got? You really will be a mediocre lawyer."

He laughed. "Seriously, what's with the names?"

"For two years I worked at Children's Hospital, and for two more I've volunteered there, spending time with the kids." She straightened the papers in front of her. "We have to be careful what we say around them. And just like the regular cuss words, the silly ones become a habit, and they just sort of come out. The nurses and I made a game of it…to see who could come up with the most creative ways to curse without actually cursing."

"I hope you won."

"The competition is ongoing."

They continued talking for a few minutes, and Lauren picked up her coffee mug to find it empty.

Andrew rose and held his hand out for it. "Here, let me. I need to order something, and I don't trust you with a hot beverage."

Lauren scowled, and he winked at her before he walked to the front counter.

He returned with two cups full to the brim, and the aroma of freshly brewed coffee drifted across the table.

"What was going on this morning? With that guy?" Andrew asked.

Confusion clouded Lauren's thoughts for a moment before she realized he must be asking about Zeke. She scrunched her nose in apology. "I can't talk about it. Patient privacy rules are pretty strict."

"Oh." Andrew took a drink of his steaming coffee. "I guess that's good to know. That you haven't been going around telling everyone how my mom asked about sex."

Lauren grinned at him even as her stomach flipped at the word coming out of his mouth. Goodness, what was she, twelve? "Never."

His eyes dropped to the tabletop, and the sudden silence seemed intensified despite the low hum of nearby conversation surrounding them.

"Are you doing okay? Really?" she asked. "Like I said before...I have a hard time believing men if they have no complaints."

He met her gaze. "Honestly? I'm tired. My appetite is weird, and certain smells bother me." He raked his fingers through his hair. "Can I be honest and say I'm dreading going bald? I know I'm a guy and I shouldn't care, but I don't think it's gonna be a good look for me."

He lowered his hand and looked away, and in that second he seemed so vulnerable and unsure, Lauren would have done just about anything to make it better. "I don't think you need to worry," she said quietly.

"What?" His eyes were back on her.

"I said I don't think you need to worry."

"What do you mean?" He lifted an eyebrow, teasing her.

She narrowed her eyes. "You know exactly what I'm saying."

"You think I'm hot?"

"I think you know how attractive you are."

Andrew's face turned serious. "Do you know how attractive *you* are?"

She felt her face warm. "I..."

"Because you are," he interrupted. "You're beautiful."

Her limbs suddenly felt weak, and she wrapped her fingers around the edge of her seat for balance.

He continued, either not noticing or not concerned that he'd unnerved her. "I've thought about you a lot since we first met. And I don't mean at the cancer center." They both glanced in the direction of the self-serve coffee area.

"Me, too," she admitted against her better judgment. It was nice to know she wasn't the only one who had replayed that morning in her head.

"Would you go out with me? For coffee, or a drink? Dinner, even?"

"We're having coffee right now."

"We're studying. This doesn't count."

"I haven't looked at my books once since you showed up."

"It wasn't agreed upon that this was a date prior to the event," he argued. "Therefore, it doesn't count."

"Not mediocre anymore," she said under her breath.

He draped one arm across the chair to his left and grinned, a triumphant glint in his eyes. "Is that a yes?"

"No."

He frowned. "You're saying no?"

"No."

His head cocked sideways. "What, then?"

Lauren wrapped her fingers around her coffee mug and looked down at her hands for a moment. What did he want from her? What could his end goal possibly be? She raised her eyes back to his incredibly handsome face.

"Why?"

# Chapter Six

"Why what?" Andrew stared at her. "Why do I want to go out with you?"

She nodded.

What kind of question was that? Who wouldn't want to go out with her? "I'm attracted to you. You make me laugh, even if it's because your jokes are terrible. You're smart, and you've devoted your life to helping people. Those are the things I know about you so far, and it's not enough. I want to know more."

She wanted to say yes. He could see it in her eyes. The way her lips tipped up into a smile, and her shoulders relaxed the tiniest bit.

She sighed. "I want to. But I don't think I should."

Now it was his turn to ask, "Why?"

"Because I work at the cancer center. It feels...I don't know...unethical, I guess. I don't want anyone to think you're getting special treatment, or get Dr. Patel in trouble."

Andrew hadn't considered any of that. "But you're not in Dr. Patel's clinic anymore, right?"

"No. But I was part of your care team at the beginning, and my name is documented in your chart. I really want to get a job there when I'm done, and I don't want to risk doing something that might be perceived as unprofessional."

He didn't want to seem pushy, but she'd said she *wanted* to. *He* wanted her to. "Is there a formal policy against it?"

"There is against physicians having relationships with patients. I don't know about the rest of us, or when it's a patient from a different clinic."

He wasn't willing to give up without hard evidence. "If we don't know for certain, can we assume there isn't?" He leaned forward, resting his forearms on the table. "Please, let me spend more time with you."

She looked at his hands, and he focused to keep them steady. He felt a little out of his element...he wasn't normally this nervous. Women rarely made him work this hard when he asked them out. That wasn't the only reason he grew uneasy, though. He didn't think he'd ever been so invested in the outcome before.

He wanted her to say *yes* so badly he ached with it.

He supposed the pain could've been related to the lymphoma, or the chemo...but he didn't think so.

"I don't know." She ran a hand along the back of her hair and circled her fingers around her ponytail, a gesture he noticed she did often. Was she nervous, too?

"What if I'd had my appointment a day later, and you'd never seen me at the cancer center? If you hadn't run out so fast and I asked you out when you spilled coffee on me, what would you have said?"

Lauren countered with a question of her own. "Didn't you just get out of a relationship? Someone named Caroline?"

Andrew was surprised she remembered Caroline's name. Caroline had been mentioned in front of her what, once? Nearly a month ago? "It's been almost two months. I'm not looking for a rebound, if that's what you're worried about."

"Was your sister right? Did she end it because of your diagnosis?" Anger flashed in her eyes, and he bit back a grin. His sisters' overprotective natures got tiresome, but Lauren feeling defensive on his behalf was strangely satisfying.

"Not exactly," he hedged.

Lauren lowered her eyes and shook her head. "I'm sorry, I don't know why I asked that. It's none of my business."

He didn't want to talk about Caroline, so he said nothing more. He watched her for a moment, unsure what else he could say to convince her. Or if he even should try to convince her. He wasn't into forcing a woman to do something.

Then again, she said she wanted to...she was just worried about her job.

Suddenly, another thought struck him. "Are you dating someone?"

Her reply was immediate. "No."

But he knew she had agreed to a date with Logan tomorrow night. She didn't know Logan and Andrew knew each other, or that Andrew had been the one to end up with her phone number. His immediate goal that night at McNellie's had been to prevent Logan from pursuing her, but later that evening he'd considered the possibilities. For himself.

After starting and deleting several texts over the course of the past two weeks, the events of this morning had finally prompted him to action. When he'd seen Lauren standing just a few feet from what appeared to be an unstable, inebriated patient, the instinct to protect her had overwhelmed him.

And then during his chemo treatment in the afternoon, he'd watched the door for her, hoping she'd pass by. When she didn't, the disappointment that had washed through him had been considerable. He realized how deeply interested he was in her, and as a cancer patient, time wasn't a guarantee he had the luxury of having.

So, he'd done what any level-headed man would do. He'd used the phone number she'd given to his best friend, pretended to be that friend, and charmed her into agreeing to go out with him. When she'd told "Logan" she was studying tonight, Andrew had a thought she might have come here. He had been studying on his couch at home and decided he could use a change of scenery.

Until this moment, though, he hadn't considered that she might be excited about the prospect of seeing Logan again. She *had* given Logan her number, after all. And had been less than thrilled that two weeks had passed before he contacted her... Had she waited in anticipation and been disappointed when he hadn't called her the next day? According to his sisters, Logan was good-looking, and Andrew knew he never had trouble with women. Could it be that Lauren's hesitation to go out with Andrew stemmed from her desire to see how it went with Logan first?

Problem was...they were one and the same.

*Shit. I've really dug myself into a hole now.*

Her quiet voice brought him out of his reverie. "I'm sorry." She gathered her belongings into a pile on the table, and she stood. The black shirt she wore brought out the brightness of her eyes, and the color was a lovely contrast against her pale skin.

*Don't go*, he wanted to say.

She took a deep breath and exhaled, her eyes on his. "I just can't." She picked up her things and turned to face the door. "I'm sorry."

Then she was gone.

*This is a mistake.*

Andrew closed his eyes and leaned his head against the headrest. Scrubbing one hand down his face, he pounded the steering wheel with the other.

He sat in the Republic parking lot. It was two minutes past seven, and because pharmacists had to be some of the most detail-oriented people on the planet, he'd bet his left arm that Lauren was already inside.

Waiting for Logan.

What the fuck had he been thinking?

An hour ago, it had been: *I have cancer. Yes, the chances of complete cure are greater than 80 percent for the type and stage I have…but 20 percent don't get there. What if I'm that 20 percent? This is not a time for fear. It's a time to take risks. To live life and go after what I want with both hands.*

Now, it was: *I'm a complete moron.*

He wouldn't stand her up, though, even if the only person it made look bad was Logan. Andrew couldn't do that to her.

*Man up and get in there.*

He slid both hands through his hair, straightened the collar of his button-down shirt, and got out of the car. His stomach was in knots.

Once inside, he stopped at the hostess stand.

"Reservation for two for Andr—I mean, Logan Davis."

The young woman at the podium referenced her book and smiled at him. "Follow me."

She led him through the maze of tables, and Andrew's palms began to sweat. He focused on breathing as his eyes darted from table to table until he saw her. In a stroke of luck she was facing away from the door and hadn't caught sight of him yet.

"I see her. Thank you," he said to the hostess, hoping that would suffice as a dismissal. He wasn't sure what kind of reception he was about to get and didn't particularly want an audience.

His eyes never strayed from Lauren's beautiful auburn hair, which she wore down in long waves. He took a deep breath and fisted his hands at his side. Approaching on her left, he stopped at the edge of the table.

She was reading a menu but looked up when she sensed his presence. Surprise registered on her face.

"Andrew?" She looked past him, then her eyes returned to his face.

He offered her a cautious smile. "So, funny story…"

Her eyes narrowed.

Andrew wiped his hands across his jeans.

"Logan's my best friend. I was with him the night you gave him your number." His pulse raced, but he forged ahead. "I told him who you were, that I knew you, and that it would be weird for me if he called you. I took your number, and for two weeks talked myself out of using it. But I couldn't do it anymore. I'm the one who texted you yesterday."

Lauren didn't respond right away. Her jaw was tight, but otherwise her face was devoid of obvious emotion.

Andrew had grown up around four women, and knew silence was deceptive. Any time he'd done something stupid, a calm demeanor from his mother had told him things were about to get very bad.

And if Valerie appeared cool and collected? Lord have mercy.

It was awkward just standing there, so he sat down across from her. "I'm sorry," he added. "I know it was wrong."

Lauren simply stared at him, her eyes moving back and forth between his, like she was searching for something. Still, she said nothing.

"Are you mad?" he asked.

She pursed her lips and took in a long, deep breath, the process seeming to take an entire minute. "Would you be?"

"Probably," he admitted.

"Then there's your answer," she said stiffly.

A strange sensation of fullness lodged in Andrew's throat. He swallowed it down. "You're right. I'm sorry to put you in this position. I should go."

He was halfway out of his chair when Lauren's hand grabbed his forearm. "Wait."

Andrew lowered himself back down. She rubbed her temple with her opposite hand, and then her green eyes met his.

"We're both already here," she said. "I'm starving. Let's at least have dinner. But this doesn't mean anything, okay?"

"Understood." He picked up his menu and offered her a small, sincere smile as a sort of peace offering.

She tentatively returned the gesture and he thought, not for the first time, how unconventional her beauty was. Her emerald-green eyes were a little too big for her face, but in a way that made it difficult to look away from them. Several other features made a fair play to steal his attention, though. The hair, for one, made her stand out like a rose among thorns. Perfectly pink lips and a delightful collection of freckles across her cheekbones. And those curves...

The server approached the table to take their drink orders, interrupting Andrew's silent appraisal. He gestured for Lauren to go first. He had avoided alcohol since he started chemo, and his stomach hadn't settled from his earlier anxiety about meeting Lauren, so he asked for water.

When the server left, Lauren asked, "Are you feeling okay?"

"I'm great."

"Are you sure? You had chemo yesterday."

"I'm sure. I have this incredible pharmacist who hooked me up with the good drugs. Plus, she's gorgeous, so there's that."

The flirtatious words just sort of came out of his mouth,

and he regretted them immediately.

Surprisingly, though, she gifted him with a genuine smile. "That has nothing to do with drugs, or how you're feeling."

Might as well take it the full mile. "I beg to differ. Being with you right now makes me feel a hell of a lot better than any drug out there ever could."

"I'm a professional. Flattery will get you nowhere, Mr. Bishop."

*Damn.* It surprised him how much he liked hearing her address him like that. "We'll see about that."

Her smile lessened a fraction. "Seriously, do you have your nausea meds with you? Just in case?"

"Seriously. Can we pretend you don't know that part about me? If we're going to have dinner together, I want you to know me apart from my diagnosis. And I want to know you apart from your role as my pharmacist."

"Oncology is a big part of my life," she said. "It's been the biggest part of my life for nearly the last two years. You can't get to know me without it."

"That's okay, just tell me the stuff that doesn't relate to me. Like the volunteer work you do at Children's Hospital."

Their drinks arrived and they placed their food order, and Lauren told him about the kids she spent time with every Saturday morning.

"At first I thought it would be awful. I mean, what could be sadder than kids with cancer?"

Andrew couldn't think of anything.

"But mostly, they're still just happy, playful kids. Usually when I'm there I hang out in the game room, where they have toys and books and video games...and if it weren't for the IV poles and bald kids, you'd have no idea it was the oncology ward of a children's hospital. There's this little boy named Max who has leukemia, he's four, and every time I see him I want to wrap him up and take him home with me. He's the happiest, silliest, funniest kid I've ever met."

"Toys and video games? Can I get my chemo over there?"

She laughed. "No. But you could volunteer if you want to. Sometimes I have a hard time getting to know the older kids. For teenagers, it's all about being able to connect with what they're going through. They don't trust me enough to let me in and get to know them."

Andrew took a drink of water. "That's not a bad idea. What do I have to do to get involved?"

"You have to pass a background check and take some required online training. I'll send you the info, and you can look into it."

He would. Even though his cancer journey was just starting, the outpouring of support from his family and friends overwhelmed him. It gave him confidence that he could make it through anything that came up, no matter how dire. If he could be that support to someone else, a kid, no less, simply because life had dealt the same hand of cards? Count him in.

Plus, it would give him the chance for more time with Lauren.

He'd take all of that he could get.

# Chapter Seven

By the time their meals arrived, they'd covered several standard first date topics.

But this wasn't a first date...she hoped she'd made that clear.

Why did it still feel like one?

They had similar taste in music, both enjoying indie and folk rock. At first Andrew didn't seem to believe she didn't like country music, but she'd insisted not everyone from Oklahoma listened to honky-tonk.

Neither had much time to read outside of work or school, but when they did, Andrew said he chose crime thrillers by authors like John Grisham and James Patterson. Lauren admitted she preferred romance novels.

"Like the kind with half-dressed men on the cover?" Andrew asked, a wide grin on his face.

"Don't you know you shouldn't judge a book by its cover?"

"That's a yes."

She speared an asparagus stalk with her fork. "Have you

traveled much?"

"A little. We took a family vacation to Hawaii when I was thirteen, and I went to London with some buddies over one spring break in college. Other than that, just places around the US. What about you?"

"If it doesn't border Oklahoma, I haven't been there."

"Really? Do you enjoy travelling?"

"I love it. I'd jump at the chance to see new places."

"Was your family not big on it?"

Lauren took a sip of wine while she considered how to answer. "My parents divorced when I was young. My mom travels a lot, but I grew up with my dad. He doesn't drift far from home." She set her glass down. "But when I'm finished with residency and get a job, I'll go places."

"I hear that. It feels impossible to do anything fun while I'm in school."

"The end is in sight for both of us." Lauren leaned back and regarded her companion—*not* her date—admiring the way his chest filled out his dress shirt and the way his jaw flexed as he chewed. *Good grief, get a hold of yourself, woman.* "So. Tell me three unique things about Andrew Bishop."

Appearing surprised, Andrew said, "Like what?"

"Anything. What makes you different from the guy at the next table over? From my ex-boyfriend? From Logan?" She winked, and he grinned. "The stranger the better."

Andrew rubbed his chin. "Wow. Uh…okay, here's one. I hate pickles."

"I ask you for a unique fact about yourself and you're giving me pickles?"

"What? My sisters love them. They think it's weird that I hate them," he said before taking a bite of steak.

Her expression went flat. "Come on, you can do better than that. Hating pickles is no big dill."

His face was blank for a beat before he laughed, a rich, throaty sound.

She smiled wide, unable to help herself. "That's one of mine. I'm a master of puns."

"Oh, I remember. Im-*port*-ant?" He shook his head. "What else have you got?"

"I asked you first." She looked down and focused on cutting a piece of chicken, like she had all the time in the world.

"Okay." He took another bite and leaned back in his chair, chewing and swallowing before he spoke again. "My favorite color is pink."

"Is not."

"I swear. Always has been. I know it's not a traditional favorite color for men, but I don't see what the big deal is. There are so many great things that are pink, like cotton candy. Shrimp scampi. A medium steak. Elvis's Cadillac."

"Tutus. Hair ribbons. Flowers..." Lauren teased.

"If you think you're the first woman to make fun of me for that, guess again."

"Well. If you like women who wear pink you'll be sorely disappointed by me. With my hair and complexion, pink and I do *not* go well together."

"Permission to flatter?" he asked.

She shook her head, despite the fact she'd love to hear what he wanted to say. "Denied."

Andrew grunted. "Fine. I'll save it for later." He pointed a finger at her. "You're up."

"I love documentaries."

"Seriously? Me too."

"Yeah? Did you see that one about the guy who walked the tightrope between the New York City skyscrapers?"

"*Man on Wire*? Loved it. Right now I'm watching one about the top chefs around the world—"

"*Chef's Table*?"

"That's it."

"I'm on episode six. I can't stop. I watched both seasons of *Making a Murderer* in a single weekend."

Andrew put his hands flat on the table. "Marry me."

Lauren froze for a split second, then burst out laughing. He grinned at her, and it was becoming increasingly difficult to remember that this was supposed to be a friendly dinner. "Okay, last one. You've got one more chance to impress me."

Andrew raised his eyes to the ceiling, and she waited patiently while he considered his options.

"This could go either way, and in most circles would be unimpressive. But I guarantee it will set me apart from Logan. And probably the guy at the next table."

She put her fork down and placed her hands in her lap, intrigued.

"I didn't kiss a girl until I was twenty."

Her mouth dropped open, and she quickly tried to recover by shifting to a neutral expression. Was he joking? She raised her chin a notch and asked, "You messing with me?"

"Not at all."

"Did you...were you kissing guys? Before that?"

Andrew coughed, his shoulders rolling forward. "No! What the hell?"

She shrugged. It was a reasonable assumption. "I just don't understand," she said. "I mean, look at you."

His eyes crinkled at the corners when he smiled. "You didn't ask for permission to flatter me."

"It isn't flattery, just an objective statement of fact. By society's standard of beauty, you're a handsome man."

"I don't care about society's standard. What about yours?"

"I like to get to know someone before I make a final decision. Personality plays a big part."

"I'm glad I tricked you into coming to dinner with me, then."

"Me, too," she said quietly, hesitant to admit it. "Are you gonna explain the no kissing thing? Or just leave me to wonder? So far I've come up with a religious pact or cystic acne."

"It was a combination of things, really. I guess the acne is the closest to the truth, because for most of middle and high school my choices were limited because of how I looked. I was exceptionally tall but couldn't keep weight on, no matter what I did. Based on how much I ate, I should have weighed three hundred pounds, but instead I was so skinny my nickname was Skeletor."

"That's terrible." Her eyes traveled across his chest and shoulders, and she added, "And hard to believe."

Did his cheeks just turn pink? "I filled out."

He most certainly had.

"I didn't have an actual girlfriend until college, and even though I could have kissed someone at a party or something before that, I guess I never liked a girl enough. I'm kind of old-fashioned and think even something as simple as a kiss should be shared with care."

Her shoulders went slack. "Are you for real?"

He looked down at his body in the chair and back to her face. "I think so."

"I didn't think men like you existed anymore."

"Honesty compels me to tell you that I'm no saint. I made up for lost time. Even so, I stand by what I said."

She didn't respond because the server chose that moment to approach the table. After a small argument, Andrew relented and allowed Lauren to pay her share, and they walked outside together. Small white lights were strung between the street lights, casting a soft glow along the sidewalk.

Andrew suggested they walk around. Lauren agreed,

because as much as it went against her better judgment, she didn't want the evening to end. Andrew was fun, easy to talk to, and a good listener. If this had been an actual date, she would have counted it as the best one she'd ever had.

A small fountain stood across the street from the restaurant, and as they approached the edge, Lauren reached into her purse. She pulled out two coins and held one out to him. "Here. Make a wish."

He took the silver coin and immediately tossed it into the water.

"What was that?" she accused, frowning. "You didn't even think about it."

It was cooler outside than she anticipated, and she shivered. Andrew removed his jacket to place it around her shoulders. Warmth and his clean, masculine scent enveloped her. He turned her around to face him and pulled the front together across her torso, tilting his chin down toward her upturned face. His brown eyes met hers intently as a gust of wind swept through, causing her hair to swirl around her face. He placed both hands on her temples and slid them down to her cheeks, taming the strands underneath his fingers.

Conscious thought hovered just out of reach.

"I didn't need to think about it," he said, his voice quiet but firm. "I already knew what I wanted to wish for."

Almost as if drawn by a magnet, she put one hand against his chest, and she wasn't certain whether it was to push him away or invite him closer. His head lowered, his eyes searching hers, probably looking for some indication of whether or not she wanted this.

*Absolutely not and a thousand times yes.*

Her other hand came up to join the first, and it landed right on top of his port. Her fingers traced the raised mound, and she pulled back with a sharp intake of breath. Her eyes went wide.

"I can't do this." She stepped back. She slipped out of his jacket and handed it to him. "I should go."

He just looked at her, his jacket held loosely by his side, disappointment in his eyes.

Unable to think of anything else to say, she turned and darted across the empty street in the direction of the parking lot. Once she reached her car, she chanced a look around, wondering if he'd come after her.

He hadn't. She should be relieved, but she felt a strange sense of loss. She didn't like it, and she forced down the sensation of deep regret as she started her car and headed home.

. . .

An hour after she got home, she sent Andrew a text message.

Lauren: *I'm sorry I left like that.*

Andrew: *Me too.*

Lauren: *I had a wonderful time tonight. It just feels wrong to get involved with you.*

Andrew: *Is your job the only thing holding you back?*

Lauren: *No. It's also because of your situation. A new relationship is the last thing you need right now. You're undergoing treatment for cancer, for crying out loud.*

Andrew: *You think I can't handle chemo and you at the same time?*

An image of Andrew appeared in her mind, standing tall over her. Large, muscular, imposing.

Lauren: *I think you should focus on what's most important.*

Andrew: *Can we be friends, at least?*

Lauren: *I'd like that.*

Andrew: *Friends with benefits?*

Lauren: *You're walking a fine line, Mr. Bishop.*

Andrew: *Friends don't address each other with such formality.*

Lauren: *Goodnight, Andrew.*

...

Sunday was Lauren's favorite day of the week. Her routine consisted of sleeping in, taking a walk around the neighborhood, and enjoying a cup of coffee at one of the shops near her house. Today was no different, and after a relaxing morning, she'd landed on her couch with her board exam study materials.

Midafternoon, her phone lit up with a text message.

Andrew: *You owe me, you know.*

Lauren: *Hello to you, too. Owe you what?*

Andrew: *Another unique fact about Lauren Taylor.*

Lauren: *I told you three.*

Andrew: *No you didn't. You gave me documentaries and puns.*

She thought back to the night before. He was right.

Lauren: *Okay. Let me think.*

Andrew: *...*

Lauren: *Don't rush me*

Andrew: *...*

Lauren: *I can flip an omelet like a boss.*

Andrew: *You're lucky I've been watching Chef's Table all day, otherwise I might be less impressed by that. I do love a good omelet.*

Lauren: *They're egg-cellent for breakfast.*

Andrew: *Nope.*

Lauren: *No?*

Andrew: *Nope.*

Lauren: *C'mon. Puns are hilarious. Try it.*

Andrew: *Definitely not*

Lauren: *You're right, it's not easy. Probably best you don't strain yourself.*
Lauren: *Hello?*
Lauren: *Are you still there?*

Andrew: *Give a man a minute to think.*
Andrew: *Okay...you really want a pizza this?*
Andrew: *I DID IT*
Andrew: *Pizza = piece of*

Lauren: *OMG you can't explain yourself*

Andrew: *I'm in the presence of pun greatness. I can't*

*help it if I doughnut belong here.*

Lauren: *You're kiwing me*

Andrew: *You butter back off, friend*

Lauren: *Do you really wanna taco 'bout this?*

Andrew: *I felt that one from my head tomatoes*

Lauren: *That was a good one. Lettuce celebrate.*

Andrew: *I'm just trying to ketchup*

Lauren: *Berry good work*
Lauren: *Wait, I want to take that one back. I can do better.*

Andrew: *No take-backs*
Andrew: *I win*

Lauren: *You win?*

Andrew: *The first ever Andrew-Lauren Pun War.*

Lauren: *You should know I took it easy on you. You're a newbie.*

Andrew: *We'll call this round one, then.*

Lauren: *To be continued…*

• • •

"What are you doing for Thanksgiving next week?" Emma swiveled in a half circle and twirled a strand of dark hair around one finger. It was Friday afternoon and the clinic was quiet. Lauren and Dr. Stanford had just seen their last patient of the day, and Emma had one left to see. Kiara had taken the week off to travel home to California, her brand-new fiancé in tow.

"Nothing."

Emma made a face. "Nothing?"

"I don't mind spending it alone. It's not worth it to travel home for just the day," Lauren said. She didn't mention that she didn't particularly want to go home. When she'd finally called her dad back, she'd caved and agreed to work as a fill-in pharmacist for two days at his store around Christmas. One trip to Oklahoma was enough. "I'm expected at Children's Hospital that Saturday, and I ended up picking up a pharmacy shift Thanksgiving morning at the adult hospital. It's not like I'm just going to sit at home all day." She leaned forward and took a bite of the pumpkin pie Mr. Jones, a long-time patient, had brought that morning. It was sweet, moist, and had the perfect amount of spice. Lauren sighed with appreciation.

A frown lingered on Emma's face. "Why don't you come to my parents' house when you get off? My mom loves you. We don't have traditional Thanksgiving food for dinner, but she's making a killer *banh xeo*. And *bun rieu*."

"That's really nice of you." Lauren smiled, flattered at the invitation when she'd spent countless holidays alone. "Can I see how I feel after my shift? I might be in the mood to just crash and watch this new documentary in my queue."

Emma rolled her eyes. "You're such a nerd."

Lauren had no argument.

One of the medical assistants walked into the room with a chart and handed it to Emma.

"Hey, could you do me a favor while I see this last patient?" Emma asked.

"Sure."

Emma held out several sheets of paper. "Andrew Bishop called and requested a copy of his original PET scan report. He didn't have an appointment, but I told him I'd run it down to infusion when he was here for chemo. Since you know him, could you take it for me?"

Lauren's muscles tensed. "What do you mean, I know him?"

"You know who he is, right? You did his chemo counseling. I can't imagine any red-blooded female would forget that face," Emma said with a laugh. "If you're busy, don't worry about it. I just thought maybe we could both get out of here a little early."

Lauren kept her face carefully disinterested and took the pages. "I can do that."

"Thanks." Emma stood up and walked out, chart in hand.

Lauren headed toward the stairwell, her heart doing a strange thump in her chest when she saw Andrew's name at the top of the page.

Andrew and Jeni were in the front of Mandi's section today, and both were looking at their phones when Lauren approached.

"Hi."

"Hey, Lauren," Jeni said.

Andrew jerked his gaze up, and a wide smile spread across his face. "Hey."

"How's it going?" Lauren's return smile was tentative. It was the first time they'd seen each other in person since the non-kiss, and she felt a little awkward.

This wasn't the first time they'd spoken though...far from it. It had been nearly two weeks since that night, and they'd texted almost every day since. Lauren never texted Andrew first, but he always seemed to find a reason to send her a message. She wasn't going to be rude and ignore him.

If she didn't initiate the communication, it wasn't as bad...right? Her entire life, Lauren had walked the straight and narrow. She'd be the first to admit she was completely out of her element with this...whatever this was.

Andrew wore a beanie on his head, and there wasn't a hint of hair near the bottom edge. He must have shaved his head.

Lucky for him and unlucky for her, he looked good in the hat. *Really* good. It was one of those oversized, slouched-types that David Beckham wore through every airport around the world.

She remembered his insecure comment about losing his hair, and she focused her eyes on his.

"We were just talking about Thanksgiving," Jeni said. She dropped her feet to the floor and sat up straight. "I prevented a mass exodus of Bishops from Nebraska to Missouri, which would have included no less than eight minivans and pickup trucks full of extended family. I used Andrew here as an excuse, and it worked like a charm."

"Who knew there would be a silver lining to having cancer?" Andrew said with a grin.

"You'd be surprised," Lauren said. "For such a terrible thing, I've heard countless stories of positive things that come from it."

"What are your holiday plans?" Jeni asked.

"I picked up a morning shift in the hospital pharmacy," Lauren replied. "I don't normally work over there, but I don't have any other plans, and I figured I could give someone else the morning off."

"And after that?"

Lauren shrugged. "I've got too much going on to travel to Oklahoma, so I'm hanging around here. I'll enjoy having an afternoon and evening off."

"You should come to my house," Jeni said.

Andrew raised an eyebrow at his sister.

"That's...very nice of you," Lauren said slowly.

"It's just going to be Andrew and me. We were going to

order pizza and watch *Parks and Recreation* reruns all night."

Seriously? She loved *Parks and Rec*.

"Doesn't that sound wonderful?" Jeni continued.

"It does, actually," Lauren said. "But I don't think I shou—"

"Just think about it, okay?" Jeni interrupted. "If you want to enjoy some time alone, I totally get it. But if you decide you want company, you're welcome to come hang out."

Lauren shifted on her feet and rubbed one forearm with the opposite hand as she considered how to politely decline.

"Don't decide right now," Andrew added. He rubbed the back of his neck, the muscles in his forearm rippling. "See how you feel after you get off work on Thursday and let me know. No big deal either way."

It would be a lot easier to say no via text message. "Okay. I'll let you know." She realized she still held his scan report in her hand. "Here's the PET scan report you asked for. Emma told me to bring it by."

Andrew took the papers. "Thanks. My mom insisted I get copies of everything."

"It's not a bad idea," Lauren agreed. "It makes things easier if you ever decide you want a second opinion about something."

"I'm not going anywhere else."

The infusion pump beeped, and Mandi promptly walked over, allowing Lauren to excuse herself.

She wove through the infusion center toward the back stairway that would take her back to clinic. Fridays were the slowest day of the week for the infusion center, and the section of chairs near the corner was empty.

Thinking she was alone as she walked through, she jumped when a voice came from behind her.

"Hey, Lauren."

Her hand flew to her chest and she spun around to find

Gavin standing near the window. He unhooked an empty saline bag from an IV pole and stuffed it into one of the bright yellow disposal buckets placed throughout the room.

"Gavin. You startled me," she said on a long exhale.

"Sorry." Finished with his task, he took three steps in her direction. "We missed you the other night. On the Plaza."

His expression was calm, but his voice held an edge. He was cocky, sure...but usually not intimidating, A tingle of unease spread down Lauren's spine at the look in his eye as he watched her.

"Oh, yeah. Did you have fun?"

"It was a blast." He paused for a beat. "What were you up to? Studying, you said?"

Lauren sensed something hinged on her response to this question, but she didn't know what else to say. "Yeah." That is what she'd planned on doing, before Logan/Andrew had asked her to dinner.

"Huh. That's weird, because I could have sworn I saw you that night."

*Bob Barker.*

"You were by the fountain with someone. He looked an awful lot like that big guy with Hodgkin's we've been treating."

Lauren's mind kicked into overdrive. How should she respond? Did it matter that she and Andrew were there together? Should she lie and say it hadn't been her? Or it hadn't been Andrew? She'd been so focused on Andrew, Gavin could have passed right by them and she wouldn't have noticed. If she tried to play it off like she hadn't been there with Andrew, and Gavin had been nearby and saw them—especially right at the almost kiss—things would look even worse.

She wasn't convinced she had anything to hide. The whole thing with Andrew felt like such a gray area. Plus, she was a terrible liar.

"Look, I don't see how this is any of your business, but I ended up going to the Plaza that night. It was a last-minute decision, and I was meeting someone. I ran into Andrew and we walked around. It was nothing."

Gavin made a humming noise between his lips. "Didn't look like nothing." His accusatory tone coupled with a lift of his eyebrow caused a spark of anger inside her.

Squaring her shoulders, she asked, "Is there something you want to say, Gavin? What are you after?"

A slight smile formed on his lips. "I just think it's interesting. You've played hard to get with me from the start, and then this guy snags you within a few weeks of showing up to your clinic. Is it because he has cancer? You feel bad for him, or something?"

"You're an asshole." The words spilled out before she could stop them. "First of all, no one has 'snagged' me. Nothing happened. Like I said, we ran into each other that night. Second, I haven't played hard to get with you, I'm just not interested. Not before, and definitely not now."

Her hands shook and her face was on fire, and she pushed past him, ducking into the stairwell. She ascended one flight and paused at the landing, attempting to calm her racing heart.

Even if she hadn't stepped over, she was walking a very fine line. On one side was a man who, against her better judgment, she wanted to get to know. On the other, her dream job. Was she playing with fire?

She wasn't sure how far she could take a friendship with Andrew without risking her career, but she did know one thing.

She had to be more careful.

# Chapter Eight

"You gonna kill me for inviting Lauren over?" Jeni asked after Lauren left.

Andrew regarded his sister, tilting his head. "Actually, no. You've proven quite useful. I think I'll keep you around. Though, I have to ask—what are you trying to do?"

"If you don't know, you're an even bigger idiot than I thought."

Andrew ignored that. "*Parks and Rec* and pizza, though? Where the hell did you come up with that?"

Jeni shrugged. "Sounds like an awesome holiday to me. And I think Lauren agreed."

"We'll see," Andrew said. He figured his chances of her actually coming were low.

Even so, seeing Lauren today was the highlight of what had otherwise been a shitty couple of weeks.

Last Monday, three days after his last chemo treatment and two days after his non-date with Lauren, Andrew had felt so awful he'd skipped his Ethics class. Even though Dan had brought him notes the next day, he still felt like it was a bad sign. That had been only the second of eight planned treatments.

Where would it go from here?

To make matters worse, last Thursday he'd woken up to find a disturbing amount of his hair still on the pillow and had immediately called Jeni. Good twin sister that she was, she'd maintained a perfectly businesslike demeanor as she'd shaved his head. She hadn't laughed, she hadn't wept all over him, she hadn't cracked jokes. She'd strode in, gotten the job done, and left for work. They both knew it sucked, but it was part of the deal.

Supposedly, it would grow back.

He'd had eight days to get used to his new look before today's chemo appointment, when he'd assumed he might see Lauren. She was probably used to seeing bald men and women…but that didn't ease his self-consciousness. He'd experimented with baseball caps and hipster-style beanies, but typically went with the latter, even indoors. November in Kansas City boasted temperatures in the forties, and Andrew wasn't prepared for how cold he would be without hair blanketing his head.

The hat he chose for today was dark gray, and as he sat in a similar-colored leather-encased chair in the chemo infusion center, he blended in quite well.

"Have you talked to Mom today?" Jeni asked from beside him. Her chair was perpendicular to his, her feet propped up on his armrest. She tapped at her phone and didn't look up when she spoke.

"No, why?" Andrew's eyes were on his phone as well as he scrolled through Instagram.

"I really did talk her out of bringing the extended family down for Thanksgiving. But she still wants to come. With Rhonda and Valerie's family…and Dad."

"I hope you told her no."

"Of course I did. But you know Mom, she's devastated we won't be together as a family. I told her there's a first for everything, and that you didn't need the commotion and stress of being around that many people. Especially on your week off, when your immune system is the weakest."

"Where did you get that idea?"

"Lauren said so."

He tried to remember anything about that…but the only thing that came to mind from that first day was an image of her red hair and the blue shirt she'd worn underneath that long white coat.

And his mother's question about sex. He'd never forget that.

"What do you need me to do?"

"Tell her you don't feel up to celebrating the holiday."

"I don't."

"I know. But she doesn't believe me."

Andrew opened his text messages. "I'm on it."

But before he could send off a message to his mother, an incoming call came through.

Andrew stared at the screen. *What the hell?* "Dad's calling me."

Jeni looked up. "So?"

"I haven't talked to him since the diagnosis."

"At all?" Her pitch rose a notch.

"Nope."

Jeni shook her head and pursed her lips. "You two are ridiculous."

Andrew didn't argue. The phone continued to vibrate in his hand.

"Aren't you going to answer it?"

"I…" Andrew paused. "I don't know."

Jeni, moving like lightning, snatched his phone and swiped the screen to answer the call, then put it back in

Andrew's hand.

He shot his sister a death glare and put the phone to his ear.

"Hello?"

"Andrew?"

"Hey, Dad."

"Are you busy?"

Andrew glanced at the IV pole attached to him. "Not at the moment."

Pause. "I uh, just wanted to call and..."

Andrew's patience with his dad was about as thin as a piece of paper. "And?"

His dad cleared his throat. "I wanted to see how you were doing."

"I'm fine."

"How's your...thing going?"

"Chemo?"

"Yeah."

"Okay."

"Good."

Andrew waited.

His dad sighed audibly. "Do you need anything?"

"No."

"Okay. Well, call if you do."

"Okay. Bye, Dad."

Andrew dropped the phone and his hands into his lap.

"That's it?" came Jeni's voice.

Andrew leaned his head against the chair and closed his eyes.

"How long are you two going to do this?" she asked.

"Do what?"

"Avoid each other. It's been *years*, Andrew. You and Dad used to be close."

"I know exactly how long it's been. Do you think I like

the way things are between us?" He cracked his knuckles. "But he refuses to support me in my decision to become an attorney. You know I tried coming home a few times after I moved away, but all he did was bitch at me the whole time, telling me I was avoiding the responsibility I had to the family business. He told me more than once how disappointed he was in me. He won't let it go, and I'm tired of being hounded, so I stopped calling. What else is there to say?"

Jeni sighed. "I don't know. I just hate seeing you two at each other's throats."

"We're not at each other's throats. We've moved on to complete avoidance."

"That's worse."

"It is what it is, Jeni. If I've come to terms with it, you can, too."

...

Despite a heaviness in his limbs, a sign of fatigue he was starting to get used to the week after chemo, Andrew spent Monday afternoon at the DA's office. He put in twelve to fifteen hours per week, and with the Thanksgiving holiday the office would be closed the latter half of the week.

Todd Griffin, a seasoned prosecutor who had been with the Kansas City DA for fifteen years, took Andrew on to help with a domestic violence case. Though Andrew was disturbed by the information in the case file, he needed to be prepared to handle cases like this one.

Their client, Isla, was a woman in her thirties whose husband had a history of assault. For several years the police had responded to incidents at their home, but Isla had never wanted to press charges. Four months ago, Isla's husband had attacked her and their seven-year-old son, which was the first time their child had incurred injuries. That, combined with

Isla's broken arm and ruptured spleen, had prompted her to move forward with protective orders and to file a lawsuit.

Each time Andrew worked on this case, he thought about his sisters and what he would do if he ever found out that a man had physically hurt them. Today, just like each time before, his blood boiled at the thought. People were meant to form partnerships and relationships based on mutual respect and love. Not out of a need to control or possess. He couldn't understand the mind-set of people like Isla's husband, and Andrew felt honored to be part of the team attempting to hold the man accountable for his actions.

During the first few months of the investigation, Andrew had attended client and witness interviews, drafted a few pretrial motions, and filed necessary paperwork at the courthouse. Todd was ruthless and detail oriented, but also patient as he'd walked Andrew through each step of the case process. He could also be laid back and funny at times, and Andrew got along with him well. He reminded Andrew of his father a little, truth be told. The way he used to be before Andrew had left home.

Andrew spent several hours that day drafting a response to a motion filed by the defense. The husband's attorney was hoping to strike the testimony of a police officer who'd initially responded to the violent incident, and the prosecution needed that piece of evidence. Just as Andrew finished up, Todd approached the desk.

"I like the new look."

Andrew cupped a hand over his bald head. This was one of the few places where it wasn't appropriate to wear a hat. "Oh, yeah. Thanks. It was time…the patchy thinning spots weren't doing it for me."

Todd nodded sagely. "I remember when Helen finally broke down and shaved her head. She cried for two days."

When Andrew had first told the staff about the

lymphoma and treatment he'd been going through, Todd had pulled him aside. He revealed that his wife had gone through chemotherapy for breast cancer several years prior. He'd insisted Andrew tell him if he ever needed anything or needed time off. Andrew had thanked him but refused to approach the internship differently than any other third year law student. He was serious about making a good impression and networking as much as possible, in hopes there would be an open position by the time he graduated.

"It's not so bad. I'm just telling myself it comes with the territory."

Todd put a hand on his shoulder. "Keep up that positive attitude and you'll do fine. Are you doing all right otherwise?"

Andrew wasn't going to be honest with the man he was trying to impress. He ignored his churning stomach and the desire to lay his head on the desk and take a nap. "I'm doing great. I can barely tell I'm getting chemo." He smiled for added emphasis, swallowing the lie.

Todd gave him a good-hearted thump on his upper back. "Glad to hear it. You've been an excellent addition to this case. You're a quick learner, and you've done good work."

"Thank you, sir." He wanted to ask if there was any chance for an open position for a new graduate come summer, but he hesitated. It was only November, and graduation was a long way off.

A lot could change between now and then.

・・・

That evening Andrew trudged up the stairs to his apartment. When he moved into this complex he'd chosen a third-floor apartment, wanting a unit with a balcony. But since beginning chemo, he'd begun to loathe these stairs.

The apartment wasn't much but was perfect for him

while in law school—kitchen, living room, two bedrooms, and a bathroom. He'd set up the extra bedroom as an office of sorts and didn't have an extra bed for guests. It had worked out when his mom and sisters were in town, because he could pawn them off on Jeni and her two-bedroom house.

Though he could have found something cheaper, the location couldn't be beat—the River Market district was eclectic and fun, full of restaurants, bars, and a huge farmers market that attracted people from all over the city in the warmer months.

He made himself a simple sandwich and crashed on his couch, remote in hand. As he had every time since their dinner together, he thought of Lauren while he scrolled through the documentaries in his queue.

Andrew: *Have you seen the new killer whale documentary?*

Several minutes passed with no response. Just when he'd decided she wasn't going to answer, his phone dinged.

Lauren: *Watched it last night. Do it.*

Andrew: *Doing it.*

Lauren: *Though, I should warn you it was a little fishy.*

Andrew: *I sea what you did there.*

Lauren: *Salmon had to say it.*

Andrew: *You've got me hooked on puns now.*

Lauren: *It wasn't on porpoise.*

Andrew: *Let's just clam down a little bit.*

Lauren: *Don't krill my vibe.*

Andrew: *Eh. When you think of a better one, let minnow.*

Lauren: *Whale done.*

Andrew: *Shell yes, it was.*

Lauren: *Water you thinking now?*

Andrew: *Damn, I can't think of any more. You win this one. How was your Monday?*

Lauren: *Pretty good, actually. Yours? How do you feel?*

Andrew: *I'm good.*

Lauren: *You sure?*

Andrew: *I'm sure. My day was busy, but I like it that way.*

Lauren: *Me too.*

Andrew: *Have a good night, hope to see you Thursday.*

She didn't reply, and he tried to think of other things. But tonight, like most others, Lauren Taylor wasn't far from his mind.

# Chapter Nine

Andrew: *Happy Turkey Day. How was work?*

Lauren stared at the message. She was curled up in her favorite navy armchair, wearing an Oklahoma City Thunder sweatshirt and leggings, a documentary about juveniles in the prison system playing on her television.

She hesitated, as she had before responding to all his messages lately. She'd been on edge since her run-in with Gavin last week. *Nothing happened that night*, she told herself. *You didn't know Andrew was the one meeting you. You stopped it before things went too far. You did nothing wrong. It might not even* be *wrong.*

Nevertheless, Gavin's words troubled her. There'd been that moment when she and Andrew had nearly kissed, and if Gavin had seen that, it would be difficult to convince anyone they were just friends. Who else had been with Gavin? Had more people from work witnessed the same thing? Would she gain a reputation around the cancer center as someone who hooked up with patients?

Earlier in the week she'd searched the institutional policies posted on the intranet and found nothing regarding pharmacist relationships with patients. As she suspected, it was a clear rule that physicians weren't to engage in a sexual relationship with a patient they were treating, but for the rest of the health care team, it was unclear. It also didn't mention patients no longer under a provider's care.

To be on the safe side, she should assume the strictest rule applied to her.

But she couldn't convince herself that she couldn't be friends with the guy. A few months ago, she'd met a twenty-four-year-old girl at the end of her treatment for acute promyelocytic leukemia, and the two had become fast friends. Lauren met her for lunch at the cancer center café several times, and now that her therapy was complete, they still spoke regularly. She didn't have to treat Andrew differently just because he was male, did she? An extremely sexy male whom she was undeniably attracted to?

Okay, maybe she should.

But she didn't want to.

There was no harm in talking to him, so long as she kept things strictly platonic.

Lauren: *Slow. How's your day going?*

Andrew: *Pretty good. I'm at Jeni's. You gonna join us for pizza?*

Lauren: *I don't think so, but I appreciate the invite.*

Andrew: *You sure? Jeni's been talking about it all day. She hasn't met many people since she moved here. I think she was looking forward to getting to know you.*

Lauren: *Give her my number. I'll hang out with her*

*anytime.*

Andrew: *Like...today?*

Lauren: *\*sigh\**

Andrew: *Come on. We're lonely over here. We're used to spending Thanksgiving with 25 people.*

Lauren: *I really shouldn't.*

Andrew: *Shouldn't or won't?*

Lauren: *Both.*

Andrew: *What you shouldn't be is alone on a holiday.*

Lauren: *Wouldn't be the first time.*

Andrew: *I don't like that. I can't possibly in good conscience allow it to happen again.*

Lauren: *I don't mind, I'm used to it.*

Andrew: *I have an idea...let's pun war for it. If you win, I'll leave you to your sad Thanksgiving by yourself. If I win, you come sit with my twin sister and me and eat pizza and watch sitcom reruns.*

Lauren: *Those sound the same.*

Andrew: *You in or not?*

Lauren: *How do we know who wins?*

Andrew: *The first person who can't come up with a response loses. Longer than a minute to respond, that's the forfeit.*

Lauren: *Fine, but I get to pick the topic.*

Andrew: *By all means.*

Lauren: *The human body.*

Andrew: *...sorry. I passed out there for a second.*

Lauren: *Not like, inappropriate stuff. I figure as a medical professional I'll win this one easy.*

Andrew: *Try me.*

Lauren: *Am I starting?*

Andrew: *Sure, go a-head.*

Lauren: *You think you're so humerus.*

Andrew: *I'm better than all the wrist.*

Lauren: *I knee-d you to take it up a notch.*

Andrew: *Whatever. I toed you I'm good at this.*

Lauren: *Psoas I was saying...*

Andrew: *(I don't know what that is but I'll trust it's a real thing) You sure can de-liver a line.*

Lauren: *That one was hard to stomach.*

Andrew: *I got your back.*

Lauren: *Hip-hip hooray!*

Andrew: *I heart-ly think that counts.*

Lauren: *I need to win this but urine my way.*

Andrew: *Eye will escort you into the house after I win.*

Lauren: *Whoa, don't ovary-act.*

Andrew: *Come on. We be-lung together.*

Lauren froze. She read the text again. *We belong together?* Her heart skipped a beat and she told it to stop being stupid.

Andrew: *TIME*
Andrew: *I WIN*

He texted an address only ten minutes from Lauren's house.

Andrew: *See you soon*

*Barbara Streisand.*

. . .

Forty-five minutes later Lauren sat in her car, around the corner from Jeni's house, at war with herself.
*You're not doing anything wrong.*
*This is a bad idea.*
*You're spending the holiday with friends.*
*You shouldn't be doing this.*
She was on unfamiliar ground, and she didn't like it. She'd never snuck out of her dad's house. She'd never gotten a speeding ticket or been arrested. Never got caught drinking before she turned twenty-one. Kept an honest approach to school—did her own work and never cheated her way through a test.

In all honesty, she never understood those who were rule-breakers and risk-takers. She'd never had the desire to do something that seemed wrong or questionable, and it had never been a temptation.

Until now.

She rubbed her face with both hands and groaned. What

was her deal? She shouldn't be here. So why had she taken a shower, carefully arranged her hair into a messy bun, and chosen a shirt that brought out her eyes?

Because she was weak. And because she *wanted* to. She wanted to spend the evening with Andrew and Jeni.

And she wasn't going to back down from her end of the bet.

*We be-lung together.*

She was disappointed in herself for allowing those words to push her mind off course. She was being stupid. His silly game threw her off, when it didn't mean anything. This was exactly why she hadn't wanted to get involved with him. She'd followed her heart once for a ridiculously handsome guy and it had ended up broken.

She was comfortable with herself, but she was no ravishing beauty. She was moderately attractive…pretty, even. Everyone raved about her unique hair color, and before having had her own chest enhanced, Emma had frequently eyed Lauren's ample breasts with envy.

She was a solid six out of ten. Maybe even a seven.

But people tended to pair up with those in their same general attractiveness category. It was how the world worked. So, in undergrad, when a perfect ten had smiled in her direction, she'd been so bewildered and flattered by the attention, she hadn't noticed the warning signs.

Here she was again, acting like the same flustered idiot she was then. Andrew, who was easily an eleven, had said something romantic via text message. Her mind had known it was a game they were playing, but her heart took over and she'd hesitated.

For a full minute.

"You're not doing anyone any good by sitting here and stewing about it. Stop being a baby and just go," she muttered, and shifted the car into drive.

She turned right onto Jeni's street and crept along, leaning forward with squinted eyes to read the house numbers as she passed. She found the correct one, fourth on the right. It was a cute craftsman-style home painted white with a wooden porch swing in the front.

A few other families must have been hosting the holiday, because the street was packed with cars. Lauren found an open spot two houses down and parked.

On a warmer day she might have ambled up the street, gathering up her courage to approach the door. But it was twenty-two degrees and windy, and each gust was like shards of ice on her face. Lauren rushed down the sidewalk and up to the blue front door.

She heard several loud voices coming from inside, but before she could fully process what that meant, the door swung open.

Chaos ensued.

A clamor of voices, mostly female, spilled from inside.

*Am I at the wrong hou*—before she could even finish her thought, a white dog burst through the open doorway. The canine slammed into Lauren's knees and knocked her backward. She hit the deck with a grunt, landing awkwardly on her left hip. Pain sliced through her wrist where she threw her hand down to brace the fall.

"Duke!" A girl who looked like Jeni shot past, chasing after the dog, who took off at a sprint down the sidewalk.

Lauren pushed herself to a sitting position as a little girl walked outside and stood at Lauren's feet.

"Hello," the girl said. Her hair was a white-blond mass of curls, and she wore a long-sleeved *Frozen* T-shirt, leopard print pants, and sparkling red shoes that reminded Lauren of the *Wizard of Oz*.

"Um. Hi?" Lauren said.

"Who are you?"

"I'm Lauren." A loud clattering sound reached Lauren's ears. "Um, is there someone named Andrew here?"

The little girl frowned. "Are you talking about Uncle Andy?"

"Probably."

Little blue eyes narrowed, and tiny hands propped on small hips. She clutched a pink purse in her fingers, and it dangled by her side. "Are you his girlfriend?"

Was this an interrogation?

"No, I'm not. But, um, is he here?"

"That depends."

"On what?"

"What you want with him."

Lauren was confused and amused at the same time. And she had no idea how to answer that.

What did she want with him?

The little girl tried a different tactic. "Do you think he's still cute with no hair?"

"Alva?" came a deep voice. "Where are you?" Andrew stepped through the doorway, and his eyes went wide. "Lauren?"

He immediately knelt down by her side. "Are you okay? Why are you on the ground?"

"Stupid...dog knocked...her down," came Jeni's breathless voice. She stepped onto the porch, pulling the shameful-looking dog by the collar. "Sorry...about that."

Jeni pushed the dog into the house and swung the little girl up into her arms. "Come on." They went inside and the door closed, leaving Lauren and Andrew alone on the porch.

Lauren's wide eyes met Andrew's. She looked at the door and the pandemonium within, and back to Andrew.

He straightened and held his hand out to her. She gripped his big, strong hand, and he pulled her to her feet with ease. His grasp lingered for a second longer than necessary before he dropped his arm to his side.

"I'm sorry," he began. "They all showed up a half hour ago. My mom and dad, Rhonda, and Valerie and her husband and kids. Even though we told them not to come. We had no idea, and I couldn't find my phone to warn you…" He trailed off. He appeared to be offering her a small smile, but it ended up more like a grimace. "At least the extended family didn't come."

Lauren brushed off her backside with a sigh and said nothing.

"I understand if you don't want to, but I'd love it if you stayed." His eyes turned soft and pleading. "When I told my mom you were coming she got so excited."

As if conjured by some spirit, the door opened to reveal Andrew's mother.

"Lauren! I'm glad you're here." The petite, gray-haired woman wrapped an arm around Lauren's shoulders and continued speaking as she pulled Lauren through the doorway.

Lauren glanced back and bugged her eyes out at Andrew, and with a grin on his face, he mouthed, *I'm sorry.*

"I could use another hand in the kitchen. We're kind of short on time. Just started getting the meal together twenty minutes ago, you know. No time for a turkey but I'm making a ham, is that okay with you?"

She opened her mouth to reply, but his mom kept going.

"Can you peel a potato, honey? That's what I really need right now. I'm working on the pies…"

Lauren's eyes darted around the living room as they passed through. Two men sat on the couch, the older one she assumed to be Andrew's dad. The other had a baby on his lap, his eyes glued to the football game on the television. Andrew's dad looked at Lauren with open curiosity, but his mother kept walking at a brisk pace, and soon Lauren found herself in the kitchen.

This was where all the commotion had stemmed from. Rhonda held a wide-legged stance in front of the sink doing dishes, and Valerie stirred something in a mixing bowl with a wooden spoon, the large white dog sitting tall nearby with his tail wagging. Jeni sat perched at the island with the little blond girl from earlier—Andrew had called her Alva?—and they were snapping the ends from long string beans.

All of the women spoke over each other, and Lauren had a hard time deciphering if it was one conversation or many.

"Hi Lauren! We're so glad you could come," Valerie said brightly.

Rhonda did a kind of head nod.

Jeni smiled widely in that way where all her teeth showed and the tendons in her neck bulged, like she was asking, "Are you freaked out yet?"

"Mom," Andrew's voice came from behind her. He must have followed them in. "Set her up over here at the table, okay?" He pulled out two chairs and sat down at the kitchen table, which was set slightly apart from the kitchen. He waved Lauren over and gestured to the empty seat.

She went gladly.

"I thought you might want a second to process." He shot her a knowing smirk. "It won't be quiet no matter where we go, but at least you'll have a little space over here."

Andrew's mom dropped a huge sack of potatoes onto the table, along with a large empty bowl and two vegetable peelers. She swiveled around to grab the trash can and set it between Andrew and Lauren's feet before returning to the flurry of activity in the kitchen.

Andrew reached for a potato with one hand and a peeler with the other, raising an eyebrow at her. "You haven't said a word since you got here."

Lauren set to work with her own peeler, scraping the skin into the trash can. "That's not true. The little girl," she jerked her head in Alva and Jeni's direction, "was interrogating me on the porch before you found us."

"I wanted to make sure she wasn't after your money," Alva said loudly.

Lauren's face heated instantly. She thought she'd spoken quiet enough that no one would hear. With her questioning and eavesdropping skills, that child was destined to be a special agent.

Andrew choked on a laugh and looked at Alva. "What? Why would you think that?"

"I overheard Mommy and Aunt Rhonda talking about your girlfriend and that she wanted you only for yo—"

"Alva!" came Valerie's sharp reprimand.

The little girl dutifully stopped speaking, but muttered something under her breath that sounded like, "It's true." Lauren glanced at Andrew. He sat very still, his attention on his sisters, both of whom avoided eye contact with him.

"How old is she?" Lauren whispered.

"Five," he said wryly. "I can't believe it either."

They peeled their potatoes in silence for a few moments.

"Andrew?" A male voice said from the living room. "You gonna come watch the game?"

"Nah, I'm good here," he called back.

"Do you usually help with Thanksgiving dinner?" Lauren asked.

"No."

"You don't have to stay here with me."

He met her gaze with dark brown eyes. "I want to."

She dropped hers back to her task. "Is that your dad in there?"

"Yeah. And Valerie's husband, David, and their one-year-old son, Charlie."

"Lauren?" Alva interrupted. "Some people think it's hard to tell me and Charlie apart. If you ever wonder, just remember that I'm bigger, and I'm a better dancer."

The entire room erupted with laughter, Lauren included, and Alva's eyes swept the room as if she couldn't understand what was funny.

"I'll remember that." Lauren fought to keep a straight face. "Thank you, Alva."

When dinner was ready, eight adults and two kids crammed themselves around the six-top table. Lauren sat squashed between Andrew and Rhonda. Andrew's left leg pressed against the length of her thigh, and she felt the contact as if no fabric were between them. She tried to conspicuously shift in the opposite direction, but then her other leg would meet Rhonda's, and she kind of thought that would be even more awkward.

Dinner conversation was lively and, having gotten used to the constant volume over the previous hour and a half, Lauren enjoyed herself immensely. She learned about what each of the sisters did for a living and asked Andrew's dad (whom she'd finally been introduced to before dinner) about his farming business. He was a man of few words but opened up about his life's work, a gleam of excitement in his eye.

Andrew remained strangely quiet during that conversation.

Jeni asked about Kansas City, and Lauren told her about the best restaurants and coffee shops, and where the best shopping venues were. She liked Jeni very much and made a mental note to suggest they get together sometime in the near future.

Halfway through the meal, Andrew's mom frowned at her son. "Andrew, you're not eating much. Are you okay?"

The table went silent.

"I'm fine."

"Do you feel sick?" Valerie asked. She sat on Andrew's opposite side and put her hand against his forehead.

Andrew gently pushed her hand away. "Seriously, I'm fine. I'm just not very hungry."

Rhonda leaned across Lauren. "You're always hungry. Are you nauseous? I can get your medicine, if you need it."

Lauren felt Andrew stiffen, and it was obvious he didn't appreciate the attention.

"You know, appetites come and go during chemo treatment. It's completely normal," Lauren said. "Andrew's been doing great, there's nothing for any of you to worry about." She paused, searching for a change of topic. "You mentioned earlier you were making a pie, Mrs. Bishop. That's my all-time favorite dessert, and I've never met a kind I didn't like. What did you make?"

It did the trick, and the conversation moved on to Mrs. Bishop's famous buttermilk pie recipe and how many times it had won awards at the Nebraska State Fair. Andrew reached his hand under the table and squeezed Lauren's fingers with his own. It was quick, the contact a mere second, but her skin tingled as if he still touched her.

After dinner, Lauren found herself on the screened-in back porch with Jeni and Duke, the big dog whom she'd learned was the family pet that refused to be left at home alone. The men insisted on doing the dishes, and the rest of the family had moved into the living room to watch a movie with the kids. Valerie discovered Andrew's phone in the pink purse Alva was carrying around and returned it to its proper owner.

The porch, outfitted with a small fireplace and a space heater, was surprisingly cozy, and the women enjoyed mugs of coffee while they chatted.

Andrew joined them not long after, and in a move that was an obvious ploy to leave them alone together, Jeni excused herself, Duke jumping off the chair to follow her.

Andrew settled on the couch next to Lauren, close but not touching. He propped his feet on the coffee table and leaned his head back, the corners of his eyes crinkling adorably as he smiled at her. "Well?"

"Your family is..."

"Loud? Overbearing? Nosy?"

"I was going to say wonderful."

A shade of relief fell over his features. "Yeah?"

Lauren nodded. She turned her upper body to face him, pulling her right knee up to her chest. "I barely know any of you, but I felt included. Like I was part of it."

"My mother has never met a stranger."

"It felt really nice."

Andrew's eyes bounced back and forth between hers. "Earlier, you said you were used to spending holidays alone. Do you mind if I ask why? What about your family?"

"No, I don't mind." Lauren took in a deep breath and exhaled. "My parents met in college. They were together for most of it, and during senior year my mom got pregnant. She had me right after graduation, and they didn't stay together long after that. My dad ended up being the one with primary custody. My mom moved to New York City for medical school, and my dad stayed in Oklahoma for pharmacy school. They met other people, remarried, and both started new families."

Lauren tucked a stray piece of hair behind her ear. "Growing up, I always felt like this extra kid that no one really knew what to do with. My parents took care of me, and I wasn't neglected or anything like that. But I always kind of thought they saw me as this mistake from their college days, and their new families were the *real* ones. Several years ago, my dad and his wife and kids went to the Caribbean over Thanksgiving. I called my mom and asked if she'd like me to spend it with her. She said yes, so I drove down to Dallas, where she lived at the time. When I showed up for dinner, she'd completely forgotten I was coming. Because she hadn't planned for me to be there, the dining room table was set up and full to the brim with her children and in-laws, and I ended up on the couch next to the kids' table.

"I didn't really have the desire to repeat that, so I've spent it alone ever since."

Andrew's jaw had drifted down as she spoke, but suddenly he snapped it shut, a muscle popping in his cheek. "What assholes." His cheeks flushed immediately and he added, "Sorry. Those are your parents and I don't even know them. But…that pisses me off."

Lauren looked at her hands. "It doesn't matter."

"Yes, it does."

She didn't know what else to say, and Andrew took the hint. "So, your dad is a pharmacist, too? Is that why you chose that career?"

"Yeah, initially," she said. "He owns an independent pharmacy in Cedar Creek and has always wanted one of his children to take over the family business. It's difficult for independent pharmacies to survive these days, with the chain stores on every corner…but he has a loyal customer base and does some unique compounding that keeps him afloat. I thought that's what I wanted to do, too.

"But once I learned about clinical pharmacy and the specialty of oncology, I never looked back. The day I told him that I didn't want to come home and work with him, with the plan of eventually owning it, was awful. He was so upset that I ended up telling him if I didn't get a job offer to stay here at the hospital I know I love, I'd consider forgoing an oncology job and move back to Cedar Creek."

"There's no way you're doing that," Andrew said tightly. "The man can't even invite you to the beach with him and his *other* family for Thanksgiving."

Lauren's lips quirked at his quick defense of her. "It wasn't that big of a deal. Was he the most involved or affectionate father? No. But he gave me a safe place to live, took me to the doctor when I was sick, and he never forgets my birthday. He paid for my school, all of it, and in a way I feel like I owe it to him. Not enough to drop my extra training right away, but in all honesty, oncology pharmacist jobs are scarce right now. If I can't land one at Coleman, I don't know that I'll have another option."

"Believe it or not, I understand how you feel. My dad wanted me to take over the family farm, and he wasn't happy when I told him I wanted to go to law school instead. It's hard to feel like you're disappointing a parent, but you gotta do what's best for you. What will make you happy."

That explained a lot about Andrew and his dad's interaction—or lack thereof—today. "We've both got daddy issues, huh?"

Andrew chuckled. "I haven't referred to it that way, but I guess so. How likely is it that you'll get a job at the cancer center?"

"Pretty good, I think. Dr. Hawthorne, the Chief of Medicine, and the Director of Pharmacy have both said they'd like to keep me on. It all depends on if the administrative and financial side of the office think I'm worth it."

"You are."

Lauren smiled. "I think it will work out. I've worked hard to create a good reputation." She met Andrew's eyes and took in his muscular form sitting so near, his handsome face focused on her.

The skin on his jaw was smooth, but he looked just as good this way as he had on the day they'd met. Without the light layer of scruff, her eyes seemed drawn straight to his lips.

She swallowed and looked away.

"I just can't mess it up."

# Chapter Ten

"What's going on with you and Lauren?"

Andrew glanced across the living room at Jeni, where she stared at him in that direct way she'd mastered as a social worker for Child Protective Services.

No time for bullshit in that line of work.

He returned his attention to the television. "What are you talking about?"

"Don't pull that with me." She was also a human lie detector, which was helpful in her job but frustrating as hell when Andrew didn't want her up in his business.

Andrew's hand went to his head, stupidly expecting to find hair to rake his fingers through. The habit hadn't faded, despite the three weeks that had passed since Jeni had shaved it off. He hadn't considered the hair on his face being affected as well, and he hadn't needed to touch a razor to his skin in that time, either.

He gave up. "I like her. A lot."

"I know."

"Is it that obvious?"

"Yes."

"She doesn't feel the same."

"Bullshit."

Andrew jerked his gaze up. Jeni's expression hadn't changed. "Why do you say that?"

"I pay attention. I'm a female, and I know what it looks like when one is interested in a guy."

"She turned me down. Said it was unethical to date me, since she's a pharmacist at the same place I'm getting chemo. And that I need to focus on getting better instead of dating."

"She's probably right, and I respect her for that," Jeni said.

On one hand, Andrew did, too. But it stopped him from getting what he wanted, and that part he didn't like.

"Doesn't change the fact that she's into you, brother. She blushes every time she sees you at the cancer center. She smiles at you like you're a man with water and she's been walking in the desert for days. She spent hours at my house last week with our crazy family, because you asked her to."

"Actually, *you* asked her to. Maybe it's you she's into."

Jeni ignored that statement and raised her eyebrows at him, pursing her lips. "What are you going to do?"

Andrew rubbed his forehead with the heel of his hand. "I don't know. As much as I want to convince her to stop worrying about the rules, I also don't want to be responsible for her losing her job. I'd never want to hurt her, and I know her career is important to her." He sighed heavily. "I'm halfway done. I have two cycles left, and when chemo is over, I'm hoping she'll reconsider. I'm trying to hold out, but I'll be damned if it's not the hardest thing I've ever done."

Jeni nodded her agreement. "Patience will serve you well with this one, I think. The right thing at the wrong time is still the wrong thing."

Andrew shot his twin an impressed look. "Listen to you,

being all insightful and stuff."

Jeni snorted and returned her attention to the television.

Andrew grinned and pulled up his email on his phone. He read through one from Todd Griffin and another from a classmate about a study group. He also received confirmation that he'd passed the background check and online training for the Children's Hospital program and that he was eligible to volunteer. He texted Lauren right away.

Andrew: *I've got good news.*

Lauren: *You passed your test?*

Andrew smiled. They'd both ended up at The Grind House two nights ago with their books—naturally it had become Andrew's favorite place to study—and he'd mentioned he had an exam the next day.

Andrew: *I did, but that's not it. I'm officially approved as a volunteer at Children's Hospital.*

Lauren: *Really? That's great! I didn't know you applied.*

Andrew: *Right after you told me about it.*

Lauren: *When are you going to go?*

Andrew: *I was hoping I could come with you. The first time, at least. I don't know what to expect. Would you mind?*

Lauren: *I don't mind. I'm going this Saturday at nine.*

Andrew: *That sounds great. Will I see you tomorrow at my appointment?*

Lauren: *Actually, I took the day off. I have a dentist*

*appointment and need to get my oil changed.*

Andrew: *I can't help with the teeth but I could change your oil. Save you a few bucks.*

Lauren: *You know how to do that?*

Andrew: *Of course.*

Lauren: *Impressive. The appointment is all set up but I'll remember that for next time.*

She likely didn't realize that meant they'd still need to be in touch several months down the road...but luckily for her, Andrew fully intended for that to be the case.

Andrew: *Should I meet you at the hospital on Saturday?*

Lauren: *Where do you live?*

Andrew: *River Market.*

Lauren: *You're close to the hospital. I guess I could pick you up on my way.*

Andrew was surprised by the offer, but sure as hell wouldn't decline it. He texted his address and said he'd see her Saturday. Jeni's dry comment came as he hit the send button. "Get that ridiculous smile off your face. You look like a fool."

He only smiled wider.

• • •

On Saturday morning, Lauren picked Andrew up at eight forty-five on the dot. She drove a black Honda Civic, and Andrew thought it fit her personality perfectly. A practical model that never seemed to go out of style.

He grinned at her after he settled in and buckled his seatbelt. "Hi."

"Hey, you."

She wore jeans that hugged her slim legs and a black Patagonia fleece. Her hair was pulled back into a loose ponytail, but a few pieces had escaped and rested along the creamy skin of her neck. He cleared his throat and looked through the windshield. "Long time, no see."

She laughed once. "It's been a week."

"A week and two days," he corrected, and immediately felt embarrassed. He didn't need to be quite so obvious about his infatuation or how much he'd missed seeing her.

"How was your appointment yesterday? And chemo?"

"Good. They said my white count was a little low—"

"What was it?" she interrupted.

"I have no idea."

"Do you have the cancer center's app on your phone? Where you can check your test results?"

"Yeah, but it's not a big deal. They said it was still okay for me to get chemo."

"With Hodgkin's we'll treat with incredibly low white blood cell counts." She stopped at a red light and looked over at him. "I'm not taking you to the hospital where you could be exposed to all sorts of weird infections until I know what your number was. Look it up or I'll call Emma and find out myself."

Andrew shifted in his seat, partially because her demanding tone was a little arousing, but also because he didn't want Lauren to call Dr. Patel's physician assistant and tell her they were together right now. Yesterday at his pre-chemo appointment, he let it slip that Lauren had spent Thanksgiving with his family. He hadn't meant to, but Emma asked how his holiday was and it just kind of came out. The look of shock on Emma's face, followed by one of suspicion, had concerned him. Worried he was going to get Lauren in trouble, he'd quickly tried to clean up his mess by explaining that Lauren and his sister had become friends, and Jeni had invited her. Then he asked some stupid question about chemo to move the conversation in another direction.

"Okay, woman," he said in a teasing voice. "Calm down, I'll look."

The light turned green and she drove forward as he pulled out his phone. He logged into the system and pulled up the lab results from yesterday.

"Which one do you want to know?"

"What's the white blood cell count?"

"One thousand eight hundred."

"What about the absolute neutrophil count?"

"I like it when you talk science to me."

She shook her head, appearing amused. "Just tell me the value, man."

"Man?"

"You called me 'woman.'"

Yes, he supposed he had.

"Okay...absolute neuro-whatever is one thousand and twenty."

Lauren pursed her pink lips together, and Andrew fisted his free hand. Damn, he wanted to kiss her.

"It would be best if your neutrophils were above fifteen hundred, but I'm okay with above one thousand."

"Great." He locked his phone and lifted his hips to slide it back into his pocket. He glanced over to see Lauren's eyes on him, but she quickly looked away, pink staining her cheeks.

He grinned.

Soon Lauren pulled into the parking garage connected to Children's Hospital. They rode the elevator to the eleventh floor, which housed walls painted floor-to-ceiling with clouds and bright flowers. Lauren greeted several people wearing scrubs as they passed.

Finally, they reached a large, open space that reminded Andrew of the youth room at the church he'd attended as a teenager. Each wall was painted a different color, and there was a television at each end of the room, flanked by overstuffed chairs and sofas. A foosball table sat against the wall, and in the middle were several stations with varying activities just as Lauren had described.

The second they entered the room, a little boy jumped up and yelled Lauren's name. He was thin, looked to be seven or eight years old, and completely bald. Based on how excited the boy was, Andrew wondered why he stood there looking at Lauren expectantly—Alva would have run and jumped into her arms by now.

That's when he noticed the IV line taped to the boy's arm, and the tall, metal pole parked next to him, a large bag of fluid swaying slightly with his movement. Lauren made a beeline for the boy and knelt down to wrap him in a hug.

Andrew's eyes scanned the room, and his chest tightened. Several children were present, ranging in age from toddler to teenager. About half were in the same situation as the boy Lauren was talking to, rolling an IV pole around wherever they went. Others had nothing visibly attached to them, but most rocked the hairless style like Andrew.

Emotion rose up inside him unbidden, and he suddenly regretted his decision to do this. These were kids…and they were going through something so horrible…it was almost too much to bear.

A hand touched his arm, and he found Lauren back at his side.

"Look at their faces," she murmured, looking up at him with worried eyes.

"What?"

"Their faces. They're smiling." She squeezed his bicep gently. Another time he would have been embarrassed that the muscle she touched was smaller than usual, because he hadn't been able to keep up his usual regimen at the gym, but right now he didn't care. She continued in a near whisper. "Yes, they have cancer. But they're happy. They're playing. Focus on their smiles, okay?"

He swallowed and nodded.

"We can leave if you want to."

"No." He swallowed again, forcing down the lump in his throat. "I'm fine."

He settled his gaze on her eyes, allowing himself to find calm in their green depths.

She smiled and tugged at his elbow. "Okay, then. Let's go color."

They joined four other children at a large circular table covered in paper, markers, colored pencils, and crayons. Lauren took charge of the conversation, introducing Andrew and herself and asking all of their names. He thought he was good with kids—he'd never had a problem with Alva or Charlie—but something about this setting and the appearance of these children threw him off-balance. Lauren was right, though—if he focused on their smiles, it was easier to see them as any other kid. Which is probably what they wanted. He knew he didn't want to be defined by his disease.

The children were talkative, and once he settled in and relaxed, Andrew found himself laughing and taking part in the silly conversations going on around him. Eventually he sat back and surveyed the room. He noticed a girl sitting near the window and paused.

She appeared to be the oldest in the room, maybe twelve or thirteen.

She wasn't smiling.

"I'll be right back," he said to Lauren. He rose and

walked to where the girl sat, stopping a few feet away.

"Hi, I'm Andrew." He held out his hand.

She looked at his hand for a second before reaching out to shake it.

She said nothing.

"May I sit?"

She shrugged and resumed looking out the window.

Andrew pulled up a chair and took in the view. "Wow. You can see a lot from up here."

No response.

He leaned past her and pressed his index finger against the glass. "See that small pink building with the bright sign? That place makes the best ice cream. And the older-looking brown one with the guitar painted on the side? I've been to like, fifty concerts there. They book the best bands...but it's standing room only, which is annoying. My feet start to hurt, but it's worth it." The girl's face hadn't changed even a millimeter, so he decided to make something up. Thinking about the woman sitting behind him, he came up with an idea. "Oh man, and the weird-shaped gray one over there? I had a job interview there once, and you know what I did? I'm in my suit, all professional and put-together with my briefcase and a latte, and I walked straight into the glass door. Spilled coffee all over myself and I looked like a complete idiot when I walked into the reception area. Didn't get the job, either."

The tiniest smile in the history of smiles formed on her face, and he counted it a success. "What's your name?" he asked.

"Jasmine."

"You don't talk much, Jasmine."

"You talk too much, Andrew."

Andrew quirked an eyebrow. "How old are you?"

"Fourteen."

"Really? I'd have guessed twelve."

That was the wrong thing to say. She scowled at him.

He tried again. "Fourteen is a good age. I learned to drive on my dad's farm when I was fourteen. Grew an entire foot. Got really into skateboarding. Ever do that?"

"No."

"Yeah, I guess it's kind of dangerous," Andrew said. He'd hit the pavement more times than he could count.

"I already have cancer," she said flatly.

"Me too."

That got her attention. Her mouth dropped open. "You do?"

He pulled the beanie off his head and rubbed a hand across his skull. "You couldn't tell?"

She shrugged. "Some guys are bald by choice." She looked down at her hands. "When you're a hairless girl, people know something's wrong with you."

Andrew frowned. "There's nothing wrong with you. If there was, that would mean there's something wrong with me, and that can't be true."

Jasmine rolled her eyes, and Andrew laughed.

She stiffened. "What's funny?"

"You just remind me of my twin sister, Jeni."

"You have a twin?"

"Yep. Do you?"

"No."

"Do you have any siblings?"

"Two younger brothers. They're annoying."

"Sisters are annoying, too. I have three."

Jasmine's expression lightened a tiny bit, as if she was accepting that she and Andrew might have things in common.

"What kind of cancer do you have?" she asked, her voice quiet.

"Lymphoma. You?"

"Neuroblastoma."

"I'll be honest, I don't know what that is." He jerked a thumb toward Lauren. "But I'll ask her about it later. She'll know."

"I've seen her here before. Is she your girlfriend?"

"No but I wish she was."

That got him a smile. "She doesn't want to be your girlfriend?" Jasmine seemed to enjoy the prospect, and Andrew was a little offended.

"Don't worry, I'm working at changing her mind."

"Good luck with that," Jasmine said dryly. "She's nice. She comes here a lot, but I don't really talk to her."

"Why not?"

Jasmine shrugged. "I don't know."

Andrew twisted in his chair. Lauren had moved on to the Lego table, joining the little boy who had called out to her when they first arrived.

"I'm going back to my room."

Andrew turned back to face Jasmine. "It was nice to meet you, Jasmine. Maybe I'll see you next time I'm here."

"Okay," was all she said.

She walked away and Andrew stayed put for several minutes, looking through the window.

When it was time to leave, Lauren and Andrew walked back the same way they came. They got into the elevator, and as the doors slid together a young woman in scrubs ran up and stuck her hand through the opening. They popped back open and she jumped into the enclosed space.

"Sorry, I didn't want to wai—hey Lauren!"

"Hi Grace," Lauren said with a smile. "How's it going?"

Grace pressed the number eight and the doors slid shut. "It's going good," she started, but then her cheerful demeanor faded. "Well, except for what happened with Kiki."

Lauren straightened, and her face paled.

Andrew immediately went on high alert.

"What about Kiki?"

Grace's mouth turned down at the corners. "I'm sorry, I thought someone would have told you. He passed away. On Wednesday. I've never seen the floor so somber, not in my seven years working here."

Lauren's sharp intake of breath was so intense, Andrew felt it in his own lungs. Her hand flew to her mouth, and he heard her whisper, "No..." behind her palm. On its own accord, his hand went to her shoulder.

The speaker dinged and the elevator doors slid open. Grace didn't move right away. Instead, she stood there with this horrified, mournful look on her face. "I'm so sorry, Lauren. It came as a shock to all of us." The doors began to close again, and Grace darted for the opening. "I have to go, but call me later and we'll talk more, okay? I'm so sorry."

Then Grace was gone and the doors closed again, leaving Andrew and Lauren alone.

"Lauren..." he began. He had no clue what had just happened or who Kiki was, and he didn't know what to say. What he knew was Lauren had cared about Kiki, and she was falling apart beside him.

Without conscious thought, he pulled her into his arms. She melted in to him, gripping his shirt in her fists as her body shook with sobs. She was several inches shorter, and he rested his chin on top of her head. He rubbed circles on her back and murmured words like, "I'm so sorry" and "It's okay," though none of it would fix a damn thing.

A light, floral scent rose from her hair, and Andrew inhaled deeply. Was it wrong of him to feel a sense of satisfaction that she was in his arms? That he was the one bringing her comfort? He hated seeing her cry with an acute fierceness, but that emotion was offset by the pleasure of finally being able to hold her.

The elevator stopped on the third floor, and the doors

opened to reveal a guy wearing a maintenance uniform, tapping at his phone. He looked up and took one step forward but paused when he saw Andrew and the crying woman in his embrace.

Andrew shot him a look that said, *Don't even think about it.*

They reached the lower level where the parking garage was located. Andrew tightened his arms around her back and dipped his head to her ear to murmur, "This is us."

She sniffed and pulled back, swiping her forearm across her eyes. Andrew felt the loss of her immediately, and he nearly pulled her back against his chest. He settled for putting his arm around her waist for support, and they walked in the direction of her car.

"I'm so sorry." Her voice shook, and she occasionally hiccupped as she inhaled. "I'm not usually like this... I'm so embarrassed."

They came to a stop by her car, and Andrew turned her to face him. He ducked low to meet her gaze directly, placing his hands on her shoulders. "Don't be ridiculous." He held out his hand. "But I'm driving."

She didn't argue and dug around in her purse for her keys. She placed them in his palm, but before she could get in on the passenger side, he pulled her in for another hug.

"I'm sorry," he said for the tenth time, but it was true. He was sorry she was hurting, and that she had a job where this probably happened often. He was sorry that in the back of his mind, he wondered if someday he would be the one she was crying over.

This time her arms wound around his waist, causing a tightening deep in his abdomen. His heart squeezed inside his chest and he closed his eyes, memorizing the feel of her like this.

"Thank you." Too soon, she pulled back and opened the

car door.

He went around to the driver's side and got in. She sat quietly beside him as he started the car and maneuvered out of the parking garage.

They didn't speak for several blocks, the soft melody of the radio the only sound.

He drove right past the entrance to his apartment complex.

She noticed. "Where are you going?"

"We need ice cream." He thought she might point out that it was only eleven-thirty in the morning or that they hadn't had lunch yet.

Instead, she nodded. "Good call."

And just like that, he fell for her a little more.

# Chapter Eleven

When Andrew pulled into Betty Rae's parking lot, Lauren offered him a small smile. "My favorite."

"Mine too."

"Though you should have told me this outing would be BYOI."

"BYOI?" he repeated.

"Bring Your Own Insulin." *Good Lord, could I sound more like a science nerd?*

But the look Andrew gave her wasn't one of forbearance. Rather, it was almost affectionate. "Is that pharmacy humor?"

She grinned. "Yeah."

When they reached the counter, he turned to her. She'd tried to wipe away her smeared eye makeup in the car, but she bet a few smudges remained. She hoped she didn't look too awful.

"Split a S'mores sundae?" he asked.

"You read my mind." She said it in a light tone, but she couldn't ignore the flutter within her ribcage. The connections forming between them today were adding up, and it was like they both knew they were nearing a tipping point.

The employee said the total and Lauren put a hand on Andrew's sternum. His heart pounded underneath her palm. "You. Go wash your hands. I've got this."

"What? No way." He pulled his wallet from the back pocket of his jeans.

She gave his chest a light shove. "I insist. You just touched all sorts of things that had grubby little hands on them, and with your white count where it is, you have to go wash your hands right this second. I'm ashamed I didn't mention it on the way out."

Andrew didn't budge.

"Andrew Nathan Bishop, so help me God, I'll make a scene if I have to."

"I'd listen to her, man," said the shop employee. He eyed Lauren warily, like she was a bomb that might explode at any minute.

Andrew lifted his hands in surrender and backed up two steps before turning around. "So damn bossy," he muttered under his breath.

"I heard that."

"I meant you to."

She let out a laugh as he disappeared into the bathroom. Lauren paid and sat in a bright yellow booth along the wall. They were the only customers, which wasn't surprising given the time of day.

When Andrew returned and the decadent sundae was between them, he confronted the elephant in the room. "Do you want to talk about it?"

Lauren sighed deeply. "I can't."

He frowned. "It's not a HIPAA violation, is it?"

She rubbed her lips together. "It sort of feels like it. Even though you're a volunteer there now, you didn't know him before... I just don't know."

"I get it," Andrew said. He scratched at his jaw. "Is there any way to, I don't know, talk about it in general terms? That might still help."

She dipped her pink spoon into the ice cream and took a bite before she replied. "As I'm sure you know, there's a fair amount of loss in my line of work."

Andrew nodded, and for a second she wondered if she should continue. Andrew had his own diagnosis to worry about…should she be talking about people dying of cancer?

As if he could read her mind, he said, "Keep going. Don't tiptoe around what happened just because of my situation. I want to know." He leaned forward, his chest touching the table between them. The booth seemed tiny with his large body across from her. "I want to know everything about you."

She dropped her gaze, hating how happy it made her when he said things like that. She wanted to collect the words and store them somewhere for safekeeping. "We cure a lot of people, too, so there's joy as well. But no matter how much we have to celebrate, it's the grief that can be crippling."

"How can you stand it?" His voice came out a little hoarse.

"I went to a lecture once, about compassion fatigue for health care providers. The way the speaker put it was so perfect, and I'll never forget it. He said when a patient dies, they go into one of three categories. Some are like a balloon released into the sky. Those are the ones that maybe we didn't treat for very long, or we played only a small part in their care. Though we're sad when they pass, they kind of float away from our memories as the days go by. Others are ones that meant a lot, and whom we got to know well. When they die, we wear them like a backpack…where they'll always be, carried around with us and never forgotten." She paused and took a deep breath. Her chin trembled, and she swallowed. "Then there's the third category. For those patients, their loss is so painful, the grief so debilitating and overwhelming, that we have to shut them away in a drawer, because thinking about them is too raw."

Tears formed behind her eyelids, and she blinked to keep them contained.

Andrew swallowed and focused on the bowl of ice cream. "This Kiki, he's in the third group?"

"Yes."

Andrew slowly scooped a bite of ice cream and put it in his mouth. He swallowed and said, "You really are amazing. I hope you know that."

She looked across the table, and the second her eyes connected with those warm brown ones, the words tumbled out. "You're pretty wonderful yourself." Another thought occurred to her, and she smiled. "I saw you talking to Jasmine. That's a feat in and of itself. I've tried to befriend that girl for months."

"I wouldn't say we're friends, but I'm working on it. She seemed sad."

"She's fourteen, and she's smart. Her disease isn't curable, and she knows it."

Andrew suddenly looked like the breath had been knocked out of him. "Fuck, this has been the most depressing day I've ever had."

Lauren leaned forward and put her hand over his. "Maybe I shouldn't have suggested you do this…"

"No." Andrew shook his head. He flipped his hand underneath hers so that their palms pressed together, and he wrapped his fingers around hers. "I didn't mean that like it sounded. It felt good, to spend time with those kids and make them laugh. I want to do it again. But it was sad at the same time. You know? I don't think I've been exposed to so much illness in a day before." He looked like he wanted to say more, but he stopped. With his free hand he tugged at the hem of his beanie. "I'm happy to have the chance to spend time with you."

She looked down, and he gave a gentle pull on her hand. When she looked up at him, the vulnerability mixed with affection in his gaze halted the breath in her throat.

Andrew took a shaky breath. "I know I shouldn't say it, but I really like you, Lauren."

She shook her head, but he kept going. "I know you don't want to do anything about it right now. I do. I'm trying my best to hold back and respect you and the job you're so good at, that you love. But I want you to know that I think you're amazing. You're funny and generous, and heart-stoppingly beautiful. So I'm giving you fair warning that when my treatment is over, this is happening."

*Oh, hell.* She could feel the flush creep up her neck and consume her face, and she closed her eyes.

"This is happening," he repeated.

She opened her eyes and nodded, agreeing wordlessly, before she slipped her hand away from his and placed it in her lap. She locked eyes with him.

"Just not yet," was her soft reply.

"I can accept that," Andrew said. "As long as I know there might be a future, I can be patient in the present."


Lauren made the trip to Cedar Creek for the holidays. She'd promised to work Christmas Eve and the day after Christmas at her dad's store, and she preferred to keep herself occupied when she was home. She also couldn't wait to catch up with her childhood friends Kate and Samantha.

Plus, after the news about Kiki and Andrew's declaration of intention toward her, it was nice to get away and take a break.

The good thing about her dad's independent pharmacy was that he set his own hours, and the store closed at six. After getting things in order and locking up on the day after Christmas, Lauren made plans to meet her friends at their coffee shop. She pulled up at Ristretto Coffee House, a business they'd opened after college. As she walked in, she saw Kate behind the coffee bar and Samantha sitting on a stool at the counter. When Samantha noticed her, she jumped to the floor with an excited screech.

"Lauren!"

"Hey, girls," Lauren exclaimed, hugging Samantha first, and then Kate, who came out to join them.

"It's so good to see you. Come on, let's go sit in the back," Kate said. She gestured to a young man working the espresso machine. "Tim's got everything handled."

Lauren followed her two oldest friends to the back corner of the sizable café.

"First things first," Lauren said after they'd settled around the table. "How's married life treating the two of you?"

Kate and Samantha had each gotten married within a few months of each other. It had been a little over a year since Lauren had come back to Cedar Creek to stand up as a bridesmaid for Kate. Samantha and her husband, Paul, had eloped and married in Vegas a few months before that, shocking everyone with the news upon their return.

They talked about married life for a while, Lauren feeling content to sit and listen to stories of the highs and occasional lows that came with new commitment. She laughed often, and, even though she loved her life in Kansas City, Kate and Samantha were the two things she missed most about Cedar Creek.

"Enough about us and our love lives," Samantha said. "We're boring old married women now. What's going on with you? Has a lucky guy snatched you up yet?"

Lauren's face warmed, and Kate picked up on it immediately.

"There is!"

"No, not exactly," Lauren hedged. This would be difficult. "I can't really talk about it."

"What? Why not?" Samantha's eyes went wide. "Is he married?"

"Goodness, no. It's just...I'm not allowed to talk about patients."

Understanding dawned on their faces.

"You have a crush on a patient?" Kate asked, keeping her voice low.

Lauren hung her head. "It's more than a crush. I'm crazy about him. He was a patient that I saw for his first appointment, but I'm in a different clinic now."

"So what's the big deal?" Samantha asked. She was, hands down, the most outgoing of the three, and had always been the type to go after what she wanted without reservation.

"I feel weird about it. I work there as a provider, and he's a patient."

"Date him and don't tell anyone about it," Samantha offered.

Kate scowled at Samantha. "You know she can't do that."

"Can't or won't?" Samantha retorted.

"Both," Lauren cut in. "It's not black and white, but it's an ethical line that I don't want to mess with. I need to keep up a good reputation to get a job there. Plus, what if he's interested in me only because of what he's going through? People become more emotional during trials like what he's dealing with. I don't want to take advantage of the position he's in."

"Okay, that's fair," Samantha acquiesced.

"But he's so wonderful. He's intelligent and driven and in his last year of law school, and he wants to work for the District

Attorney's office. He's funny and he makes me laugh, and he's so kind and thoughtful. He has a big family, all sisters, and he loves them so much. He's great with his niece and nephew, and he signed up to be a volunteer at Children's Hospital with me. He's got a good heart." She paused, realizing how good it felt to finally tell someone about him. Even if she couldn't tell them everything, like his name. She hadn't realized how hard it had been to keep her feelings to herself. "Plus, he's easily the hottest man I've ever laid eyes on."

She propped her elbow on the table and placed her forehead in her palm. "But it's getting harder and harder to convince myself that I'm supposed to stay away from him. Every time I see him, a little piece of my restraint falls away and I'm one step closer to giving in."

"Oh, that's delicious." Samantha nodded with an appreciative grin. "Building the sexual tension. I love it."

"How much longer will he be getting chemo?" Kate's eyes went wide with realization. "Oh, for the love, don't tell me if he's terminal." Her chin trembled. "I couldn't handle that."

Even thinking such a thing was like a jagged knife right through Lauren's heart. She took in a shaky breath. "Cancer makes no promises. But statistically, the odds are good he'll be cured. He has three treatments left, which will take six weeks. Then, hopefully, he'll be done for good."

"And then you can hit that." Samantha waggled her eyebrows up and down.

Kate shot Samantha an exasperated frown. "What is *wrong* with you?"

"What?"

Lauren grinned. "I've missed you guys."

"Us, too," Kate said.

"Any chance you'll end up back here in Oklahoma?" Samantha asked.

Lauren thought of the day she'd spent at her dad's

pharmacy. It had been kind of nice and not too busy, probably because it was right after a holiday. But it reminded her of the monotony of that job, and how much of it was spent on things that didn't directly relate to patient care, like dealing with insurance rejections and product inventory. She hated that part. She loved that her time spent at Coleman was with patients or teaching in some capacity—like lecturing to other health care providers or having pharmacy students on rotation. She thought of her homey neighborhood and how much she enjoyed Kansas City. Of Emma, and Kiara, and Mandi.

And of Andrew.

"I don't think so," Lauren said truthfully. "Not if I can help it."

· · ·

Andrew: *How was your Christmas?*

Lauren: *Uneventful. Nice. Yours?*

Andrew: *Jeni and I drove to Nebraska to stay for a few days. It's exhausting. But I would have regretted not coming. Alva's been asking about you.*

Lauren: *She has? I didn't think she liked me.*

Andrew: *She's just protective of her super awesome Uncle Andy.*

Lauren: *She'd be effective in law enforcement.*

Andrew: *Or as a dancer.*

Lauren: *OMG, what?*

Andrew: *What?*

Lauren: *It's like you just suggested your niece become a stripper.*

Andrew: *WHAT*
Andrew: *NO*
Andrew: *I meant like a ballerina*
Andrew: *MAYBE a backup dancer, if the group was cool. Like JT or TSwift.*

Lauren: *\*facepalm\**

Andrew: *That's it. I'm calling you.*

Lauren did a double take at the screen. He was going to what?

Then his name flashed across the screen as an incoming call. She stared. They'd never spoken on the phone before. She didn't know why but she searched the room, hoping to find some magic answer on the walls. She was sitting on the bed in her old room—the décor exactly the same as she'd left it when she graduated. The members of the Black Eyed Peas stared at her from a poster tacked to the wall. Fergie offered no help.

She blinked and accepted the call.

"Hi Andy."

"Only Alva calls me that."

"Okay, Mr. Bishop."

"Much better."

"Why are you calling me?"

"It's clear my texts were being misconstrued. I thought it might be easier this way."

"I see."

He paused. "I wanted to hear your voice."

She swallowed. "I see."

"Are you still in Oklahoma?"

"Yeah. I'll drive back early tomorrow."

"Was your dad happy to see you this time?"

"He's always happy to see me. He's buttering me up so I'll come work for him."

"I don't know how to respond to that without sounding like a dick, so I'll keep quiet."

Lauren leaned her head back. "I have a question that might make me sound like one, but I've been wondering about it for a while."

Andrew chuckled. "Nothing could make you sound like a dick. What is it?"

Lauren wasn't so sure. "Well, when you mentioned Alva, I remembered something she said at Thanksgiving. About your ex-girlfriend wanting you only for your money."

"Are you asking if I'm rich?"

"No. I couldn't care less about that."

"I know you don't. You're asking about my ex, then?"

"Was she talking about Caroline?"

"Probably. I never asked more about it, but I don't think it's true. I mean, my dad's farm does well, and as an attorney I'll make a decent living, but nothing over the top. Caroline was far from perfect, but I don't think she was a gold digger. None of my sisters ever liked her, so I'm sure they were just being catty and Alva overhead."

"Gotta be careful around kids," Lauren said. She'd picked up on that fact quickly, during her time at Children's. "How long were you together?"

"Six months. We broke up a month before I met you. I should have known it wouldn't work, with the way my sisters felt about her. Caroline disliked them as much as they disliked her, which was the main reason we broke up. I realized I didn't want to be with someone who didn't get along with them."

"I can't imagine someone not liking your family."

"And that's one of the many reasons I like you so much."

Lauren smiled widely, thankful that he couldn't see her and she didn't have to hide her emotions. Maybe they should restrict their interactions to phone only until his fourth cycle was over, at which point she could jump on him and kiss him all over.

"Curiosity compels me to ask if you've been in a lot of relationships," she said.

"Only one other that was serious. We dated for a year in undergrad, but went our separate ways, as usually happens with college romances."

Lauren snorted, and Andrew paused. "What was that?"

Lauren scrunched up her nose. "I just...had a bad experience in college. Saying Will and I *went our separate ways* would be putting it nicely."

There was a beat of silence. "Something tells me I'll want to kick someone's ass if I say this, but I'm going to need more information."

Lauren flopped onto the bed on her back, looking up at the ceiling. "There was this guy I met in undergrad, Will Gearhart—"

"Hold up. Did you say Will Gearhart? Like, pro football player Will Gearhart?"

"You've heard of him?"

"Everyone's heard of him. Six years ago he was the first round NFL draft pick. He's on my fantasy team."

"Yeah." Lauren was unimpressed with those stats. Will's success on the field was no concern of hers. "Anyway. He was kind of an unusual college athlete...his major was Biochemistry. He said he wanted to be a doctor if football didn't work out.

"He and I shared several upper level science courses our junior year. I knew who he was, of course. He was KU's star quarterback and generally recognized by all females as the hottest guy to ever grace the halls of campus. We ran in completely different crowds, and he didn't know me from Eve. But one day, about a third of the way through the semester, I walked into the organic chemistry lab we shared, and there he was, waiting at my table.

"He told me my partner had dropped the class, and that he asked the professor if he could switch partners to be with me. Said he noticed me on the first day and had been waiting for an excuse to talk to me.

"I was so flattered, it didn't occur to me to be skeptical of his motives. He was smooth as butter. He said nice things to me, made me laugh, touched me in—"

"I don't want those kind of details," came Andrew's hard voice.

"I meant he found excuses to touch me in class...but okay. The other touching came late—"

"*Stop.*"

"Okay, jeez. Anyway, after a few weeks he asked me out, and we started dating. Once, I asked why we weren't going to any of the big football parties I'd heard so much about, and he said I was too nice a girl to be exposed to the stuff that went on there. He said I was different, and he didn't want to treat me like his previous girlfriends.

"Like an idiot, I believed him, and I fell hard. That is, until the last week of the semester. The night after our lab final, I went to his house to surprise him with a bottle of wine to celebrate the semester being over and found him hooking up with another girl. Apparently, he'd been running around with her the entire time he was seeing me. He'd been close to failing the class and paid my old lab partner to drop so he could team up with me, as the one with the highest grade. He used me to pass the class, so he wouldn't lose his football scholarship. He broke it off with me right then and there."

The other end of the line was silent.

"Andrew?"

Andrew made a choking sound. "I'm gonna have to call you back."

The line went dead.

Lauren lowered the phone and looked at the screen, dumbfounded. What had just happened?

She sat up and crossed her legs. When he didn't call back after a few minutes, she texted him.

Lauren: *Is everything okay?*

He didn't reply, so she waited. Maybe she shouldn't have told him about Will. It had happened a long time ago. But because Will was in the public eye, she was constantly inundated with images on social media of the first man she'd given her heart to—with beautiful actresses or models on his arm. Reminding her that he'd used her.

She opened Instagram and swiped through several photos, barely seeing what was passing across the screen.

What was Andrew doing?

Finally, he called her back.

"Andrew?"

"Sorry about that." His words were clipped, his breathing heavy.

"Where did you go?"

"First, I got onto my Fantasy Football app and benched that fucker. Then I found my Gearhart jersey, went outside and threw it in the trash, and took to the punching bag my dad has in the garage to try to calm down."

"Oh." Lauren chewed on her bottom lip. A warm sensation settled in her belly. "Did it work?"

"No."

"Oh."

"I can't believe he did that to you. How any man could treat you that way is just… It makes me so fucking mad. I don't think I've ever been this angry."

"You don't need to be," Lauren said in as soothing a tone as she could muster. She'd never heard him talk that way and, though a small (okay, medium-sized) part of her was thrilled that he was so indignant on her behalf, she didn't want him to be upset. "I'm sorry I told you. Even though it probably would have come up eventually, since Will's the reason I hadn't planned on giving you a chance in the first place—"

"Whoa, what?"

Lauren toyed with the edge of the comforter. "Ever since that happened with Will, I've only had bad experiences with men. I've kind of sworn off really attractive guys in particular. You know, the super-hot ones who have no business living among us mortals. I'd pretty much decided guys like that were all conceited tools that existed only to use and break the hearts of average-looking women like me."

The other end of the line was dead silent. A few indecipherable sounds came through, and then finally, Andrew spoke, his voice low. "Average-looking?"

"You know what I mean. I know I'm not ugly, but I'm nothing special. I don't typically attract the attention of men like you unless they want something from me."

"I..." he said, then stopped.

The sigh that came through the speaker was so heavy, she felt the weight on her own chest.

"Lauren." The rough, husky tone of his voice sent a tingle down her spine. "If you only knew what happens to me every time I look at you..."

He trailed off, and Lauren's pulse picked up speed. She closed her eyes and placed her hand across her chest, feeling the pound of her heart underneath her palm. No one had ever made her feel this way, of that she was certain.

"If I could act on my thoughts, you'd *never* doubt the attraction I have to you," he said. "But I have to be honest. I do want something from you."

Lauren waited in silence, not confident in her ability to speak.

"I want your words, your breath, and your touch. Your thoughts and ideas, and your ridiculous puns. I want to know every dream and desire you have so I can give them to you. Every single one."

Silence.

Or, what she thought was silence.

"Are you crying?" he asked.

"N-no."

"Damn, I wish you weren't six hours away. Why are you crying?"

"T-that is so s-sweet." She swept a finger under her eye to catch a tear. "I don't know what to do when you say things like that. No one's ever said things like that to me."

"Then everyone else is an idiot. I mean every word. And I think you're incredibly beautiful, do you hear me?"

"I hear you," she whispered. Her feelings for this man overwhelmed her, and it was both wonderful and frustrating. She let out an irritated groan. "Alex Trebek," she muttered.

"Did you just cuss at me? After I said nice things?" An air of humor was back in his tone.

"Yes."

"Why?"

"Because this sucks, Andrew!" She jumped off the bed and paced around the small room. "Why couldn't I have met you before? Or some other way? Why did you have to be a patient?"

"Believe me, I'd prefer if I hadn't met you the way I did, either."

Lauren froze mid-step. Had she seriously just complained to him about the fact that he had cancer? "Oh my gosh...I'm sorry. I wasn't thinking—"

"Lauren, I'm messing with you. Finish what you were

saying."

She resumed pacing but chose her words with care. "I like you, Andrew. I liked you from the beginning, and those feelings grow stronger every day. But I shouldn't like you. Not like that, and not right now. And it's hard."

"I know exactly how hard it is," he said dryly.

Lauren slapped her hand over her mouth. "Andrew Bishop!"

He chuckled, and she was relieved to hear the sound. "You set me up for that one."

She supposed she had.

"I've liked you from the beginning, too. From before you were my pharmacist." He paused, and they seemed to inhale simultaneous breaths. "You had me at William Shatner."

# Chapter Twelve

Andrew didn't see Lauren again until his next chemo appointment. If it weren't for her, he'd probably dread the way he spent the afternoon every other Friday. But as it was, he looked forward to them the same way he had Saturday morning cartoons as a kid.

He was coming back from the restroom, pulling his IV pole behind him, when he found her at his chair talking to Jeni. He paused at the edge of a pull-around curtain, just out of view, wanting to just look at her for a minute.

She wore dress slacks and a fitted black sweater, and her hair was down, which drove him crazy with the desire to bury his hands in it. Damn, she was beautiful.

"This morning was crazy," Lauren was saying. "Clinic was super busy. I'm headed down for lunch and wanted to check in on my way. What about you? Andrew said you had a nice Christmas in Nebraska?"

From her chair, Jeni extended her legs straight and crossed her ankles, then folded her arms across her chest. She regarded Lauren with one eyebrow raised. "It was good...

until the family got into a huge argument. Because of you."

"What?" Lauren asked, her voice shrill. "What do you mean, because of me?"

*Shit.* Andrew hadn't planned on Lauren knowing anything about that, but before he could reach them and stop her, Jeni kept going.

"You should know the Bishops have been die-hard Denver Broncos fans for decades. We drive out for a game at least once a year. But suddenly after Christmas Andrew went on a rampage through the house and took out anything Broncos-related he could find and demanded we choose a different team. 'At least as long as Gearhart is on it,' he said.

"He wouldn't say why, just that the guy had done something pretty shitty in college involving you. Most of us were on board without a second thought. But a few were resistant. You've gotta understand, that's been our team forever. Since way before Gearhart came along. That kind of loyalty isn't something you can just turn off, you know? No matter how much we like you."

"Of course, I would never ask you to—"

Andrew came up behind Lauren, but she still hadn't noticed him.

Jeni held up a hand. "I know you wouldn't. I'm with Andrew on this. I don't know what happened, but I haven't seen Andrew that angry in a long time. So, it must have been bad. Either that, or he cares a lot about you."

"It's both." His voice behind Lauren made her jump. He smiled and brushed his hand across her arm as he walked past, maneuvering his IV pole back into place next to the chair. He bent over to plug it into the wall, and when he stood back up and turned to sit down, Lauren's cheeks were flushed.

"You..." she swallowed. "Um, you look very nice today."

He grinned, pleased that she seemed flustered. He'd dressed up in a full suit today, the jacket resting on the arm of his chair. The white dress shirt he wore was partially unbuttoned for access to his port.

"I've got a mock trial in class this afternoon, and I wasn't sure if I'd have time to change." His eyes moved across her face, lingering on her hair. His voice was low when he said, "You look...very nice, too." He paused and lowered his chin a notch. "Very."

"Oh, for heaven's sake," Jeni cut in. "This is painful to watch."

Lauren scrunched her nose, the color on her cheeks deepening. He loved when she blushed.

Andrew regarded his sister. "I don't recall asking you to be here."

"You can't come to chemo alone."

"Sure I can."

"No, you can't. Lauren said so."

Andrew's gaze flicked to hers. "You did?"

"I said it's best to have someone with you, but the only time it was required was that first time, in case you had a reaction to any of the drugs." She cocked an eyebrow and put a hand on her hip. "Were you not paying attention when I taught you about chemo?"

He opted for honesty. "Not to your words."

Jeni smacked him on the shoulder. "You're such a jerk," she muttered.

Andrew's eyes didn't leave Lauren's.

She ran a hand down her hair with a small smile. "I'd better get going. I just wanted to stop by and make sure everything was going okay." Her expression transformed to a frown. "I didn't even ask that. How are you feeling? Any nausea? Diarrhea? Headaches?"

Andrew blinked. "No, none of your business, and no."

"I'm a medical professional. Everything is my business."

"Not that."

It looked like she was going to argue, but she just squared her shoulders. "Fine. Good luck on your trial. I hope you win." She turned to Jeni. "See you Saturday?"

Andrew spoke before Jeni could respond. "I can't believe you two are hanging out without me."

Jeni imparted her perfected eye roll. "You see her all the time."

"I do not."

"Okay, but you talk to her all the time."

Andrew shrugged and smiled at Lauren.

She smiled back. "We're going shopping," Lauren said. "You'd hate it."

"I wouldn't hate anything, so long as I was with you."

Apparently today he was just going to put it all out there.

"Stop it," Jeni whined. "You'd better get going, Lauren. I think he's about to recite the poem he wrote about you."

With a wide smile, Lauren left and Andrew's eyes followed her as she walked away. Just as she was about to turn the corner, that stocky blond nurse came up behind her. He seemed to whisper something in Lauren's ear, and Andrew's hands gripped the arms of his chair.

Lauren turned and took a step backward. She glanced in Andrew's direction for a split second, then back at the guy. She gestured to the exit and moved to walk away, but he must have said something else, because Lauren slowly twisted toward him once more.

Her cheeks were flushed, but in a completely different way than they had been just moments before with Andrew. She looked pissed. They spoke back and forth, and the guy gave her a slow, theatrical nod, bringing to mind a villain in an action film, contemplating his next move.

Andrew didn't like what he was seeing, but he felt helpless to do anything about it. They were in a room full of people, and Lauren and the nurse were just talking. If the dude put a hand on her, Andrew would be out of his chair and across the room in two seconds flat.

Surely the guy wasn't that stupid.

After a few more words—heated ones, by the looks of it—Lauren finally made her escape, glancing once more at Andrew before she disappeared.

Andrew stared at the male nurse, who suddenly turned his head and made eye contact with him. A smug grin spread across the guy's face before he walked off.

Andrew frowned.

*What the fuck was that?*

• • •

Two weeks later, Andrew dropped his dumbbells onto the weight rack.

"I'm out, man," he called out.

"Already?" Logan looked up from his crouched position near the bench press.

"I'm spent." He hated that, and hated saying it out loud even more. Especially at the gym, when his regular workout buddies were around. They'd noticed the change in his physique and energy level, not to mention his lack of hair, and Andrew had eventually told them what was going on. They were good guys and were supportive, but he still hated appearing sick and weak. The fatigue worsened with each cycle, and it wasn't just for a few days anymore. He was tired all the time.

Logan stood. "Need anything?"

"Nah. I'm heading home. I'll talk to you later."

"Okay. See ya."

Andrew drove home and crashed on his couch for a few hours, a textbook open in his lap. Right when he thought he couldn't keep his eyes open any longer, his phone dinged.

Lauren: *Hi.*

Andrew perked up immediately. She'd never texted him first. Plus, she'd been distant in the two weeks since his last chemo treatment, and he'd been miserable. He'd been concerned after seeing her talking to that nurse but had decided not to ask her about it. What if there was something going on between them? If there was, was it even Andrew's business? She wasn't his girlfriend, and he had no right to question her.

He also worried he had been too forward that day, too honest about the way he felt...and with Jeni there to hear it all. Though he'd kind of thought it would make Lauren feel better that there was a witness. To ensure he kept to his word and didn't act on his constant desire to pull her into his arms and kiss her.

Andrew: *Hey you.*

Lauren: *Chemo tomorrow?*

Andrew: *Yep. Second to last one. *fist pump**

Lauren: *That's great. I'm going to Children's on Saturday, but in the afternoon. Did you want to come?*

Andrew hadn't been back as a volunteer since that first day with Lauren. It had gotten to him more than he thought it would, and he'd made excuses to avoid going. But he'd thought about Jasmine a lot and wanted to try again.

Andrew: *Yes. What time?*

Lauren: *I'll pick you up at 1:45.*

Andrew: *Sounds good. You doing okay? Haven't*

*talked to you much.*

Lauren: *I know, sorry. I'm good. I'll see you Saturday, okay?*

Did that mean he wouldn't be seeing her tomorrow at the cancer center? He hoped not, but he didn't want to push it. He'd be with her Saturday, and he'd take what he could get.

Andrew: *Yeah, see you Saturday.*

It started to snow as he stood outside waiting for her, and she picked him up at exactly a quarter till two. When the first few minutes were strained with an air of awkwardness, Andrew said, "Do we need to talk about my bowel movements? Will that loosen things up between us?"

Lauren laughed so hard, Andrew had to reach over and take the steering wheel to keep them on the road.

"Don't do that," she chastised, still giggling. "Not while I'm driving, and it's snowing."

"You're right, I'm sorry," he said with a smile. "I didn't think you'd find it so funny. You have asked about that before, you know." In a more serious tone, he asked, "Is everything okay? You've seemed...different these last two weeks."

Her laughter slowed, and she looked...guilty? Ashamed? He wasn't certain. "You noticed, huh?"

He lifted an eyebrow to say, *Hell yes, I noticed.*

"I'm sorry. I just..." she trailed off.

"Did I say something to upset you? Scare you off? If I did, I'm sorry. I just figured we both know what's going on here and how we feel. Even though we can't do anything about it, we might as well be honest—"

"I disagree."

He frowned. "With which part?"

"Verbalizing how we feel about each other makes it that much harder to keep things under control." She halted and swallowed, like she was hesitant to continue.

*Please don't stop. I want this to spiral out of control more than I've ever wanted anything.*

She stopped at the entrance of the parking garage and looked him straight in the eye. "When you say things about how nice I look or that you want to spend time with me, it makes it nearly impossible for me to hide how I feel."

She pulled forward, and he wanted to point out that *she* was the first one to comment on his appearance that day and had basically undressed him with her eyes. He shifted in his seat, remembering the look in her eyes.

He was also tempted to say that she had looked exceptionally beautiful, wearing that black sweater that clung to her curves and her vibrant hair loose and begging for his hands to bury themselves in the thick mass.

"I'm sorry about that." *No, I'm not.* "I'm not trying to put you in a bad spot. I'm not used to having to keep that kind of thing hidden, and it's not easy. I want you to know what I'm thinking. And"—he pulled at the edge of the red hat he wore—"I don't want you to hide it."

She pulled into an empty spot and put the car in park. She looked over at him, her expression softening. "The second problem is people are starting to notice."

"What are you talking about?"

"One of the nurses, Gavin? He stopped me after I visited you that day. Asked if something was going on between us."

The dickhead had a name. Gavin.

"Is that the blond one?" he asked, to be sure. "I saw you two talking."

"Yeah. He called me unprofessional, told me to be careful, and that I could get reported for inappropriate behavior with a patient."

Red hot anger shot through Andrew like a lightning bolt. "He's threatening you?"

"I don't think it's that, exactly. I don't get a dangerous vibe from him, but he's definitely acting like a jerk. I'm not sure what his deal is."

"He likes you." Of that, Andrew had no doubt.

Lauren's lip curled. "He has asked me out before. Several times. He never seems content with the fact that I'm not interested."

"I'll be happy to make it clear."

She nudged him across the console with her elbow. "That wouldn't make us seem less involved at all," she said dryly.

She was right.

"What can I do?"

She looked down at her hands and sighed. "You can ignore me until you're done with chemo."

There was no way in hell. "I can't do that."

Was that relief he saw reflected on her face?

"Just…don't treat me any differently than you would anyone else at the cancer center. Like Dr. Patel, or Emma. Don't look at me differently and don't talk to me differently. Can you do that?"

He wasn't sure. "I'll try my level best."

She nodded and opened her car door to get out. He opened his as well, and they met at the trunk of the car.

"I don't think it matters how I look at you, though."

"Why do you say that?" she asked as they walked to the hospital entrance.

He gazed down at her. "I can guarantee I'm not the first patient to check you out when you're not paying attention."

She muttered something he couldn't quite catch, and her cheeks flushed. They rode together in the elevator in charged silence, along with an oblivious man wearing scrubs and a white coat.

They spent several hours with the kids, and Andrew was glad when Jasmine joined the group half an hour after he arrived. She looked as sullen as the first time he'd met her, but he also detected a hint of insecurity. She went to the same chair by the window as last time, and he joined her.

"Hey, kid," Andrew greeted.

Jasmine scowled. "I'm not a kid."

"How old did you say you were? Twelve?"

"*Fourteen.*"

"Oh, yeah." He grinned and she ignored him. "What are we gonna do today?"

"I'm looking out the window. I don't know what you're doing."

"What are you looking at?"

"Anything but you."

Andrew let that pass. "See that tall silver one? The ninth floor is the law firm where I worked last year."

"You're a lawyer?"

"Almost. I'm in my last year of school."

"My mom says lawyers are liars."

"Some of them are."

Jasmine continued to stare out the window.

Andrew put his forearms on his knees. "What do you want to be when you grow up?"

Jasmine's eyes flashed to his. "I won't grow up."

Andrew's stomach dropped. *Shit.* Lauren had said Jasmine was terminal... He hadn't given any thought to the words he said. He wished the ground would open up and swallow him whole, but at the same time he wanted to fold this young, thin girl up in his arms and give her a hug.

But she'd probably kick him in the shin if he tried.

He swallowed, holding back his emotions. "Okay. What do you want to be tomorrow?"

She frowned. "What do you mean, what do I want to be tomorrow?"

"Don't people say we should live every day like it's our last? Make each one count? People like us, who have cancer, should probably take that advice pretty seriously. If you could be something else, instead of a cancer patient, what would it be?"

Jasmine's dark eyes dropped to her hands. "I don't know. I guess I'd want to be a regular kid. Ride the bus, go to school. Eat lunch in the cafeteria. Play soccer after class. Eat dinner with my family and watch TV until it was time for bed."

Andrew sat beside her, not speaking, ideas spinning in his brain. Finally, he said, "That sounds like a good day. When were you diagnosed, Jasmine?"

"A year ago."

"Before that, what did you want to be when you grew up?"

"An artist."

"That's cool. What kind? Drawing, painting? Something else?"

"I like to paint."

"Don't they have painting supplies here?" Andrew twisted in his chair and pointedly looked at the art supply cabinet.

Jasmine shrugged. "Yeah."

"Then tomorrow, I think you should be an artist."

# Chapter Thirteen

Lauren had a smile on her face when she and Andrew made their way down to the parking garage. There were no sudden announcements that a patient passed away, and she'd watched Andrew build a friendship with Jasmine. Lauren had spent most of the day at the Lego table but kept an eye on them throughout the afternoon. It appeared Jasmine made Andrew work pretty hard, but eventually he'd convinced her to play Mario Kart. They played game after game—complete with Jasmine's laugh and trash talk—and Andrew even forfeited his red hat as a prize when she beat him two games in a row.

Lauren had been so engrossed in the kids and watching Andrew and Jasmine that she hadn't noticed how the weather had changed.

"It's really coming down out there," Andrew said as they entered the parking garage, the open-air walls allowing gusts of white flurries to blow inside.

Lauren's eyes went wide. "Oh, my goodness, it is."

Andrew held out his hand. "I grew up in Nebraska. I'm a master at driving in snow."

Relief rushed through her. "I hate driving in it." She handed over her keys, and once again Andrew drove her car in the direction of his apartment.

The roads were slick, and they drove at a near crawl, the ten-minute drive taking double that amount of time. Lauren remained quiet next to Andrew, allowing him to focus on the surrounding cars, her body tensing up with each slide across the ice.

When he finally pulled into a visitor parking spot outside his building, he turned off the ignition and angled his torso to face Lauren.

"You're not driving home in this. Come inside." Before she could argue, Andrew got out and walked around to her side of the car, opened the door, and held out his hand.

"I can drive myself home." She looked at the dark gray sky and blinked. "It's not that bad."

Andrew stared at her. "You said you didn't like driving in snow. I've done it hundreds of times, and even I had trouble maintaining control. Your car isn't made for conditions like this. Quit being stubborn and come in. Jasmine stole my hat and I don't have any hair and it's freezing out here."

"Fine." She grabbed her purse and got out, nearly falling right on her ass the minute she stepped onto the icy asphalt.

"Whoa," Andrew said, grabbing her around the waist. Her hands flung out to grip his biceps, releasing him when she regained balance. He was a little slower to take his hands from her body, and the sensation unnerved her.

"Take my hand," he said, his tone brooking no argument.

She slipped her hand in his and focused on taking slow, steady steps to the stairwell, which thankfully was covered and dry.

To her disappointment, he released her hand as they climbed to the third floor. He unlocked the door and held it open, gesturing for her to precede him.

"This is really nice," Lauren said. The front door opened directly into the living room outfitted with furniture typical of a single guy. A dark gray couch faced a large flat-screen TV flanked by shelving. The living room opened to the kitchen, separated by a wood table with four chairs. The entire wall to her right was exposed red brick, giving off a trendy vibe.

She glanced at Andrew, taking him in with the space. While he looked every bit the part of the young, confident, professional male, she still didn't think he quite fit in here. Not completely. The more she got to know him, the more she saw the boy who grew up on a farm in a tiny town in Nebraska, surrounded by his family, hard work, and traditional values.

He caught her staring and tilted his head to the side in question. She looked away to survey the art and photographs hanging on the walls and knelt to examine the books on his bookshelf. Mostly textbooks and crime fiction novels, just like he'd said. She shifted slightly to the left and found a large stand full of DVDs.

"Wow. I didn't know they made these anymore."

Andrew laughed. "Besides documentaries, I love movies. I stream nowadays," he said in a tone that indicated he knew that was the "cool" thing to do, "but when I was in high school and early college I ended up with a pretty serious collection of discs."

"Uh-huh," she said with a grin, turning back to the assortment in front of her. She gasped and pulled one off the shelf. "Oh my gosh, you have *Love Actually*? I adore this movie."

"Let's watch it."

"Really?"

"What else are we going to do?" Andrew gestured to the living room window. "Doesn't look like it's gonna clear up anytime soon, might as well do something to pass the time."

As soon as the words were out of his mouth, thoughts of

alternative ways she and Andrew could pass the time invaded Lauren's mind. Heat spread through her body, and she pulled her bottom lip between her teeth, looking up at him from her crouched position.

He stood with his hands clenched at his sides, his intense eyes on her.

"A movie sounds good," she said, her voice a notch higher than usual. She stood and grasped the edge of the bookshelf, her legs a little unsteady.

Andrew took the DVD case from her, seemingly careful not to touch her as he did. She was thankful, because in that moment, she wasn't sure she could control herself if she felt his skin against hers.

As he bent over to put the DVD in, Lauren's stomach growled, and she checked the clock on the cable box.

"Why don't we eat something first? It's after six."

"Sure." He crossed into the kitchen and opened a cabinet. "Let's see...I've got stuff for spaghetti, sandwiches..." He moved on to the refrigerator. "Frozen pizza..."

She sidled up beside him and ducked underneath his arm to peer into the fridge. She didn't miss the grin on his face when she pressed up against his side.

Her expression mirrored his.

She moved a few things around and excitement filled her. "Can I make you an omelet? Breakfast for dinner?"

"You trying to show off your flipping skills?"

"Maybe."

He chuckled. "Sounds great."

He reached for the carton of eggs, and she inhaled his woodsy, masculine scent as he did. She grabbed a bag of spinach, tomatoes, and shredded cheese. After he helped her locate all the utensils and cookware she would need, he took a seat at the table and watched her work.

They chatted while she cooked and while they ate.

Though he complimented the meal and thanked her, he didn't eat much. Maybe half of his omelet...but she didn't take it personally. People's taste buds went haywire during chemo, and appetites came and went.

"Got anything sweet?" Lauren asked when she finished. She had a bad habit of eating a handful of M&M's after a meal.

"Sorry, I don't think I do. I try not to keep that stuff around. I don't have any self-control."

She pursed her lips, and her eyes dropped to his flat midsection. "So that's why your body looks like that."

Andrew laughed. "Flattering me again?"

She didn't respond to that and instead said, "I don't have self-control, either, and that includes at the grocery store. I can't seem to stop myself when I want something."

"I find that hard to believe. You're demonstrating excellent self-control when it comes to our situation. It's taking super-human strength on my part to keep you at arm's length."

"It's an illusion," she said quietly. She paused and toyed with a lock of her hair. "Besides, my problem is...once I start, I can't stop. I think it helps that I haven't tasted you yet. I don't know what I'm missing."

*Did I really just say that?* Judging by Andrew's expression he was surprised, too, his chest rising and falling with each breath. He groaned and leaned his head back against the chair, his eyes on the ceiling.

Lauren jumped up from her chair, nearly knocking it to the floor. "I'll, um...just—" She picked up both of their plates and walked them to the sink.

Andrew remained seated for a moment before he joined her and nudged her aside. "The cook doesn't clean."

After the dishes were done, they found themselves on opposite ends of the couch, talking. She made sure to keep plenty of space between them.

"What made you want to go to law school?"

Andrew cast his gaze across the room, like he was considering how to respond. "It's kind of a long story."

"That's okay."

His eyes came back to hers. "When I was a senior in high school, Jeni and I were in a bad car accident. A drunk driver swerved into our lane and hit us on the front driver side. Jeni was in much worse shape than I was, and her injuries, plus the condition of the vehicle, prevented her from being able to get out of the car. I could, though, and after making sure she was alive and breathing, I went to check on the guy who hit us.

"He reeked of alcohol, and there's no doubt in my mind he'd been drinking. When the cops arrived, they performed a Breathalyzer and he blew a zero-point-two, which is miles above the legal limit."

Lauren's hand had come up to cover her mouth. "Was Jeni okay? I mean...I know she is now...that's probably a stupid question. But it sounds awful. How bad was it?"

"A broken leg, concussion, and several torn ligaments in her shoulder. She was the star of the softball team, and it ruined her chances to finish the season, and she lost her scholarship to play for Oklahoma."

"Poor Jeni."

Andrew nodded. "The dumbass that hit us? He ended up getting away with it. All because he had an attorney who did some digging around and found that the Breathalyzer machine the police officer used was a week late for calibration. One week, and it was thrown out as evidence. There was no proof that he was under the influence, even though I smelled it and saw it with my own eyes, and he wasn't charged with a DUI."

"I can't believe that! How is that even possible?"

"He had a damn good attorney, that's how. That's not the

worst of it. Three weeks after the guy was released, he did it again, and that time he killed somebody."

Lauren gasped. "Someone you knew?"

Andrew shook his head. "No. But I couldn't shake this intense anger and a feeling of regret, that there was something I could have said or done through the proceedings, even just as a witness and victim of the crash, that would have either put him behind bars or had his license revoked. And maybe that person would still be alive.

"So that's what originally prompted my interest in law. I wanted to be on the other side of things, representing victims like Jeni and myself, making sure criminals like him weren't being set free because of a *technicality*. The more I've learned about the system, the more I've seen the other side of the coin, too, where innocent people are wrongly convicted. And I feel strongly about that, too, that someone needs to stand up for them. It's hard to do both, but I think our justice system should be able to function in a way that's honest and fair, and in all things, seeks the truth. I want to help get us there."

"That's incredible, Andrew." How was it that one man could be so wonderful? "I can see you doing exactly that. Dedicating your life to protecting people."

"While you dedicate your life to saving people."

She looked down. "I don't save them all."

"There's more than one way to save someone," he said softly.

She smiled but didn't look at him.

After a moment, he changed the subject. "Tell me what's so great about Coleman Cancer Center. Why do you want to stay here so badly?"

"So many things. The pharmacy department is advanced, and I love the involvement I have in patient care. There are hospitals where clinical pharmacists don't exist, and at a place like that I wouldn't be able to have the direct patient contact that I love so much."

"I like that part, too," he put in.

"Yeah, yeah," she said with a grin. "My coworkers are incredible. I've never worked with a group of people who cared so much about the patients they see. It inspires me every day. No matter which clinic I'm in, we're like a family, celebrating the successes of some patients and being there for one another when things don't turn out well for others. And aside from that, they're fun, interesting people. Several of the physicians are from other countries, and it's fascinating to hear what those places are like. Makes me want to visit them all someday."

"That's cool," Andrew agreed. "I'd love to travel more."

"Someday," she said wistfully. "Where will you go first? When you're a big-time lawyer and can do what you want and take vacations and stuff?"

"It'll be a while before I work my way up and can do what I want. But…I'd have to say New York City."

"Really? I was expecting you to say somewhere exotic."

"Why?"

She shrugged. "I don't know. I'm with you, though. I want to go to New York, too. Go to a Broadway show."

"Have dinner in Chinatown," he said.

"Ride the subway."

"Go for a run in Central Park."

"Shop at Tiffany's."

"Whoa, there. Big spender."

She laughed. "You only live once, right? What would you drop a lot of cash on?"

Andrew stroked his chin. "A few weeks ago, I would have said season tickets to the Broncos for my whole family. Now, I'm not so sure."

Lauren frowned. "Stop that. Don't overhaul your family's favorite team just because the quarterback is a jerk. I'm sure there's a player on every NFL team who has done something sketchy for the sake of his game."

"He's not just a jerk. He was a jerk to *you*. I refuse to support him or the team he plays for."

She pursed her lips, irritated more at herself by the pleasure she felt in that, than at Andrew for being so ridiculous about it.

But was it time to let go a little, and face the truth?

Whether she wanted them to or not, her walls against him were crumbling, and it was only a matter of time before nothing was left.

# Chapter Fourteen

They kept talking for hours, though Andrew couldn't have put his finger on exactly what they talked about. They simply talked. They talked about high school, about their hobbies and their best friends. She told him about Kate and Samantha, her closest friends from Cedar Creek, and he told her about some of his childhood buddies and the friends he'd made when he moved to Kansas City. They talked more about music, because they both loved it, and discovered they'd been at several of the same concerts that had been in Kansas City over the last few years.

"I wonder if we ever crossed paths," Andrew mused.

"I doubt it. I think I'd remember...you're pretty noteworthy."

He laughed. He adored her pun addiction. "And you're nothing but treble."

She lifted one shoulder even as she grinned. "But if we had, do you think things would have turned out differently?" she asked.

"Maybe. If I'd asked you out back then, you'd have had

no reason to turn me down. How refreshing." He grinned.

"I still would have turned you down," she returned. "You're too attractive, remember?"

"I wouldn't have given up easily. Just like now, I'd have tried to change your mind."

"I hate to admit it's working."

"Good."

His gaze roamed over her, and for a split second he considered moving closer to her, to see how she would respond. Would she scold him, or smile up at him, pleased he'd made the first move?

He thought back to the words she'd said just a few short hours ago.

She hadn't tasted him *yet*.

He couldn't do this much longer. He couldn't take his eyes off her, from the way her breathing sped up as her gaze met his, her lip once again tucked behind white teeth. Damn, he wanted his teeth to be the one nipping at her mouth, his tongue following in the wake to soothe her skin. He craved it like he was an alcoholic and she was a bottle of fine whisky.

A slight wave of nausea passed over him, reminding him that had he been alone tonight, he would have skipped dinner altogether. But she'd been so excited about cooking for him, and she'd probably been starving. She hadn't received chemo yesterday, after all. Though the queasy sensation was there and gone, he hesitated. "Should we start the movie?"

"Sure."

Andrew picked up the remote. "Let the record state I didn't pick this movie. It's romantic, and I'm not sure you'll be able to keep your hands to yourself. I promise I'll be good, but if you suddenly feel the need to come on to me, I won't say no."

Lauren shot him a wry glance. "I'll try to control myself."

As the movie played, Andrew's mouth felt dry, and his

stomach churned. *Please, not now.* He tried desperately to focus on the movie, like he could use mind over matter to control his body's response to the poison that had been shot into his veins yesterday. His favorite part of the movie was coming up, where Andrew Lincoln's character comes to Kiera Knightley's door and holds up signs to tell her that he's always been in love with her.

He and Lauren had inched closer together throughout the movie, and he felt her hand cover his. His heart thumped in his chest, and he wasn't sure if it was because of the nausea or her proximity. Probably both.

He slowly turned his head and found her eyes on him, her gaze focused and her chin tilted up. Her fingers trailed up his forearm, caressed his bicep, and curled around his neck, while she simultaneously shifted onto her knees to bring her face closer to his.

Holy shit, he wanted this so much. He wanted her so much. His body vibrated with it, ached with it. He gently cupped his hand around the back of her head and pressed his forehead to hers, and his stomach heaved.

*NO.* He leapt off the couch and lunged for the hallway, barely getting the bathroom door closed behind him before his knees hit the tile. The burning, cramping sensation in his abdomen intensified tenfold, and he felt light-headed as the bile rose in the back of his throat. As the first wave of his stomach's contents were expelled, the door opened and Lauren was at his side, her hand on his back.

"N-no," he shook his head, pushing her away with his left arm. "Leave, please." His right hand gripped the edge of the toilet and he spit, the acidic taste bringing on another wretch.

She didn't leave, and instead began hastily rifling through his drawers. "Did you take anything today? Where's your ondansetron?"

"Lauren, get out of here," he ground out, mortified

beyond measure as he vomited again.

"I know I sent in prochlorperazine, where is it?" Her pitch was rising, like she was getting panicked.

He began to sweat, and his stomach cramped again, and the desperation in his chest boiled over. He wanted her gone, far away from him when he was like this. When he was weak and sick and disgusting. He tried one last time, thinking of nothing but isolating himself. "Lauren, get the fuck out!"

He couldn't see her reaction because his head was once again over the toilet, but he heard the door close. When he could breathe, he looked up and found himself alone in the bathroom. He closed his eyes and hung his head, rocking back on his haunches. He yanked the bath towel from where it hung on the wall and wiped his mouth.

When he was sure his stomach had nothing else to throw up, he pushed himself backward and leaned his back against the bathtub. He covered his face with trembling hands and waited until his heartbeat returned to a normal rhythm and his breathing evened out.

After several minutes he flushed the toilet and stood. He refused to look at himself in the mirror as he covered his toothbrush generously with toothpaste, knowing he might never leave the bathroom if he saw his reflection. He scrubbed his mouth thoroughly and rinsed, and then did it again.

When he opened the door and took in the woman before him, his heart shattered into a million pieces. Lauren was curled against the wall across from the bathroom door, her knees pulled to her chest, her head bent forward. One hand was clasped around the back of her neck, gripping so hard her knuckles were white, and the other covered her eyes.

She was crying.

Andrew's own vision blurred as he lowered himself to the floor. He sat beside her for a moment without speaking, the echo of her halted breathing the only sound in the hallway.

He swallowed, the crisp taste of spearmint flooding his senses. His shoulders felt heavy as he put his arm around her. He half expected her to pull away, but she didn't. She didn't respond at all.

He pulled her closer to him, side by side, their ribs, hips, and thighs pressed together. "I'm sorry," he whispered in a broken voice.

She hiccupped and curled into him, burying her face in his shirt.

"I'm sorry," he said again, reaching across to embrace her fully with both arms. She stretched across his body to hug him back and held tight, allowing her bent knees to fall to the side and rest across his legs.

They remained that way for a long time. Not speaking, holding each other, her tears subsiding and her breath returning to normal. He stroked her hair and rubbed her back, feeling his heart swell with emotion. When she hadn't moved in a while he peeked at her face.

She'd fallen asleep against his chest. He released a slow, steady exhale. What just happened had been horrible, but he felt strangely content in this moment. He kept his arms around her body and leaned his head back against the wall, and eventually sleep pulled him under.

Several hours later, Andrew woke with a major crick in his neck. He and Lauren were still in the hallway of his apartment—he sat with his legs extended and his back against the wall; Lauren was curled into a ball, pressed against his body with her arms loosely around him.

He blinked and scrubbed a hand down his face as the events of the night before rushed back to him.

Lauren cooking dinner. Talking for hours. Watching

*Love Actually*, and Lauren finally making a move to kiss him. His body choosing that exact moment to fail him, and him yelling at her.

Making her cry.

He closed his eyes. His body hurt, and so did his heart.

He opened them again and gazed down at the beautiful woman lying across him. Her dark eyelashes lay across her lightly freckled cheek, and her thick hair was swept back and bunched near his ribs. She'd taken her shoes off when they came in, and her feet looked so tiny and feminine.

He chuckled at himself. He had it bad if he was admiring her feet, of all things.

He wanted her more than he'd ever wanted a woman in his life. And not only physically, though that was an extremely powerful desire. He wanted to be *hers*. The one she called when she was upset or excited. He wanted her face to light up when she saw him, like he knew his did when he laid eyes on her. He wanted to hold her hand in public and kiss her in the coffee line at The Grind House. He wanted everyone to know that they were together, and that she was his.

A line had been crossed. He didn't know if it was the hours of conversation, the near-kiss during the movie, or holding her after such a raw display of vulnerability. Maybe it was something else entirely.

But he was done pretending.

He also felt confident, for the first time, that she felt the same. She'd seen him at his worst last night…and not just on his knees getting sick. He'd yelled at her to get out—no, to get *the fuck* out—and leave him alone. And yet, she was still here, wrapped around him.

She stirred, her arm brushing his groin as she moved, and he quickly cleared his throat to wake her up completely. He put his hands on her shoulders and helped her sit up.

She rubbed her eyes and yawned, her hair tumbling

across her shoulders. She lifted her eyes to meet his, and he smiled tentatively, suddenly feeling both nervous and lighter at the same time.

"Good morning," she said, her low, sleepy voice sending a shock of desire through him. "Jeez, I'm sorry I fell asleep on you in the hallway. That had to have been miserable."

"It was the furthest thing from miserable."

She returned his smile and stood up, holding her hand out to him.

He stood up with her and let her use the bathroom while he went to the kitchen to make coffee. When she joined him, he handed her a full mug.

"I used some of your toothpaste, I hope that's okay," she said.

"I'm surprised there was any left. I brushed the hell out of my teeth last night."

Her gaze was intent on his, and he appreciated that she didn't shy away from his reference to what happened.

"How do you feel this morning?" she asked.

"I'm a little achy, but it's always like that through the weekend after chemo. Other than that, I'm great."

"Good." Her chest rose with her inhale. "I'm sorry."

"You have nothing to be sorry for."

"Yes, I do. I shouldn't have followed you in there like that, and I should have left the second you asked me to..." She shook her head.

"You were trying to help. I shouldn't have spoken to you like I did."

"I don't blame you. If I'd been the one getting sick and you came in? I would have freaked out. I wouldn't want you to see me like that. But it's my job, my entire life's work, to make sure people don't go through what you did last night. And of all people, you're the one I failed." Tears welled up in her eyes. "I had no idea you were having so much trouble after chemo, there are so many other things that can help… other medications you can try—"

Andrew shook his head. "I don't want more drugs. I don't even take the ones I have. That doesn't happen every time, I promise. I don't feel great for a few days, I'll admit. But there's been only one other time I've gotten sick like that."

She just looked at him with those big green eyes, and a tear slipped down her cheek. "I hate this. I hate it that you're sick. I wish I could take it from you. Or even better, that it never happened."

"Don't say that." He walked around the kitchen island, coming to stand directly in front of her. "I don't wish that. I may never have met you."

"You technically met me at the coffee shop, before you ever came to the cancer center."

He reached out and took one of her hands. "The only reason I stopped at The Grind House was because it was on my way to the cancer center. Plus, you said yourself you wouldn't have given me a chance, based on that encounter alone. If God hadn't forced your hand by putting me in your clinic, you'd never have looked at me twice."

Her eyelids lowered marginally, and she bit her lip, causing his gaze to drop to her mouth. "I would have looked. I might have never spoken to you, but I definitely would have looked."

He grinned, and she tilted her face up to his. Feeling bold, he moved a few inches closer, his eyes moving between her eyes and her lips. Her grip on his hand tightened.

He slowly lowered his head, watching her, waiting for an indication it wasn't what she wanted.

"Lauren?" It was a question and a warning.

Her breath hitched, her pupils dilated, and her eyes darted to his mouth. He let go of her hand and put one arm around her, his heart beating erratically in his chest. The air sizzled between them, like a firework about to go off. There was nothing he wanted more than this woman standing before him, and he was done waiting.

"I have one treatment left. In less than two weeks, it will be over. I know I said I wouldn't make a move until I was done, but I don't think I can do it anymore." He brushed her auburn hair back from her face. "If you want me to stop, tell me now."

# Chapter Fifteen

For once, Lauren didn't think about all the reasons this was a bad idea. Or at least she ignored them, pushing them deep down. Instead, she thought about how much she loved being this close to Andrew and how she wanted him closer.

He spread one hand across her upper back, his fingers spanning the width between her shoulder blades. His other hand brushed the hair away from her face, starting ever so gently at her forehead, leaving a trail of fire across her skin as he smoothed it back.

His proximity was dizzying, and her heart was like a drum in her chest, vibrating through her ribcage. Her breath came quickly, her breasts brushing his hard chest with each upward movement.

He towered over her, his eyes locked on hers, and it might have been uncomfortable if it wasn't so intense. She couldn't form a coherent thought to save her life.

"Andrew..." she whispered. She wasn't telling him to stop, that was for sure. Her fingers gripped his arms tighter, her action completing the thought she couldn't seem to say.

He closed his eyes.

"I have to." His breath caressed her cheek as he spoke, and a shiver ran through her, down her spine and to the tips of her toes. He touched his forehead to hers. "I *have* to." His lower lip pressed upward against her top one. It wasn't a kiss, exactly…his mouth was open slightly and so was hers, and they weren't properly aligned. But the feeling of him against her, his nose brushing hers as he shifted to slide both of his lips fully across hers, was earth-shattering. It seared her soul, burning her inhibitions to ash.

She leaned in to him, molding her mouth to his, their lips becoming the single most important connection between them, despite his arms crushing her body close. A kiss could say so many things, and these words had been denied far too long.

*I think about you always.*
*I care about you.*
*I've been wanting you.*
*I adore you.*

She lost herself in his kiss, his smell, his breath. His tongue swept into her mouth and she moaned, letting him in completely. He released a low growl from deep within his throat, and suddenly his hands gripped her hips and she felt herself being lifted into the air. Her butt hit the granite, and he moved between her legs, putting her at the perfect height. Face-to-face, she tilted her head and kissed him deeply.

He pulled her to the edge of the countertop and their hips came together, her legs wrapping around his waist. She arched herself against his broad torso as they kissed feverishly, stopping only for brief seconds to take in ragged breaths.

Andrew's hands were everywhere and nowhere at once; the second she sensed his touch in one place he moved to another. Her face, her hair, her waist. A few times his lips dipped to her neck or collarbone, only to return to her lips within seconds.

"Never stop kissing me," he breathed into her mouth. "Never."

She didn't stop. Not for a long, long time.

Finally, she mustered the resolve to pull back, but she left her hands where they gripped Andrew's waist. That part of him was as hard and muscled as she'd imagined. Damn him and his healthy eating habits.

His warm brown eyes were full of passion and affection. She blinked, taking in the gravity of what she'd done.

She tucked her lips between her teeth and furrowed her brow. "Oops."

He stared at her for a moment, then threw his head back and laughed.

She couldn't help but start giggling, too.

"I don't think I've ever had that response after kissing a woman."

"What's the standard one? They probably rip off all of their clothes, don't they? Wait," she quickly added. "Don't answer that. I don't want to know."

Andrew's laughter came to an abrupt halt and his eyes met hers, his gaze smoldering.

"You know, it's weird." He traced her cheekbone with his thumb. "I know I've kissed other women before you, but I can't seem to remember a single thing about them."

She leaned in to his caress.

"You're all I think about," he said.

"It's the same for me," she admitted. "No matter how hard I try to stop it."

He kissed her softly, and her pulse was like fire in her veins. She slid her fingers around to his lower back, gripping the waistband of his jeans. A low rumble rose from his chest, and he fisted his hands in her hair.

"This is..." He tore his mouth away, and his forehead came to rest on her shoulder. "I can't even describe this."

"Consuming," Lauren supplied, and he nodded, tilting his head to brush his lips against her neck. "What..." Her voice wavered when he sucked on a particularly sensitive area of skin near her throat. "What are we going to do?"

Andrew lifted his head. "What do you mean?"

"How are we going to do this? Your last chemo is in twelve days. I don't want to be with you publicly until then, and to be safe, I don't want to tell anyone until after your scan."

Andrew searched her face. "We can't go back to the way things were. I can't." He brushed his fingers across her lips. "Not after this."

Lauren couldn't, either. "We have to be careful. Especially at the cancer center, but in public, too. We can't go on dates or show outward affection when we're around people. You never know who could see us..." She thought of Gavin and his warning.

"I'm all for lying low until after the scan. You'll just move in here, yeah? We'll hole ourselves up at my apartment for the next two weeks. I mean, if you insist, we don't even have to leave my bed." He grinned and winked, a boyish, hopeful gleam in his eye.

She smacked him on the shoulder, smiling. "I still have to work, big man. And you don't get me in your bed yet."

"That's fine." His expression turned serious. "I was kidding about that part. I'm in no hurry. I want to take this slow, do it right." He stopped for a second and gripped the back of his neck with one hand, suddenly appearing vulnerable. "I chose you even when you weren't an option. I won't do anything to mess this up now that you've chosen me, too."

"Andrew," she murmured, reaching up to tug at his hand.

He let her bring it between them, where she pressed it against her chest. "My heart chose you a long time ago. Even if it took my mind a while to catch up."

Lauren didn't make it home that day, and not because a foot of snow covered the ground.

She and Andrew were all over each other all day, kissing, touching, and tangled up together. Lauren had, without question, never enjoyed kissing someone so much. He alternated between slow, languorous minutes where he took his time learning what she liked and how she responded, and greedy, hungry kisses where it seemed he couldn't get enough.

She'd never felt so safe and *wanted*. Was this how it felt, to be in a real relationship? With someone who cared about you, who maybe even loved you? It felt surreal, the joy inside her, ready to burst at any moment.

No wonder people loved falling in love.

Lauren saw Andrew every day the following week. After work on Friday, she tried to keep her distance so she could get some things done.

Key word: tried.

Andrew: *Come over.*

Lauren: *Can't, I need to study.*

Andrew: *Study over here.*

Lauren: *You know that's not what I'll end up doing.*

Andrew: *I can control myself.*
Andrew: *Promise*
Andrew: *I miss you.*

Lauren: *You said we'd study last night, and when you came over you pinned me to my couch for two hours.*

Andrew: *Funny, I didn't hear you complaining.*

Lauren: *Duh*
Lauren: *Regardless, I really have to study tonight.*

Andrew: *I want to see you. I should study too. The Grind House?*

Lauren: *Can you keep your hands to yourself?*

Andrew: *I can be discreet.*

Lauren: *That's not the same thing.*

Andrew: *It's a risk you'll have to take.*

Lauren: *I'm not going until you promise me you'll be good.*

Andrew: *No one's even going to be paying attention to us. But I promise that if someone looks at us, they'll have no idea about the dirty thoughts running through my head.*

Lauren: *...*

Andrew: *Fine. I'll be good, I promise.*

Lauren: *Okay. I'll be there in twenty.*

Nineteen minutes later, Lauren walked into The Grind House to find Andrew already at a table. He'd done well, grabbing a two-top near the back corner, partially hidden from the busiest part of the café.

His eyes tracked her as she made her way to him, a sweet

smile on his face. He tugged the gray knit hat a little farther down on his head as she approached. Tempted to forgo her own rule and give him a quick peck, she steeled herself at the last second and sat down across from him.

"Hi."

"Hi."

The air between them sparked with energy, and she wondered how long they'd last.

"I got us coffee." Andrew pushed a mug in her direction.

She smiled. "Thanks." She pulled out her notebook and laptop, powering it on. She felt his gaze still on her. "Are you going to study or not?"

He flattened his lips to hide his grin and obediently shifted his eyes to the open laptop sitting before him.

To help her focus on the material and not on Andrew, she plugged in her headphones and started her reading playlist, consisting mainly of classical piano music. She got in a solid half hour of studying before it all went to hell.

It started with Andrew's foot. The concept of "playing footsie" with someone had always seemed a little ridiculous, because how on earth could touching someone's feet with your own be a turn-on? When both parties were wearing socks and shoes, no less?

Well. She had some things to learn.

When his shoe first slid along the inside of hers, she looked up to find him watching her, his brown eyes dark in the dimly lit corner of the coffee shop. She tried to keep her attention on her study guide, but then he nudged her foot to the left, forcing her legs apart. Butterflies filled her belly and swarmed aggressively when his knee pushed between her thighs.

"Andrew," she chastised.

His eyes went wide in an innocent expression saying, *what did I do?*

Lauren arched an eyebrow. He knew exactly what he was

doing. He halted his movement but left his leg where it was. Five minutes later her phone lit up with a text message.

Andrew: *You look really beautiful.*

Lauren: *Thank you. We're supposed to be studying.*

Andrew: *Don't I look cute, too?*

She kept her attention on her phone, feeling his eyes on her.

Lauren: *You're easily the hottest guy here. There's a girl to your left who keeps checking you out, and it's all I can do to stay on my side of the table. She needs to know you're taken.*

Andrew: *I support whatever you need to do, even if it means jumping over the table to maul me.*

Lauren looked up with a laugh. "Maul you?"

"A man can hope." He waggled his eyebrows and tapped at his screen again.

Andrew: *And Lauren? I'm taken whether she knows it or not.*

That did funny things to her heart, and she lifted her eyes once more, letting all the emotions she felt for him shine through. She was still aware of their situation, though, and where they were. When his hand slid across the table in her direction she shook her head, dropping her gaze back to her phone.

Lauren: *Apparently, I'm territorial. Who knew?*

Andrew: *I like it.*

Lauren: *I like you.*

Andrew: *I'm dying to kiss you.*

Lauren: *I love it when you wear that hoodie. You wore it the first day we met.*

Andrew's foot curved around her ankle, entwining their legs together. Breathing became a little more difficult.

Andrew: *I remember everything about you from that day. Your laugh, the way you wore your hair. Your freckles and the way you blushed when you "accidentally" ran into me.*

Lauren: *Yes. It was my brilliant attempt to get you to notice me. I was hoping for a second-degree burn but the coffee wasn't hot enough.*

Andrew: *Lukewarm did the trick.*

Lauren: *Tell me truthfully. Did you see the picture on my phone? Before the coffee incident?*

Andrew: *The breasts? I most certainly did.*

Lauren: *They weren't mine, you know.*

Andrew: *…I can't think of a gentlemanly way to say that I know they weren't yours.*

Lauren: *Oh.*
Lauren: *You know, if you wanted to be a little ungentlemanly…sometimes…that would be okay.*

Andrew shot to his feet. He slammed his laptop closed and was standing next to her chair with his belongings in one hand in fifteen seconds flat. "We're leaving."

Lauren blinked, only now processing where she'd allowed their text conversation to go, and taking in his large body looming over her. "We are?"

He leaned down to speak directly into her ear, his breath tickling the tiny hairs on her neck. "If we don't, I'm going to maul you right here in front of everyone."

Her mouth went dry, and she ran her tongue across her bottom lip to moisten the surface. Andrew's mouth dropped open slightly as he watched her.

She cleared her throat. "Right. Let's go."

. . .

Exactly one week later, Lauren sat in front of her computer at work, typing progress notes for the patients she'd seen that morning. She heard a feminine groan from behind her and swiveled around.

"I've lost it," Kiara said, throwing her hands in the air.

"What?" Lauren asked.

"My momentum."

From Lauren's other side, Emma laughed. "No kidding. It's Friday, we're all a little fried."

"We've got two patients left this morning and none this afternoon," came Dr. Patel's voice from across the room. "I know you've got it in you."

"Speak for yourself," Dr. Stanford grumbled, and Lauren nodded. Their afternoon was booked solid.

As Lauren typed a note to document the chemo education she'd just finished, she heard Dr. Patel and Emma converse about Andrew, who was there for a routine visit.

She felt a jolt of anticipation run through her at the sound of his name. She hadn't seen him for three days because she'd come down with a virus and didn't want to expose him. He wasn't happy about it and had let her know via text and through her front door when he brought soup and tea to her house. It had nearly killed her, as she'd slumped against the other side of the door, to not open it and fall into his arms. But his recent lab work had shown a low white blood cell count, and protecting him from whatever bug she had was more important than her desire to touch him.

Today she finally felt back to normal, and her fever was gone. She couldn't wait to see him, and she tried to act normal as she eavesdropped.

"Kiara, be sure we have a PET scan scheduled for Bishop next week," Dr. Patel said. "If things have gone as planned, he won't need more chemo."

"I'm on it," Kiara replied, and picked up the phone.

Emma looked around. "Where's my damn stethoscope?"

Lauren gave her the side-eye. "Around your neck."

Emma's hand flew to the curve of her shoulder, and she smiled sheepishly. "Oh. Thanks."

Dr. Patel and Emma finished reviewing the patient charts and went into their respective exam rooms. Lauren listened while Kiara spoke to radiology and scheduled Andrew's PET scan, and made a mental note that it would be next Thursday at seven-thirty in the morning.

He'd hate having to be there so early, but at least he wouldn't have to go all morning without eating. She'd remind him of that when he complained.

Emma was back in the workroom after only ten minutes, reporting that Andrew was doing well. She put her hands on the back of Lauren's chair, turning Lauren around to face her. Emma looked her right in the eye and said, "He said he had a medication question, and asked if any pharmacists were around. I told him I'd send you in."

Emma had both hands on the armrests of Lauren's chair, leaning toward her, her head angled to one side.

Lauren glanced at Kiara, who wasn't paying them a lick

of attention, and back to Emma, who continued to stare at her. Was Emma acting weird, or was she imagining things?

She scooted her chair to the left so she could stand. Dr. Stanford had just gone to see a follow-up patient, and Lauren had finished the note she was working on. "Sure, I'll see what he needs."

Emma muttered something under her breath that sounded almost like "I bet you will," but when Lauren looked back at her, she'd moved on to Kiara. Lauren shrugged it off and entered the hallway.

Anticipation spread through her as she checked the board and went to the room he was in. She knocked on the door before entering, as she did every time she went to see a patient, and walked in.

Andrew was alone.

Lauren closed the door behind her and walked forward two steps, then stopped.

The expression on Andrew's face was unlike anything she'd ever seen. His eyes trailed down her body and back up, slowly.

"What?"

Andrew shook his head as if to clear his vision. "You're wearing scrubs."

She fidgeted. "So?"

"I've never seen you in scrubs before."

"I woke up late," she said defensively, her eyebrows furrowing slightly when Andrew stood up. She loved how tall he was. "*Someone* kept me up late texting, and I didn't have time to—"

"Let me stop you right there," Andrew interrupted. "What I should have led with is how hot you look in scrubs."

Lauren's cheeks warmed. "Oh." She backed up a step as he closed in on her. "Andrew, what are you doing?"

His hands came up to rest on her waist. He looked down

at her. "I don't know," he said quietly. "I'm so glad it was you. I took a chance. I've missed you. How do you feel?"

"Great," she whispered. She needed to stop this. Move away from him, away from his hands and his scent and his intense eyes. But it was hard to breathe now that his thumbs were sliding up and down along her hips. "Andrew…" she whispered. Her heart rate sped up and her breath joined the race. "I can't… we can't. I'm at work. If someone saw us like this…" Speaking the words aloud restored some of her willpower, and she gently slid his hands away from her body. The loss of the warmth of his fingers almost made her want to cry.

Andrew dropped his hands to his sides, then lifted one closed fist to his mouth. He shook his head slowly. "But…the scrubs…"

Lauren laughed a little. "What's the deal? You have a fetish or something?"

Andrew swallowed. "I had it bad for Isabel Stephens."

"From *Grey's Anatomy*?"

"I binge-watched it a few summers ago. Couldn't get over how hot she looked in those blue scrubs…with that drawstring that's so easy to tug loose…and I don't know how it's possible, but you look ten times sexier than she ever did." Andrew's eyelids lowered slightly, and his free hand inched toward her waist.

"Andrew, you're not taking my pants off!"

He jerked his hand away, and his eyes widened. "Shit, I'm sorry. You'd better go." He moved back a step. "And don't wear those around me again, unless we're *not here*."

A tingle shot down her spine, and the temperature in the room seemed to increase by ten degrees. Andrew's gaze was hot on hers, and his nostrils flared slightly with his heavy breathing. Suddenly he was right in front of her again. He softly touched her face, sliding his fingers across her cheek.

"Just a quick kiss," he said. "Then you can get back to

work."

"That's not a good idea." Still, she leaned closer.

"I know. But I can't..."

Lauren's protest died on her lips, because suddenly his were pressed against them, causing the most wonderful friction and sending her stomach into a free fall.

The door opened.

Lauren pushed Andrew back at the same time he lurched away from her.

Kiara froze with the door partially open.

It looked bad. Even if Kiara hadn't seen the actual kiss—and that was a big IF—the scene now was just as bad. Lauren's back was against the wall, her cheeks flushed and her hands shaking. Andrew stood awkwardly in the middle of the room looking like a child caught with his hand in the cookie jar.

"I—" Andrew began.

"I'll come back," Kiara interrupted. With a purse of her lips and a disapproving glance at Lauren, she shut the door.

Lauren's hands flew to cover her mouth. "Oh no." Her voice came out muffled.

Andrew moved farther away from her. "I'm so sorry. Shit, Lauren, I'm sorry."

Fear automatically coiled in her stomach, even though it had been Kiara. Kiara was her friend...she wouldn't say anything. Right?

"I can fix this. I see Kiara every time I'm here; she likes me. She likes Jeni. I'll talk to her," Andrew spit the words out rapid fire.

Lauren held up a hand. "No, please don't talk to her about it. Let me. She's my friend...I think it will be okay." She gave him a stern look. "But see? We *can't do that*."

He sat down, still looking like a little boy who knew he'd been caught and was bravely awaiting his punishment. Lauren wouldn't have pegged him as a back-talker, though.

"We can't do that *today*. After today I won't need chemo anymore."

"You don't know that. We won't know until after your scan next week. Which is Thursday at seven thirty, by the way."

"Damn, that's early." He rested his elbows on his knees. "You keep talking about my PET scan like you don't think it's going to be good. Is there something that makes you think we didn't get it all?"

Lauren was torn, the girlfriend part of her wanting to do nothing but assure him all would be well, and the oncology provider part of her wanting to prepare him for every possible outcome. She went with a mixture of both.

"Of course not. I think it will be perfect." She prayed for it every day. "But it's possible you'll need more chemo. It's a small possibility, but it's there."

"I can't think like that. I've focused on today for months, knowing this would be my last one. I've kept this to myself, and saying it will probably piss you off, but chemo sucks. It *really* sucks, and I don't want any more of it."

"You're right. That does piss me off." Lauren clenched her teeth. "Let us help you, you big, stubborn man!"

Andrew smiled at her. "You've helped me more than you'll ever know, my beautiful girl."

His words and the soft expression in his eyes made Lauren's knees go weak. But he didn't stop there, and the next sentence out of his mouth made her heart seize up, but not in a good way.

"You've been the perfect distraction during this miserable process and taken my mind off the worst thing I've ever been through."

Lauren felt like she'd been punched in the stomach, and all the air left her lungs. She blinked. "Is that all I've been? A distraction?"

Andrew's expression turned horrified. "That's not what I—"

"Stop." Lauren put her hand on the door handle. "I need to get out of here and talk to Kiara. There's no telling what she thinks we're doing in here."

Andrew stood up. "Wait—"

"No. Not right now, we'll talk later." Lauren slipped through the door and shut it behind her. Her hands trembled, and her eyes filled with hot tears.

*Not now. Keep it together. Focus on what happened before he called you a distraction... You can deal with that later.*

Lauren dreaded facing Kiara and felt like she was walking straight toward a firing squad. As she feared, when she entered the workroom, Kiara and Emma were waiting, the room otherwise empty. Both were unsmiling with arms crossed in front of their chests, eyebrows raised.

Lauren opened her mouth to speak, but Emma cut her off. "Are you insane?" She turned to Kiara. "Also, I told you so."

Lauren's eyes widened at that last comment. "What do you mean, 'you told her so?' How long have you known?"

Kiara's head whipped toward Lauren. "How long has there been something for her to know about?"

Lauren lifted a hand and rubbed her forehead, trying to ignore the sensation of a knife in her heart. She needed to deal with what Kiara saw before processing what Andrew had just said.

"I didn't mean for it to happen." She spoke quietly, aware that someone could enter the room at any minute. "I told him multiple times that I couldn't get involved with him. And for the longest time nothing...inappropriate happened. We did start talking, and became friends, and I saw him a few times outside of work at Children's Hospital—"

"And you spent Thanksgiving with his family," Emma cut in.

"How did you know about that?" Lauren squeaked.

"Why do I not know *any* of this?" Kiara whined.

Emma uncrossed her arms and propped her hands on her hips.

"His sister, Jeni, invited me over for Thanksgiving. I said no, but then I just sort of found myself there..." Lauren lowered herself into her usual chair and slumped her shoulders. She looked between her two friends, knowing they were responding this way out of concern. "You guys, I've tried so hard to be professional, and ignore the way I feel about him. It's the hardest thing I've ever done in my life. I love it here, and I want to stay so badly, and I'm so terrified of what could happen if someone finds ou—" She stopped short when Dr. Patel came in.

"Kiara, can you make a renal ultrasound appointment for Mrs. Garcia? I'm not sure why her creatinine keeps rising... um, why is everyone staring at me?"

The three women were grouped in the middle of the floor and had all gone silent and focused on Dr. Patel when she entered.

*Mothersmucker.* Lauren froze. She was never cool in situations like this.

Kiara's eyes widened.

Emma spoke quietly and smoothly. "Don't mind us, Lauren was just telling us about a date she had this weekend. One that went horribly wrong." She gave Lauren a hard look. "We'll pick it back up, later."

Dr. Patel accepted this, and Kiara returned to her computer. Lauren breathed a sigh of relief, though it was short-lived.

This conversation was far from over.

# Chapter Sixteen

The pounding started at five-thirty. Not the pounding in Andrew's head...that had begun the second Lauren had walked out of his exam room. This was the beat of his fist against her front door. "Lauren!"

Nothing.

"Let me in. I'm not leaving until you talk to me. You're not a distract—"

Lauren pulled open the door, and he stopped mid-sentence. She seemed so small, as he stood with one hand gripping the doorframe above his head. The other was in a fist, poised to hit the door again, and he dropped it to his side. The sky behind him was gray and the ground covered in snow, creating a scene as dismal as the air between them. She still wore her blue scrubs. Still looked beautiful.

"Get in here, it's freezing," Lauren snapped. "Why aren't you wearing a hat?"

He walked past her without responding. He went straight to her living room and stopped in the middle, turning to face her. She stood behind the couch, resting her hands on the back, like she wanted something between them, or something to hold on to.

He tucked his hands into his front pockets. "I've been calling you all day."

"I know."

"Did you get in trouble at work?"

"No."

"Lauren, please. Tell me what happened. Tell me I didn't fuck everything up for you, and for us."

She sighed and walked around the couch to sit down. "Kiara and Emma won't say anything. No one else knows. They agree it's questionable for me to be with you, and it just reminded me of the reasons why I was hesitant in the first place." She blinked, a tear streaming down her cheek. "But I don't think it matters, because even though I think you're worth it, I don't think we feel the same—"

"Lauren," he choked out. He lurched forward and dropped to his knees in front of her. He took her hands in his. "Please, I beg you. Hear me. What I said, about you being a distraction—I didn't mean it like it sounded. The second I saw your face I knew what you thought, and it nearly killed me."

He pressed her palm flat against his firm chest, so she would feel his pounding heart. "What I meant was that I don't know how I ever would have gotten through this without you. From the first time I saw you, you've been this bright light of beauty and joy, making this dark road bearable. When I'm so tired I can barely walk up the stairs to my apartment, or when I don't eat for two days because my stomach is on fire…I think about you, and the next time I get to see you. I tell myself it's worth it to push through, because not only do I want to see you at my next visit, I want to see you next month. Next year. Five years from now. When I want to quit, I tell myself it's not an option, because I can see the life I want to live, and I want you to be in it. Beyond all this. Beyond chemo, and scans, and lab work every week that tells me I need to be careful who I see and what I do. I want to get past all this and for you to still be there, by my side.

"If all you are is a distraction, I hope you'll be that for the rest of my life. Be my distraction on the hard days when work gets me down. When I lose a case, or when I don't get the promotion I wanted. Be my distraction when my sisters drive me to the brink of insanity and I need someone to bring me back. Be my distraction when we turn on the news and when the world is falling apart and it's hard to see the good in it. If you're there, I'll have faith that God is real and that He still cares."

Tears streamed down her cheeks and he cupped her face, wiping them away with his thumbs. "I can't do this without you, Lauren."

"Yes, you can." Her voice wavered, and her bright green eyes looked deep into his. "But I don't want you to."

Andrew's eyes closed, and he mouthed a wordless *thank you* before he crushed her to his chest. They held each other tightly for a long moment, Andrew still on his knees, Lauren supported by his arms around her.

Andrew pulled back and kissed her softly, reverently. He didn't think he'd ever tire of kissing her, of touching her.

He worked his way down the column of her throat, loving the way her breath hitched with each press of his lips. Her hands roamed his shoulders and arms, causing goosebumps to break out along his skin.

Just when he'd made his way back up, his phone rang. Lauren tried to move away, but he held firm.

"Ignore it," he said against her mouth.

The tone stopped for a few seconds, then started up again.

With a muttered curse, Andrew rocked back on his heels

and reached into his pocket.

"What the hell do you want, Logan?"

Lauren watched with an amused expression while Andrew listened to Logan's proposition. "I'm at Lauren's. I know. *I know.* I'll ask her, okay? She had a long day, and I'm not going anywhere without her. I'll let you know."

He ended the call and looked at her. "Logan wants to go out tonight to celebrate my last chemo. What do you think?"

Lauren thought for a moment. She gifted him with a wide smile, the first he'd seen since she first walked into his exam room that morning.

"I'm in."

...

The following Wednesday, Andrew found himself sitting on a rickety wooden bench, hunched over his feet to make sure the laces were tight.

"Ready?" Lauren asked.

"No."

"Come on. Stand up already."

"Don't rush me, woman."

"They're tight enough, I promise. I won't let you fall."

Andrew gave her the side-eye. "If I go down, there's no way your tiny body can stop me."

Lauren put her hands on her hips, wobbling slightly. "I'm hardly tiny."

"Compared to me you are."

"Being a giant is no excuse. Stand up and let's get out there. The couple's song is about to start. I always had to sit this one out as a kid, because I never had a boyfriend to skate with. Let me have my moment."

Andrew groaned. "Fine." He was happy to share firsts with her and give her a reason to feel like she was proving a point to all the assholes who'd passed her by. He had no idea how rolling around a skating rink hand in hand with him would do that, but it hadn't been up to him. She'd insisted they do something fun tonight to keep his mind off the PET scan tomorrow morning, and he'd let her pick the activity.

It was working—he'd only thought about his scan twice. He pushed himself up from the bench, his arms immediately flailing.

Lauren blinked, keeping her expression flat. "We're on carpet. You can't be off-balance yet."

"Are you going to be heckling me all night?"

"Probably."

"Maybe I'm just trying to throw you off. Once I get out there, you'll be blown away by my blazing speed."

"*Pfft.* Get inline, buddy," she said with a wink.

He laughed and shrugged. "That's how I roll."

"See? You're having fun already." She grabbed his hand, and they began the awkward clomp across the carpeted floor to the rink entrance. "I had a feeling this would be a wheelie good time."

"Stop. I can't handle it." He also couldn't handle how good she looked in black leggings. Thank God she had a long sweater that covered her perfect backside. He wouldn't mind a better view, but there were a lot of teenage boys here, and a surprising number of other couples his and Lauren's age— Was hanging out at the skating rink coming back in style?— and he would've had to spend the entire evening standing behind her if he thought they were checking her out.

He took a few rotations around the floor to get the hang of it. He hadn't spent time at a skating rink as a kid, but he had gotten a pair of roller blades for his tenth birthday and had worn them out that summer. Somehow his body remembered the basics, and soon he and Lauren were flying around the outside, hand in hand.

She looked up at him and laughed, and he smiled down at her, feeling ridiculous and happy. The DJ announced it was time for the couple's song, and those who were with someone paired up across the floor while others went for the exit to wait it out. Lauren squeezed his hand, and the first notes of a Khalid song came across the speakers.

The lights went low, and a few colored beams strobed across the floor, passing across the bodies of the skaters who circled the rink. The beat of the song, the feel of Lauren's hand wrapped around his, and the sudden darkness in the room did something to him. When they came around a narrow curve near the wall, on the opposite side of the benches and social area, Andrew veered off course, successfully slowing enough that when his shoulder hit the wall it barely stung. Following his momentum, Lauren collided with him, cushioned by his body.

She yelped as their skates crashed together. He put his arms around her as he braced his back against the wall to keep them on their feet.

"Are you okay?" she asked, trying to pull back and look up at him. "Did you lose control?"

Andrew gazed down at her in the darkness. The music pulsed around them and people continued to glide by, either not noticing them embracing in the corner, or not caring.

"Yeah. I kind of think I have." He kissed her, loving the way she responded with enthusiasm, even here. He wasn't typically one to put on public displays of affection, but he'd also never been this into a woman before. He forgot about everything else when he was with her. They could have done anything tonight, and as long as she was there, he wouldn't worry about tomorrow.

When he traced the seam of her lips with his tongue she sighed, opening to him, and a passing skater called out, "Get a room!"

They broke apart, Andrew's eyes searching the crowd for whoever had said that, wanting to tell him to mind his own damn business. Lauren giggled and pressed her face to his chest.

The song ended and the lights flipped on. Lauren slid back a few inches and grabbed his hand, her eyes bright and happy.

"Come on," she said. "Let's skate some more, and then we'll go get ice cream."

Andrew didn't want to move an inch from this spot. He wanted to stay here and hold her but he sighed and said, "Okay, gorgeous. You lead, I'll follow."

It was one of the truest statements he'd ever said.

...

The next morning, Lauren was waiting for him immediately after his PET scan, and her presence gave him strength. A year ago, if someone had told him he would live his life in sections of time—revolving around chemo appointments and scans, he'd have looked at them like they were crazy. But here he was, doing exactly that. And he prayed that after today, he'd be finished with it all.

She walked him to his car in the parking garage, keeping what felt like yards between them. Once there, he pulled her between his car and the one parked beside him, so they were completely hidden. He kissed her hard before he let her go, trying to convey what he felt through his touch. Her cheeks were pink when he released her, and she wobbled a step, grabbing his arm.

Pleased with himself, he smiled at her. She knocked him off-balance, too, but he was better at hiding it. "Thanks for coming with me. I hope the rest of your day is great."

"You too. I'll talk to you tonight?"

"Definitely."

She pressed another kiss to his lips and turned to walk back into the building. Andrew leaned against his pickup truck, watching her. He had no idea how he'd gotten so lucky, but he wasn't about to question it.

It wasn't until late that afternoon, when he received a phone call from Dr. Patel, that he learned his luck had run out.

He'd just left the DA's office and was sitting in his car when the phone rang. He recognized the number as one from the cancer center, and a brick settled low in his stomach. Why were they calling so soon? Was that bad?

"Hello?"

"This is Dr. Patel, is this Andrew?"

"It's me."

"I'm calling about your PET scan from this morning. There has been a good response to the chemo, but unfortunately there are still two bright spots on the scan..."

Andrew's vision went fuzzy, and he had difficulty focusing on what she was saying. He heard things like "two additional cycles of chemo" and "still a chance of complete remission" and "another scan in two months."

"Andrew, are you there?"

"I'm here. Sorry. It's just, not what I was expecting, I guess."

"I know it's hard to hear that the scan results weren't as good as they could have been. But sometimes we need a little additional kick to get it all. The odds are still good we can get you into remission with two more cycles. I'll ask Kiara to schedule you to see me next week, and we can look at the scan together and discuss it in more detail, okay?"

"Okay. Thanks, Dr. Patel."

Andrew sat in his car, staring at nothing. The fuzzy, numb feeling he'd had while talking to the doctor faded, replaced by the urge to move. To do something.

He felt antsy, almost to the point of desperation.

He pulled up a contact on his phone and put the car in drive. It rang a few times before the other person picked up.

"Hello?"

"It's me. Can you meet me at McNellie's?"

Andrew was sitting at the bar when Logan walked up. He gestured to the two beers sitting in front of Andrew.

"One of those for me?"

"Nope." Andrew finished off the one that was nearly empty, pushed the glass to the other side of the bar, and went for the second.

Logan raised an eyebrow and took the stool next to Andrew.

One of the regular bartenders came over and put the empty glass in the sink. Andrew didn't miss the wide-eyed look she shot Logan, but he did ignore it.

"What can I get you, Logan?"

"I guess I'll have what he's having." Logan jerked a thumb in Andrew's direction. "But just one. Looks like I'll be driving tonight."

Andrew grunted and took another long pull.

"What's going on, man?"

Andrew kept his eyes on the wooden bar top. "Got my scan results. There's still cancer, and I have to get more chemo."

"Shit. Man, I'm sorry." Logan put a hand on Andrew's shoulder. "That sucks, Andrew."

Andrew nodded, not sure he could respond and keep it together.

Logan removed his hand and sat beside him for a few

minutes. His beer arrived, and they silently watched the basketball game on the television mounted above the bar.

"How much more? Chemo, I mean?"

"Two more cycles."

"That's not so bad."

Andrew glared at his friend.

"Don't look at me like that. You got this. You've made it this far, you can do two more."

They sat like that, side by side at the bar, barely speaking, for two hours. Andrew didn't want to talk, and Logan was a good enough friend to know it. He simply sat there, a silent show of support, and Andrew was grateful for it.

But just like the lucky feeling he had this morning, his gratitude for Logan was short-lived.

When Jeni sidled in on his other side and asked how many drinks he'd had, Andrew turned to Logan.

"Seriously? You called my sister?"

"No," Logan said. "I texted her."

Andrew rolled his eyes.

Jeni prodded Andrew's bicep. "You didn't answer my question."

"It was a stupid question."

"Why didn't you call me? You know I'm here to talk."

"I don't want to talk."

"It's better to sit and sulk in silence, drinking away your sorrows?"

"Sure. I feel better."

"You look terrible."

Was she always this annoying? "Thank you, dear sister."

"It's not the end of the world, Andrew. You'll get through this like you did the others. Now snap out of it."

"No cancer, no opinion."

That shut her up. For a few minutes, at least.

He really hadn't had that much to drink. He'd been

here three hours and had nursed four beers. He was a big guy, and even though he'd lost some of his bulk over the last few months, he'd never been a cheap drunk. He barely felt anything.

Jeni ordered a drink, and Andrew sat between his best friend and his twin sister, ignoring both of them as they spent the next half hour trying to cheer him up.

Nothing would lift his spirits tonight.

"Andrew?"

Except her.

Just the sound of his name coming from her lips soothed him. The tension in his muscles released, flowing out of him, a river of fear and disappointment. Andrew swiveled on his chair to find Lauren standing there, so beautiful it almost hurt to look at her.

She held her hand out. "Are you okay?"

He grasped it with his own and pulled her to him, hugging her close. He'd initially called Logan instead of Lauren, because he'd wanted to shield her from the bad news for a little longer. But now that she was here, he realized she was the only one he really wanted to see.

Damn, she smelled good. And her body felt so good, pressed up against him. Lush and soft, and so deliciously curvy.

He spoke into her hair. "How did you...?"

"Jeni texted me."

"Did she tell you?"

"About the scan? Yes. Don't worry, it doesn't mean—"

Andrew shook his head against her neck. "I don't want to talk about it right now."

"Okay."

He pulled back a little. Her green eyes met his, and she kept her hands wrapped around his neck.

"Can we leave?" he asked.

"Sure. I'm driving, though."

When he stood, he suddenly realized how much liquid he'd consumed. "I need to hit the men's room, then we can go."

She nodded and edged up onto his vacated seat to wait.

When Andrew came out of the men's room, he stopped cold in his tracks. Lauren had her hand on Logan's arm, laughing at something he was saying. Logan was smiling at her and said something else, eliciting a new laugh from her. She leaned over and put her forehead on his shoulder, shaking with laughter.

Red-hot jealousy unlike anything Andrew had ever experienced jolted down his spine like a bolt of lightning. Bitterness swept through him at the memory of the night Logan had proudly boasted getting the phone number from a redhead named Lauren.

It had been a while since he'd thought about that night and the fact that Lauren had talked to Logan—probably even flirted with him and asked him to call her. She'd agreed to go on a date with him, too, even after thinking he'd brushed her off for weeks before contacting her.

Did she regret not having a chance with Logan? Logan was healthy and strong. She wouldn't see him kneeling on the bathroom floor or touch the raised imprint of a medical device under his skin. She could run her fingers through the thick hair on his head and wouldn't have to worry about what his blood counts were before they went somewhere.

When he took her number away from Logan, Andrew had taken that choice from her.

Pain clenched Andrew's heart, and he ground his teeth so hard his jaw hurt. He forced himself to approach the smiling couple, and Jeni, who was chuckling along with them.

Lauren saw him and sat up straight, a twinkle in her eye. "Andrew, Logan was just telling me—"

"Can we leave now?" Andrew interrupted.

His harsh tone didn't go unnoticed, and Lauren's smile faded. Logan watched him warily, while Jeni scowled and shook her head.

"Um, sure," Lauren said quietly. She grabbed her purse from the bar and waved goodbye.

Andrew walked too fast for her to keep up, but he didn't slow.

She reached for his hand and tugged. "Slow down."

He pushed the door open and scanned the lot for her car. He pulled his hand from her grasp, trying not to let her hurt expression get to him.

"Where are we going?" she asked, starting the car.

"Just take me home," he bit out.

Lauren eyed him sideways but didn't argue, and they drove to his apartment in charged silence. When she pulled into a parking space and turned off the car, she reached for the door handle.

He shook his head. "I'm good. You don't have to come in. You can go back to the bar and hang out with Logan." He didn't look at her.

A small part of his brain told him he was being unreasonable, but he couldn't stop himself. He got out of the car and slammed the door, not looking back as he took long strides to the stairwell. He heard her get out and run up the steps behind him. He increased his pace, but she caught up when he stopped to unlock the door.

She pushed past him into his apartment, throwing her purse onto the coffee table.

"Andrew, what's wrong? Why would you say something like that?"

"You looked pretty cozy at the bar with Logan." His breath came heavy, from virtually running up three flights of stairs and from the weight sitting on his chest. "I thought maybe you'd like to spend more time with him. See if it could go anywhere. You were interested in him once before, after all. I'm the one who forced your hand in my direction."

Lauren's mouth dropped open, her green eyes flashing with anger. "We were talking about *you*. He was telling me a story about the two of you being stupid on some guy's night out. I was never interested in Logan. I didn't give him my number that night, Emma did. She gave it to him, and I didn't want to hurt his feelings by taking it back. I figured I could at least give him a chance. But then it turned out to be you, and do you know what I felt? Relief. Relief and joy. You've always been the one I wanted, Andrew. From the moment I saw you."

He wanted to believe her, to believe the words she said were true. But how could they be? He was sick and broken and wasting away. *What woman wants this?*

No. She was just trying to make him feel better. Chemo had ravaged his body, and now he had to take more of it. Overwhelmed with anger and sadness, he reached one hand behind his neck and tore his shirt over his head, tossing it on the couch.

"Look at me," he said harshly. In a jerky motion, he waved a hand from his head and down his torso. "How can you be attracted to this? I'm bald, I'm as pale as that vampire kid my sisters used to be obsessed with, and I've lost thirty pounds. Nothing about me is the same. Dammit, I hardly even feel like a man."

Lauren stared at him, her bright eyes devouring him. "Are you serious? You're honestly asking me how I could be attracted to you?"

Andrew just looked at her, feeling exposed and resentful. He'd never wanted to be proved wrong so much in his life.

"Do you want to know the things I first noticed about you?" She paused, and he wasn't sure if she actually expected him to answer. He didn't, and she continued on. "I noticed you were tall, I thought at least a foot taller than me. I've always had a thing for exceptionally tall men. I noticed that you had warm, kind brown eyes. I noticed your lips and your big, masculine hands."

He swallowed, clenching those hands into fists by his side.

"Yes, I noticed your hair, because you had beautiful, thick, brown hair that looked like it would be soft to the touch. But you know what? You also look ridiculously hot when you wear those beanies, and even better when you're not wearing one because you've given it to a little girl with cancer to make her happy. Jasmine wears that stupid hat every single day, did you know that? I'm getting off target, because that gets into how much I adore the person you are inside, but that's not what you're asking about, is it?"

He didn't answer that question, either.

"The first day I laid eyes on you, I thought you were the sexiest man I'd ever seen. You're *still* the sexiest man I've ever seen. None of that has changed, except the fact that I'm no longer satisfied just *noticing* those things about you. I don't want to only be attracted to you, I want to be wrapped up in you. I want your huge body towering over me as you put your arms around me. Your eyes looking at me and seeing me for who I am. I want your hands touching me, caressing me." Her voice became a whisper and she swayed toward him, and everything in him wanted to believe her, that she wanted him, even now.

His heart pounded against his ribcage, and he noticed her own chest moving up and down with unsteady breaths. He remained in place, desperate to touch her but worried he'd upset her with his outburst.

She took two steps in his direction, placing her hand on the smooth, hairless skin of his chest. The feel of her warm touch was everything he needed right then, and a tremor ran through him.

"I want your lips on mine," she whispered. "All the time."

His gaze collided with hers, and he couldn't have looked away even if the room caught fire.

It felt as if he needed her like the very air he breathed.

He touched her face with his left hand, sliding his palm across her cool cheek. His fingers threaded through her hair, and she shivered. Two thoughts ran through his mind as he lowered his head: how badly he wanted her, and how even though he didn't deserve her, he couldn't live without her.

# Chapter Seventeen

Andrew wound his right arm around her waist, pulling her body flush against his, soft against hard. He kissed her softly, a slight caress, and she felt the power restrained deep inside him. He was holding back.

Lauren wanted none of it.

"Andrew," she whispered against his lips, curling her hands around his shoulders. She arched into him and nipped at his bottom lip. Asking him to let go.

He groaned, moving one arm around her shoulders and hooking the other beneath her knees. He swung her up and carried her to his bedroom, never breaking contact from her mouth. He laid her down on top of the comforter and crawled over her, caging her in between his hands and knees. He slanted his mouth over hers, kissing her deeply, running one hand down the length of her body. Her arms wound around his torso, her nails lightly trailing the bare skin of his back.

"I want to make love to you so badly it hurts," he said, his voice thick with emotion. "But I'm so fucking tired, and I'm a little drunk, and I'm not going there until I know I can give you the best I've got." He wove their fingers together and pressed them into the mattress, on either side of her head. "But I am going to kiss the hell out of you."

She lifted her head to brush his ear with her soft lips. "Never stop," she said, her voice breaking.

He made a sound deep in the back of his throat before taking her mouth in a rough kiss. A few minutes passed, the sounds of their heavy breathing echoing against the walls. She pulled her hands away from his fingers and ran them all over his back and shoulders.

"Do you have any idea what I feel for you?" he asked.

She nodded. "I feel it."

He lifted his hips, shooting her a strange look. "I can't help it."

Lauren laughed, curling her fingers through the belt loops of his jeans. She pulled him back down to her, loving that she affected him like that. It made her feel powerful, and *wanted*. "I meant I can feel the emotion behind it. That you care for me."

He relaxed against her, still keeping his weight on his arms, his expression softening. "Can't help that, either."

She pushed against his chest, rolling them to the side and switching positions. He kept his arms around her when he landed on his back, and she stretched out beside him, her body half on top of his. His skin was warm and smooth, and he smelled so good she wanted to wrap herself up in it. Her hair fell down across his chest, and with a shaking hand he gathered it behind her head.

With one hand she stroked his face and could hardly believe he looked at her with such affection. "But you, you idiot man, apparently don't know what I feel for you."

He opened his mouth, but she put her lips on his. She kissed him for several minutes and moved her lips to his ear. "I love you."

Andrew froze for a second, then jerked up on his elbows, the movement startling her. She pulled back, and he searched her face.

She smiled and nodded, understanding the question in his eyes. "I really do."

He dropped onto his back and took her face gently between his hands, punctuating each sentence with a kiss. "I love you, Lauren. I love you. So damn much. You're mine, and I'm never letting you go."

On Saturday morning, Lauren and Andrew spent several hours at Children's. At first, she was worried he might not want to go, with the recent scan results and news about needing more chemo.

"Are you sure?" she'd asked. "I can go on my own this time. Give you a day to relax and recharge."

"I had my little pity party. I'm done," he said. "Nothing makes me believe I can keep doing this more than those kids. If they can handle it, so can I."

An hour into their visit, they were seated around a round table with several kids, playing a farm animal variation of Go Fish. After the first two rounds, Andrew had persuaded Jasmine to join in. He'd flipped his chair around backward and leaned his chest against the backrest, his long legs bracketing either side and his hands holding his set of cards on the table, looking just as focused as if it were a professional game of poker. He'd changed things up and worn a Royals baseball cap today, which he'd also turned backward after the first game, declaring things were "getting competitive."

Lauren watched as he leaned to his left, where Jasmine sat, eying her cards.

"*Psst*," he whispered loudly. "Got any horses in there?"

She frowned. "It's not your turn."

"I'm just planning my next move. Help a guy out."

Jasmine narrowed her eyes and pulled her cards to her chest. "Go away, cheater."

Andrew sat back with wide eyes, feigning shock. "I thought we were friends."

She shrugged one shoulder. "When I beat you, I'll take that hat."

Lauren giggled, and Andrew glanced over at her, a happy grin on his face. "Whose turn is it?"

Jake, an eight-year-old boy whom Lauren had met a few weeks ago, spoke up. "Mine. Lauren, do you have any cows?"

*Dagnabbit.* She had three. She scowled and handed him the cards, muttering, "This is udder nonsense."

Andrew burst out laughing.

"What's so funny?" Jasmine asked.

"This girl." Andrew jerked an elbow at Lauren, and amusement lit up his eyes. "She quacks me up."

Jasmine's lips quirked, but she rolled her eyes. "You're not funny."

Andrew huffed once, then he looked at Lauren with disbelief. "She's goat to be kidding, right? That was a good one."

The look of indignation on his face forced a chuckle from her. He was adorable. She reached over and lightly pinched his muscular forearm. "You think you're so a-moo-zing, don't you?"

Jasmine laughed at that, and Andrew dropped his cards on the table. "No way. My goat one was better than that."

Still smiling, Jasmine glanced at Lauren. "Yours was so funny it gave me goose bumps."

Lauren nodded appreciatively, and Jasmine returned a conspiratorial grin. It was the first smile she'd ever received from Jasmine, and she felt a sense of accomplishment. Even if she'd required Andrew's help to get it.

It took Andrew a minute to process, but then he held up his hand. "Nice."

Jasmine slapped her hand against his, her expression pleased with just a touch of embarrassment.

They resumed playing and Jake won the game, but because the little boy was already wearing a hat and Jasmine had more points than Andrew, he still relinquished his hat to her. He plopped it onto her head before excusing himself to the refreshment area for a drink.

The other kids left the table, and only Jasmine and Lauren remained.

"He really likes you," Jasmine said quietly.

Lauren smiled. "You think so?"

She nodded. "He told me. But even if he hadn't, it's pretty obvious."

Lauren gathered the cards in a pile and stuffed them into the small box. "Is it obvious that I like him, too?"

"Um, yeah."

The way Jasmine said it made Lauren laugh.

Then Jasmine's expression turned serious. "He's cool. You're really lucky."

A lump suddenly formed in Lauren's throat. She tried to swallow it down, then met Jasmine's dark eyes. "I think so, too."

Lucky didn't even begin to cover it.

• • •

On Wednesday, the midday break in patient visits was just long enough for Lauren, Emma, and Kiara to grab lunch together.

"What's everyone doing for Valentine's Day?" Emma asked, stabbing at her salad with a fork.

"Nate and I are staying in," Kiara said. "Making dinner and watching movies."

"Lame. What about you, Lauren?"

Lauren still felt a little weird talking about Andrew openly at work but tried to ignore the niggling sensation of unease. These were her friends, and everything was out in the open between the three of them. Plus, they currently sat in the noisy café and no one paid them any attention. "Same, actually. We're stopping by the Valentine's party at Children's, but then I'm going to try to make Andrew dinner."

Emma curled her lip in mock disgust. "Is this what happens when you fall in love? Things get boring?"

Kiara smirked and took a drink of water. "Nothing boring about naked dinner and a movie."

"Naked?" Emma trilled. "You definitely did not say that the first time."

"Didn't I?"

Lauren laughed at her friends, choosing not to involve herself in the direction the conversation had gone. She dipped a French fry in ketchup. "I actually wanted your opinion on what I should wear," she said. "Be honest...do you think I can pull off pink?"

Emma winced, and Kiara looked away, scratching the back of her neck.

Lauren took no offense, as that had been her initial thought, too. "Can I show you?" She unlocked her phone and pulled up a selfie she'd taken in the dressing room. "It's not like a bright pink, and I thought it wasn't too bad..."

Emma grabbed the phone and her eyes went wide. "Wow."

Kiara leaned over to look. "Hot damn. Who would have thought? You make that sweater look good."

Lauren grinned. "Thanks, girls." Pleased, she put her phone away and pointed at Emma. "What about you? Any

Valentine's plans?"

Emma's face turned red, and she shrugged. "Maybe."

Lauren and Kiara snapped to attention.

"You do!"

"With whom?"

Emma scrunched her nose. "I've been flirting with this guy at the gym for weeks, and last week he finally asked for my number. We've been talking on the phone for at least an hour every night, and he asked if he could take me to dinner."

"Emma, that's great," Lauren exclaimed. "Tell us about him. Is he funny? What does he do for a living? Is he cute? Does he have a nice squat?"

Kiara groaned, and Emma nodded vehemently. "He certainly does."

Emma filled them in on everything she knew about him, and Lauren hoped things went well for them tomorrow night. She hadn't seen Emma this excited about a guy in...well, ever.

"I can't wait to hear how it goes," Lauren said. "I'll expect a full rundown on Friday morning."

"Right back at you," Emma said.

"Andrew has an appointment Friday, we could just ask him," Kiara joked.

"Don't you dare," Lauren sputtered.

Emma shook her head. "I'd never ask my patient about their love life. That would be awkward as hell."

Lauren agreed. She looked between her friends, worry etched between her eyebrows. "But promise me you'll take good care of him, okay?"

"We always do."


Andrew: *Whatcha doing?*

Lauren: *Standing in the spice aisle at the grocery store.*

Andrew: *Getting stuff for tomorrow night?*

Lauren: *Yep. Prepare yourself for the most average homemade meal you've ever tasted.*

Andrew: *I can't wait.*

Lauren: *Me neither.*

Andrew: *The spice aisle, huh? Is it chili in there?*

Lauren: *A little, but I can dill with it.*

Andrew: *(you already used that one on me but I'll let it slide)*
Andrew: *Good. Curry on.*

Lauren: *It's about thyme I found someone who loves puns as much as I do.*

Andrew: *We're mint to be.*

Lauren: *I clove you so much.*

Andrew: *I clove you, too.*

• • •

On Valentine's Day, a beautiful bouquet of flowers arrived with Lauren's name on it. It wasn't signed but had a terrible hand-drawn picture of what looked like a deer and the words, "I'm so fawned of you."

She would keep it forever.

She left work early to pick up Andrew and head to the Valentine's party at Children's Hospital. She sent him a text message when she pulled in and put the car in park to wait.

A few moments later she watched him come down the stairs, a little slower than she'd have expected. Usually the days before a treatment were when he felt the best...but then again, the toll of chemo could build over time. He wouldn't want her to mention it or ask if he was all right, so she focused on the rest of him, which looked damn good. He wore fitted jeans and a deep burgundy sweater, and the signature gray hat he seemed to favor. He opened the car door and sat down.

"Sorry I wasn't ready, I fell asle—"

His voice came to an abrupt halt when he looked at her. She smiled.

His brown eyes drank her in. "You're wearing pink."

"I thought it would be festive. You know, for Valentine's."

"You remember pink is my favorite color, right?"

She nodded. "I remember."

He rubbed the side of his jaw with one hand. "What I remember is you saying you didn't wear pink well."

She quirked an eyebrow. She still didn't think it was the most flattering hue for her, but as Emma and Kiara had confirmed, this particular blush-colored sweater seemed to compliment her auburn hair quite well. She'd thought of Andrew when she bought it and had been waiting for an excuse to wear it for him. "Do you agree?"

"I think it's a good thing you texted me to come down, because if you'd come up we wouldn't have left my apartment."

Lauren couldn't stop her smile from widening to ridiculous proportions. She reached across and put her hand on his thigh. "You look great."

He moved her hand away, entwining their fingers and resting both on the console. "We're going to a place with kids...I need you to keep your hands to yourself for a bit. Okay?"

"Okay, big man."

The game room at the hospital was filled with heart-shaped balloons and decorations, and upbeat music streamed from a large speaker in the corner. The room was full of patients, their families, and volunteers. Tables were set up for face painting, Valentine's Day card designs, and jewelry making.

Lauren and Andrew stuck together for a few minutes but eventually separated, visiting with the kids and parents they'd gotten to know. Lauren noticed Jasmine enter the room, wearing Andrew's red hat, and didn't miss the small smile on the girl's face when she saw him. He waved at her enthusiastically and met her in the middle of the room. He pulled a red envelope out of his back pocket and gave it to her, bowing with a flourish. Jasmine blushed and sheepishly handed him a white piece of paper.

Lauren couldn't quite see what was on it, but she fell in love with Andrew a little more. His heart was so generous and caring, and though he'd never admit to it, he felt deeply. Not only for the kids he'd gotten to know here, Jasmine especially, but about life in general. He was affected by good music. Romantic movies. The things happening in the lives of the people he knew. He was good, and wanted to spread that goodness beyond himself.

He was an incredible man, and he would be a wonderful father someday.

When it was time to leave, Lauren took his hand in hers as they walked down the long, colorful hallway. She hoped the elevator would arrive empty and got her wish. The second the doors closed, she pushed Andrew against the wall and locked her arms around his neck.

"You're so amazing." She kissed him.

"And hot." She kissed him again.

"I love how sweet you are with Jasmine." Again.

"Why are you so wonderful?" She kissed him once more

and pulled back.

He blinked at her, looking a little dazed.

"I asked you a question," she said with a grin.

"You expect me to think right now? You just attacked me in an elevator."

She kissed him again and stepped away as the doors opened, and he draped his arm around her shoulders as they walked to the car.

"What did Jasmine give you?" she asked.

He held up the white rectangle, which turned out to be a section of thin canvas rather than paper. On it was a painted image of an outdoor landscape with mountains and a bright blue sky.

"That's beautiful. Did she make that?"

Andrew smiled, a proud gleam in his eye. "Yep. She's an artist." His voice wavered when he said "artist." He cleared his throat and looked away, and she didn't bring attention to his obvious emotion.

They drove back to her house hand in hand, and Lauren couldn't wipe the smile off her face. She'd never been in a relationship over Valentine's Day before. Had never even spent it with a male who was a friend, much less one she cared so much about. She'd never really understood what the fuss was about, until today. Everything seemed more romantic, simply because it was a day recognized by the whole world as one dedicated to love. Every touch, every word, every thought seemed permeated with Andrew and what she felt for him.

As they approached her house, she slowed, coming to a stop next to her mailbox. She rolled her window down.

"I don't know why I do this every time I come home," she said. "I never get mail."

Sure enough, it was empty, and she closed the metal door and pulled her car into the driveway.

"Do you want mail?"

"Sometimes. When I bought this house, I was most excited about having a real mailbox. Isn't that stupid? I guess I thought having one meant I had a real home. But, since everything's online, it's always empty."

"That's not stupid," Andrew said quietly.

They got out of the car, and she grabbed his hand, smiling up at him. "But my house won't be empty tonight. I'm glad you're here."

She cooked fajitas, because he'd said it was his favorite food, imagining he might be able to feel the love she put into the meal's preparation. She'd certainly felt his affection with the flowers that morning, and the several silly love-related puns he'd sent her in text messages throughout the day. And in every brush of his fingertips around her waist as she cooked.

Andrew coughed a few times during dinner, and she worried she'd made the meal a little too spicy, but he assured her it was perfect. He had two servings, so she figured it couldn't have been too awful.

Instead of a movie they watched a documentary about the Seven Wonders of the World—not romantic by any means, but perfect for them. They watched it in her bedroom, side by side on her bed, her head on his chest. Toward the end of the film, Lauren registered Andrew's breathing had sped up. She lifted her head. "You okay?"

He smiled. "I'm good. I was just thinking about how pretty you are in pink and wondering how much longer this damn documentary was going to last before I could do this."

He pulled her on top of him, her legs straddling his thighs, and slid both of his hands into her hair, pulling her face down to his. He kissed her thoroughly, and soon she, too, was breathing heavily.

Sometime later they lay beside each other, both on their backs. Andrew had one of her hands in both of his, toying with her fingers.

"Do you think we'll get married?"

Lauren froze. "You're not asking me, are you?"

"Not right now."

"Oh. In that case...I'd say maybe."

"Maybe?"

"What do you want me to say? That's not a good question to pose theoretically."

"What if it wasn't theoretical? What if I was asking you to marry me?"

"Are you?"

"No."

"Andrew!"

"What? I'm just curious what your answer *would* be."

"Why are you even thinking about that?"

"Because I love you. Isn't that what people in love should think about? The next steps?"

"Probably."

"So?"

"I already told you. Maybe."

"You're infuriating. You know that?"

"You should have thought about that before theoretically asking me to marry you."

"Probably so."

"What else have you thought about? About us?" she asked, admiring his masculine hands as they massaged her fingers.

"Honestly?"

"Yeah."

"Sex."

"Is that so?" Lauren's face warmed, and he tightened his arm around her.

"Do you think about that?" he asked.

"Of course I do."

"Is it okay that we haven't? Yet? I just want our first time to be perfect, and I'm terrified I'll have a repeat of the night before we kissed. And I'm so tired all the time, which pisses me off. But also, I'm a little worried that it would, um... expose you. To the chemo, somehow. Is that possible?"

Lauren propped her chin on his chest. His left arm was folded behind his head, and he looked down at her with questioning eyes.

"It's possible, yes. I never got to this part in your chemo education," she pinched him in the ribs, and he flinched and laughed, "but I usually make sure men know to wear condoms. To protect their partner."

Andrew nodded, his smile fading. "Even that wouldn't protect you one hundred percent, though. I'd rather wait until I'm done and it's completely safe, if that's okay with you. I mean, to be clear, I don't *want* to wait, but I think we should wait. You know?"

Lauren shifted higher on his chest and planted a sweet kiss on his lips. "I do know." She pushed herself to a sitting position beside him, folding her legs together. "Actually, I'd kind of thought the next guy I slept with would be my husband."

Andrew's eyes met hers, and he tilted his head to the side, waiting for her to continue.

"Um, Will was...my first, and when I realized it meant nothing to him, I was devastated. After that I thought maybe I'd wait until I was married, because then I'd know I wasn't being used, and that the man I was with wanted me for more than my body." She shrugged and added, "Or my chemistry skills."

Andrew shot up to a sitting position. "Are you fucking kidding me?" His jaw went taut, and he swung his legs off the edge of the bed, his back to her. "I'm going to kill that son-of-a—"

"Andrew," Lauren put a gentle hand on his back, where the muscles were bunched and tense. "Don't worry about that; I was just trying to explain why I'm waiting now."

"Don't worry about it?" he bit out. He stood, flexing his fingers. "I'm so pissed I can't see straight."

Lauren scrambled to the edge of the bed and got up on her knees. She grabbed his hand and pulled him close to her, turning his body to face her. His face was like stone.

"Look at me," she said, and he did. "Don't let that bother you. I'm over it, okay? I learned something from it. And now I have you, and you're better than anything I could have ever imagined."

Andrew's expression softened marginally, and he put one hand on her hip. "It bothers me. I can't help it."

She kissed him once and said, "I don't want to think about Will anymore. It's Valentine's Day, and I'm with the man I love."

Still on her knees, with him standing at the edge of the bed, their faces were almost level. She pressed herself against him, moving his arms to circle her waist. He looked down at her with heavy-lidded eyes, but the muscles in his cheek remained clenched.

Lauren dipped her head to kiss the hollow of his throat, then moved her lips to his earlobe. "Andrew," she whispered, feeling a tremor run through him. "Aren't I supposed to be your distraction?"

All at once, his body relaxed, and he nodded. He dropped his head to her shoulder, tightening his embrace. "Distract me."

...

The next morning, Lauren searched for any plausible reason she might need to be in the infusion center around the same time as Andrew's appointment. She searched her current patient roster and found one she'd needed to call and check in with, anyway.

She took the back stairwell and wove her way through several occupied infusion chairs. Before seeking out either of the patients she hoped to see, she turned down a short hallway just off the infusion suite for a cup of coffee.

When she came out of the empty break room she almost had a repeat of her first meeting with Andrew. She caught herself just short of colliding with a large male chest, but this one belonged to Gavin.

"Whoa. Hey, Lauren." Gavin grabbed her by the upper arms. He flashed white teeth in a cocky grin.

*Be nice.* "Hey, Gavin."

She backed out of his grip and moved to slide past him, but he put a hand on her elbow.

"Hey, can we talk for a second?"

Lauren glanced around the hallway. They were alone. She hadn't forgotten about the last time he cornered her, making accusations about her and Andrew's relationship, and she didn't want anyone to overhear. "About what?"

"I wanted to say I'm sorry. About the last time we talked, and calling you unprofessional. You're great with our patients and have made a big difference here at the cancer center." He raked a hand through his hair. "I think it's pretty obvious I like you. I have since the start, and I think I was jealous. I acted like an asshole, and I'm sorry."

Something inside Lauren told her not to trust him, but when she met his ice blue gaze, it surprised her to find he looked sincere. "I appreciate that. Apology accepted."

"I know I messed up, but I really would like the chance to take you out." He angled his body, forcing her to take a step back, and her left shoulder hit the wall. "Please? Would you give me a chance to get to know you, and show you I really am a nice guy?"

Lauren felt a little like she was caged in, and she didn't like it. She tried to step to the right, but he blocked her. He put a hand against the wall near her head, his thick, veiny forearm at eye level.

"There's something between us," he said in a low voice. He reached up with his other hand and rubbed a section of her hair between his thumb and forefinger. Nausea swirled in her stomach. "There's no way I'm the only one who feels it."

Lauren straightened her spine and batted his hand away. "I'm sorry, Gavin, but there's nothing here. I'm not playing games with you, I'm just not interested." Lauren tried to keep her voice firm, but her pitch kept rising, which happened when she was nervous or uncomfortable.

"But we'd be so good together," Gavin continued, crowding even closer to her.

Lauren looked him right in the eye. "Gavin, you're the one being unprofessional. Please move and don't ask me out again."

A new voice came from the end of the hallway. "You heard her. Back the fuck up before I put you on the ground."

# Chapter Eighteen

Gavin twisted around and Lauren's head jerked to the end of the hallway, where Andrew stood with his legs planted, one slightly in front of the other, his arms at his sides. He took a deep breath and tried to stay calm, but one wrong move on that asshole's part and Andrew would lose his shit.

He and Jeni had been headed to Mandi's section for his treatment. Andrew had to stop in the restroom, and on his way back through the infusion center, he thought he heard Lauren's voice. His heart had leapt because he'd missed her this morning, and he wanted to see her.

When he'd turned down the short hallway in the back corner of the infusion center, the scene in front of him had made him see red. The woman he loved stood with her back against the wall, her beautiful face pale and her posture tense. A man hovered over her, one arm appearing to block her exit, the other touching her hair, and his head bent close to hers.

Too damn close.

Images of Isla's injuries flashed through his mind—photographs of bruises and lacerations, proof of the things a man could do to a woman when he wanted control and possession.

Andrew didn't understand the desire to control this woman, but he sure as hell wanted to protect her. If anyone tried to hurt her, they'd have to get through him first.

Gavin wasn't stupid and did as he was told. "Relax, buddy. We're just talking."

Andrew took three purposeful steps forward.

Gavin remained where he was, having given Lauren space but still within arm's reach.

The adrenaline coursing through Andrew's body clouded his vision, and he held his jaw so tight the muscles burned. "The hell it isn't. If I ever hear about you bothering her again—"

"Andrew," Lauren said, widening her eyes at him. He stopped short at her tone and turned his head in her direction. *Don't*, she mouthed.

Gavin looked between them. "There *is* something going on between you two, isn't there?"

Andrew crossed his arms in front of his chest. "Fuck off."

Lauren closed her eyes and sighed.

Gavin smirked. "Got it. Well, good for you two." He looked at Andrew. "Sorry I stepped on your toes, dude. I didn't know."

Andrew's arms twitched with the need to grab the guy and shove him against the wall. He focused on taking measured breaths and rolled his shoulders. "It's not my feet I'm worried about. It was pretty clear she was saying no before I happened to walk by. I suggest you move on, now and for good."

Gavin raised his eyebrows and made a slight bow before he sauntered off. The slight grin on his face concerned Andrew, but he had something more important to focus on right now. He went to Lauren immediately. "Are you okay?"

"Why did you do that?" she snapped.

His head jerked back. "Seriously? He was basically forcing himself on you."

"There are fifty people right outside the hallway. He wouldn't have done anything, and I was handling it."

"You were handling it? Is that why he had his hand on you, touching your hair? That asshole doesn't deserve to breathe the same air as you." Andrew moved closer to her, a fire consuming his entire being. Despite her angry tone, she swayed toward him, her green eyes locked on his. Her body language, the opposite of what he'd seen in response to Gavin standing near her, encouraged him to surge on. "That's *my* hair he was stroking. *My* breath he was stealing. You're not the only territorial one here, Lauren."

Her face softened, but then she lifted a hand and rubbed her eyes. "He's a petty man, Andrew. He's the last person I wanted to find out about us. When I thought your chemo was done I kind of let my guard down, but now that you need more treatment…" She shook her head. "Just to be a jerk he could report me, and my job could be in jeopardy. You can't go around making a scene like that here."

Andrew gently cupped a hand around her elbow. "I—I'm sorry. I didn't know we still needed to be so careful, but no one else was even around." His eyes searched hers, back and forth. A thick strand of her vibrant hair fell across her shoulder, and he thought of Gavin's fingers touching it. "Actually, no. I'm sorry for how I went about it, but I won't apologize for stepping in to defend you. I'll always do that, no matter what."

"I don't need you to protect me. I can take care of myself. I've been doing things on my own my whole life."

He slid his hand down her arm to take her hand. "But now you don't have to. I'm here."

She yanked her hand back. "I don't need you, don't you understand? I want you, Andrew. But I don't need you."

*Wow.*

Andrew felt that like a punch in the gut, and he swayed back a few inches. "You don't need me," he repeated.

"What I need is to keep my job here, so I don't end up back in Oklahoma at a job I'll hate. And you may have just ruined that."

Indignation flared alongside his earlier anger, which hadn't faded. "It takes two to do what we've been doing, you know," he pointed out. "And if you're so good at handling things on your own, why would you ever work for your dad? If you hate the idea so much, and know you won't be happy, why would you allow yourself to be manipulated into going back? I'm clearly not the only man trying to be a part of your life. But I'm damn sure the only one who cares about your happiness."

"If you cared about my happiness, you wouldn't have potentially gotten me fired!"

Andrew scrubbed a hand down his face. "Lauren, I walked past and saw you against the wall, looking scared, with a man over you. Touching you. Not moving an inch when you asked him to back away. The only thought in my head was to get him away from you, and there was nothing in that moment that could have stopped me. *Nothing.* If you lose your job because of what I did, I'll feel terrible, and I'll do whatever I can to make it right. There's nothing wrong with two consenting adults seeing each other, even if I am a patient here. I'd never intentionally do anything to hurt you, surely you know that."

Lauren blinked, her expression unreadable. "Look, I have to go. I have a patient to see, and then I need to find Emma. See if she thinks I need to tell Dr. Hawthorne what happened."

He let out a heavy breath. "Seriously? You're walking away from me right now?"

"We'll talk later."

He opened his mouth to say more, but Lauren brushed past him, the familiar scent of her shampoo flooding his heightened senses. She didn't look back and disappeared around the corner.

Alone in the dim hallway, Andrew pressed a palm against his temple. He made his way back through the infusion center, finding Jeni settled in for the several-hour treatment.

"You okay?" she asked. "You were gone a long time."

*No.* "I'm fine."

Andrew thought of nothing else during his treatment. By the time he got home late in the afternoon, he'd nearly worked himself into a state of panic. His body had never felt this on edge. He was so consumed with thoughts of Lauren that it was several hours before he realized what he was feeling was more than anxiety.

Fear took over. He called Lauren, but she didn't answer. He tried his sister, and she answered on the third ring.

"Jeni? Something's wrong."

. . .

Andrew lay there, waiting. Taking in the white walls and sheets and the embarrassingly thin white hospital gown he was wearing.

His chest felt tight, like someone's fist was squeezing his lungs. He alternated breathing through his mouth and nose, but one didn't seem better than the other. His heart beat furiously in his chest, and he wasn't sure if that was from nerves or because something was seriously wrong. Maybe both.

Jeni sat in the mauve chair to the right of the hospital bed, perched on the edge, her knees bouncing up and down. He'd begged her not to call their family until they knew what was wrong, and as far as he knew she'd complied. He had heard her call Lauren, though.

So he waited.

He didn't have to for much longer. Only a few more minutes passed before the door opened and Lauren tentatively peeked her head in. Her eyes found Andrew, propped up in the bed, the sheet up to his waist. Her eyes swept his entire body, like she was looking for physical evidence of something, and then came back to his. She walked completely into the room and closed the door behind her.

She wore a hooded KU sweatshirt and her hair was piled on top of her head, and he wanted nothing more than to get up and go to her and tug her into his arms. She looked so familiar and comforting, and he willed her to come closer to him. He wasn't sure if she was still upset with him, though, so he said nothing.

Maybe it would help that he was in the hospital. It would get him a pity kiss at least, surely.

Lauren addressed Jeni. "What do we know?"

"They said it could either be a blood clot, pneumonia, or a side effect from one of his chemo drugs."

Lauren nodded. "Bleomycin. It can cause pulmonary toxicity." She shot a glare in Andrew's direction—*what was that for?*—and then returned her gaze back to Jeni. "Have they done a chest X-ray yet? A CT scan? Did they start any medications?"

"They did a lot of tests and took some blood. That's it."

At that moment the door opened, almost hitting Lauren in the back. She darted to the side, and the nurse taking care of Andrew walked in. The nurse took Andrew's vitals for what felt like the thousandth time since he'd been here, and Lauren sat in a chair against the wall.

"The CT was clear, so no blood clot," the nurse said. When Andrew didn't reply, she added, "That's a good thing."

He nodded, forcing himself to tear his gaze away from Lauren and focus on the nurse. She was an older woman, with long gray hair pulled back, and a stern countenance. "Great." He took a breath. He was so short of breath, he had difficulty saying more than a few words at a time. "What...now?"

"We're still waiting on some other test results, which will probably be another hour." She finished taking his blood pressure and pulse and made some notes on the laptop she'd brought in with her. "When we have more information the on-call physician will be in to talk to you. Until then, can I get you anything?"

Andrew shook his head and thanked her, and she left.

He looked at Lauren. "Come here."

He was desperate for contact with her. He felt terrible that his actions may have put her job at risk, but he'd meant what he said—he'd do it again every time. There was no way he'd let that jackass talk to her like that or bully her into going out with him.

Andrew hadn't bullied her. He'd tricked her.

Huge difference.

She stood and came to his bedside. Her moss colored eyes were filled with tears, and her chin trembled. He lifted his hand and she took it immediately, a tear spilling over and sliding down her cheek.

"Jeni," he began, able to get only a few words out between breaths. "Make...yourself scarce, will you?" He paused and winked at Lauren. "She doesn't...need to see us...making out."

"There won't be any making out," Lauren countered.

"That's...debatable."

"I'm definitely leaving." Jeni stood with a huff. She eyed him sternly. "You have twenty minutes."

When the door closed behind her, Andrew tugged on Lauren's hand, and she sat on the bed, her hip curving into his side.

"You're so...beautiful," he began, every few words punctuated with an inhale, "you take...my breath away."

"That's the bleomycin."

He shook his head. "It's...you."

Another tear fell, and he reached up with his opposite hand to wipe it away with his thumb. "Don't cry. I'm...fine."

She took a stuttered breath. "It's the bleomycin. It has to be. I can't believe I didn't see it before." Her eyes clamped shut with frustration, and she shook her head. "Yesterday, you were coughing at dinner, and when we were watching the documentary, I noticed you were breathing hard." She opened her eyes and regarded him, her cheeks reddening. "Like a complete idiot, a self-absorbed idiot, I thought it was because of me. I can't believe I didn't even think about it...I..." She started to cry in earnest.

"Please...stop," Andrew begged. He reached for her and pulled her against his chest. "Don't cry."

She wedged herself into the single bed with him, and he held her, kissing her hair, her forehead, her eyelids...wherever he could reach.

"Why didn't you say anything? Tell me you were having symptoms?" She sniffled. "I told you this could happen and that it was important to catch it early!"

"You did?"

She glared at him. "You really did not listen to a word I said that day, did you?"

"I...told you. Was busy...trying not to...stare at your mouth...and chest. A man...can only take...so much."

"Well, now look where we are." She closed her eyes. "This is my fault. I never should have gotten involved. If I hadn't done your education that da—"

"Kiss me," he demanded. "Stop...talking crazy...and kiss me."

Wiping a tear from her cheek, Lauren tilted her face up and brushed his lips with hers, and it felt so right. It was as if the world had been spinning off its axis and had been put back in position. His body tightened, and he silently willed it to stay calm.

"You can't...tell me this...is wrong," he breathed. "If being...together...is wrong...I don't want...to be right."

She didn't respond and instead lay her forehead against his chest. His heart sped up, fear and anxiety churning in his gut.

Something was off. He could feel it.

"Tell me...you love me," he said, unable to find even an ounce of pride. He needed to hear her say it, tell him that she was his.

She lifted her head, tears continuing to slowly stream down her face. His shirt was damp where she'd rested her head. "I love you." One of her hands touched his face, her fingers brushing what would have been his hairline. "But..."

"No." He shook his head, his own eyes burning. "No buts...not right now. Please."

She stayed right where she was, stretched out alongside him on the bed, looking at him with sad eyes. She did as he asked and didn't say anything more. It was almost worse that she didn't argue and tell him the "but" was something silly like, *but you look ridiculous in this hospital gown.* The fact that she stopped told him it wasn't something he wanted to hear.

"Just...stay with me."

She probably thought he meant stay with him now, in this room, on this bed. And he'd take that.

But what he really meant was that he wanted her to stay with him for all time. Forever.

No matter how long his forever was.

Suddenly, it hit him.

Was that fair to her? To ask her to stay with him when his life was so precarious? If the cancer didn't kill him, it became painfully obvious today the chemo could. Or some other complication from his treatment. Was he hurting her, by asking her to walk this road with him?

Most days he'd envisioned them continuing a life together outside of this...outside of his illness and all that came with it. He pictured them beyond this, when it was over and they could live a normal life together.

But that wasn't a guarantee, was it? Plan A hadn't worked to cure him. What if Plan B didn't work, either? What if the rest of his life—with the length of that life in question—was consumed by doctor visits, medication, and weakness? He couldn't give her everything she wanted, everything she deserved, from a sickbed. Hell, he couldn't even make love to her properly.

Her arms tightened around his torso, and the lump in his throat nearly choked him. He willed his eyes to stay dry, his emotions to stay composed. He just felt so much... everything...for her. He *felt* for her. In every sense of the word. And he couldn't imagine doing this without her.

But for her sake, maybe he needed to try.


Turned out, it was the bleomycin. His chest X-ray had shown what they called "infiltrates," but his white count was normal and, without a fever, they were pretty confident it wasn't pneumonia.

They administered several doses of steroids, and his breathing eventually improved. He wouldn't receive the bleomycin again, and his remaining chemo treatments would have three drugs instead of four.

Lauren and Jeni stayed with him overnight and try as he

might to get Lauren to sleep in the bed with him, she refused.

"I shouldn't stay at all," she'd said. "If any of the nurses I know see me, they'll wonder why I'm here."

"If you think you should go, I understand," he'd said.

Her expression had been torn but her voice was sure. "I'm not leaving."

Both women attempted to find comfortable positions using the couch and armchair in the room, and as he watched from the bed, Andrew had never felt more like a douche in his life.

He also felt incredibly lucky.

Lauren left shortly before he was discharged Saturday afternoon. Andrew didn't speak to her again that day, and by Sunday he'd come to a few realizations.

One, he loved her more than he knew it was possible to love someone.

Two, he wanted to be with her forever. Marry her. Have children with her.

Three, he didn't know if number two would ever happen for him.

Four, until he knew he could offer her a full life, he didn't deserve to have her now.

Three times now, she'd cried because of him. Because of his illness and the difficulties of her job circumstances. He'd been selfish to push her into this relationship, when she'd made it clear it wasn't something she was comfortable doing in her position. He'd cared only about how much he wanted her. He knew there were times he made her happy, and that she wanted to be with him, too. But being with him wasn't the only thing that brought her happiness.

There was her job, and her friends. Her favorite ice cream sundae from Betty Rae's. The barista at The Grind House who knew her name and her regular drink. The bookstore on Second Street that she liked to browse for hours, sometimes accidentally buying the same book twice because it looked so good but she never had time to read. So many things about her life in Kansas City made her happy, and she'd told him her job at Coleman was what could keep her here. Let her continue this life and put down roots here.

She'd told him that starting a relationship with him could risk that and, like an asshole, he'd done it anyway.

All those things together brought him to her doorstep that Sunday afternoon. It was sunny but still cold, typical for March. Teasing everyone with impending spring but still sending down a freezing wind from the north. During the drive to her house he thought about the fact that he'd been diagnosed in October. He'd spent the last six months of his life facing something horrible and gaining the most beautiful thing he'd ever known.

Taking as deep a breath as he could while recovering from the injury to his lungs, he knocked on the door. He waited a full minute before knocking again, but still she didn't answer. He glanced around her porch and sat on the single step down to the sidewalk. He bent his knees and propped his elbow on one, laying his forehead in his palm.

There was only one thing to do.

He pulled his phone out of his pocket and called her.

# Chapter Nineteen

Lauren dropped her eyes from the road to see who was calling.

*Andrew.* His name on the screen simultaneously caused her heart to soar and her stomach to drop.

"Hello?" Her voice sounded tentative even to her own ears.

"Hey," came his deep voice. "Where are you?"

"Driving."

"Where are you going?"

"Nowhere. I like to take a drive when I need to think. I'm somewhere north of town. I don't even know."

"What are you thinking about?"

"Us."

There was a pause at the other end of the line. "I'm at your house."

"You are?" She looked at the passing street sign. "I'm sorry. I think I'm like thirty minutes away."

"It's okay. It might be easier to talk about this over the phone anyway."

"Talk about what?"

"Us." His voice cracked.

She didn't say anything for several seconds, and neither did he. Neither of them wanted to be the one to say it. To be the one to break both their hearts.

"You don't want to be together anymore?" she finally asked.

She imagined him alone at her house. Was he pacing on the porch? Sitting in his car? She considered telling him to wait there until she could meet him, thinking it might be easier to talk in person. She quickly erased the thought.

Nothing would make this easy.

"That couldn't be further from the truth, but all I've thought about up to this point is what I want. That's the problem. When I think about what's best for you, and what you want out of life, I can't possibly allow this to continue. It's not fair to you. I've asked you to risk your career and your happiness to be with me, and I can't do that anymore. I won't."

"Andrew." Tears burned behind her eyelids. "I may have risked my job to be with you, but never my happiness. I've never felt so much joy, or"—she paused, searching for the right word—"fulfillment as I have since I met you. Never in my life have I felt cherished and valued. Until you. So don't say I risked that to be with you. Do you hear me?"

"Yeah." His voice sounded far away.

"You got under my skin in the most wonderful way, and I fell in love with you. I know I got upset about the Gavin thing the other day, but then you got sick…and I realized I want you more than my job. But I feel at least partly responsible for what happened. You were having symptoms, and I didn't see them because I was blurring the lines of your cancer care and our relationship. If I'd put it all together and said something to you, maybe you would have realized something was off.

If I'd been paying attention to what was going on with your health instead of being so wrapped up in my feelings for you, I could have prevented it. I'll never forgive myself for it, and I can't let it happen again. I care more about you being alive than I do about being with you."

"What happened on Friday is *not* your fault. How can you even think that?"

"Don't try to convince me otherwise, it will only piss me off. You didn't know, so you get a free pass. But I knew. I *know*, Andrew. I know what bleomycin can do, and what the symptoms are. When I think back on it, I noticed several things that should have set off alarm bells in my head, and I missed them all. Every single fucking one."

There was a beat of silence. "Did you just say fuck?"

A small part of her wanted to smile, but she couldn't. "Focus, Andrew."

"Fine. I'll never blame you for that, as long as I live."

"That will make one of us."

"So that's it? We're breaking up because you're blaming yourself because I experienced a well-known side effect from chemo that probably would have happened anyway? That's bullshit."

"I thought we were breaking up because you think you make me unhappy. That's even shittier bullshit."

Another pause. "Who are you and what have you done with Lauren Taylor?"

"Don't make a joke."

"I'm not joking. You're freaking me out."

"You're pissing me off."

"I can tell." A rustling noise came through the speaker, like he was shifting position. "What makes you think things would be any different if we weren't together? You not pointing out my symptoms is the same as if I had no girlfriend at all. If you hadn't been with me, the end is the same."

"Did Emma ask you if you'd had any shortness of breath or difficulty breathing when she examined you on Friday?"

"Yeah, she did."

"What did you say?"

"I said no."

Exactly as she suspected. "Did you even think about it?"

"Of course I did. I thought about the night before when we were all over each other and how she didn't need to know about that kind of heavy breathing."

"My point exactly," she nearly yelled. "If you'd been sitting at home on your couch with the same difficulty taking in a breath, you'd have said something, right?"

"Maybe, but that's ridiculous. Are you saying that anyone who gets this chemo regimen can't hook up with their significant other because they might mistake a chemo side effect for being turned on?"

"I'm not talking about other people. I'm talking about us, and what happened, and I missed it. And that could be directly responsible for you getting the drug again, when you were already showing signs of toxicity." She turned into a small parking lot and put the car in park. She couldn't pay attention to the road any longer. She was nauseous and cold, and her heart felt like a stone inside her chest. "I just think it's best if we back off for now. Stay away from each other for the time being, while you finish your treatment."

"I still love you," he said.

She closed her eyes. "I love you, too."

"Then why are we doing this?" It sounded like he was asking himself as much as her.

"I don't know why you're doing it, but I'm doing it because I want you to live."

"It feels like this is what will kill me. Not the cancer, not the chemo. Being away from you is what will do it." He sniffed once. "But I don't want to do this to you anymore.

Drag you along in my misery and pain. It's selfish and unfair and I won't."

"I hate you when you say things like that."

"I hate myself when I think about what I've put you through."

She sighed, long and heavy, the sound of her breath echoing inside the car. "Any tears I've cried over you have been because I care so much. Surely you understand that."

He made a noncommittal noise.

They sat there, he at her house and she in her car, with phones to their ears and saying nothing. Was he wishing she'd change her mind, like she wished he would? Hoping she'd say this was stupid and ridiculous, and could they forget the last ten minutes ever happened?

Maybe he was, maybe he wasn't. She'd never know.

Tears fell freely from her eyes, and she didn't want him to hear her fall apart. "I need to go. I'll talk to you later, okay?"

"When?" he asked, but she'd already lowered the phone from her ear.

She hung up, dropped the phone on the passenger seat, and let herself cry.

The two weeks that followed were the worst of Lauren's life. Worse than the days after discovering Will's infidelity and deception. She'd thought she'd loved Will and that she knew what it was to have her heart broken.

Losing Andrew was a hundred times worse.

She called her friend Kate a few times, needing someone to talk to, but she wished she had someone to hug and talk to face-to-face. The fact that she didn't feel she could be that open with Emma or Kiara about it just made her feel more isolated.

She spoke to her dad once, and he excitedly described a new electronic dispensing machine he'd purchased for the pharmacy that would speed up the process for both the pharmacists and technicians. Between the uncertainty of where her job stood at Coleman and the loneliness she felt, Lauren had an unusual sensation of homesickness for her uncomplicated prior life in Oklahoma. She'd been an outsider in her family, true. But she had good friends and had never suffered acute pain like this. Before, she'd focused on the negative aspects of working with her dad. But now, she was considering the positives, and there were more than she thought.

Then, on Friday morning, two weeks after the run-in between Andrew and Gavin and when Andrew was admitted to the hospital, Lauren had an email waiting in her inbox. Dr. Hawthorne wanted to meet with her, but he didn't specify why.

So here she was, about to step off the elevator and head to Dr. Hawthorne's office, terrified of what she was about to hear.

His door was open, and she stopped short of entering, knocking lightly on the frame.

Dr. Hawthorne's gray head tilted up from where it had been bent over paperwork on his desk. He stood and motioned her inside.

"Lauren, come in. Is it two o'clock already?" He pulled out a chair on the opposite side of his desk for her and closed the door before he returned to his seat. "How's your day going?"

"Well, and yours?"

"Busy, but I like it that way." He smiled at her. "Well, let's get straight to it. You've been a wonderful asset to this institution, and instrumental in improving patient care and safety. We'd like to offer you a full-time position here at

Coleman, as the Clinical Pharmacy Specialist in the leukemia and lymphoma clinic."

His words were so unexpected, and the release of tension in her muscles so sudden, she nearly slid to the floor. A wide smile spread across her face. "Really?" Part of her had thought Gavin had reported her, and this meeting would be a serious discussion about her involvement with patients for the rest of her residency contract. Minus a permanent job offer. "That's such great news. I'd be thrilled to be a part of this group. I've learned so much, and I respect the mission of the center and the strides being taken to improve the quality of care for patients with cancer. I've never been happier since starting my residency here."

Dr. Hawthorne leaned back in his chair. "I take it you accept the position, then?"

She thought of her dad, prepared for the familiar rush of guilt. But now that the opportunity to continue the job she loved was in front of her, she felt nothing but excitement and certainty.

"Yes, I happily accept." She and the Director of Pharmacy had previously discussed the salary and benefits that would be offered if the position was approved, and knowing she would stay in the lymphoma clinic had answered her final question.

"Wonderful. I'll have Sandra in HR reach out with the required paperwork to get the process started."

"Um, Dr. Hawthorne? There's one more thing I'd like to talk to you about, if I could." She swallowed, terrified to bring it up but knowing she wouldn't feel right if she didn't. Even though she and Andrew had broken up, it was still possible for Dr. Hawthorne to learn of the short-lived relationship.

The older man steepled his fingers. "Of course."

She willed herself to stay calm and her lunch to stay down. She didn't remember ever feeling this nervous. "I want to be completely honest and tell you I became romantically involved with a patient. I was only part of his care team for one day, before I moved to another service, and we didn't start seeing each other until after that. It was near the end of his treatment, when we thought he wouldn't be receiving chemotherapy anymore. Unfortunately he had some residual disease on his scan, and he's still receiving chemotherapy. The relationship has...ended." She took in a shaky breath. "Before we move forward with the job offer, I wanted to make sure you were aware, and that I recognize it was unprofessional of me."

Dr. Hawthorne's face remained calm as he listened. When she stopped, he said, "I appreciate your candor, Lauren. It's not easy sometimes, being in our position. It's a delicate balance, the care we have for our patients, and the time we spend with them, while keeping it professional at all times. Important, but difficult."

Her heart was in her throat and she held her breath, unsure where he was going with this. He swiveled in his chair and pointed to a framed photo on his desk.

"See that woman right there? That's my wife, Karen. She was the nurse in my clinic when I was a fellow at Memorial Sloan. It wasn't convenient or appropriate for me to fall in love with her, either, but I was helpless against that woman." The look in his eye when he spoke about her confirmed his obvious affection for his wife. "I've met with several providers who have worked with you, including Emma, Dr. Patel, and Dr. Stanford. None had a single negative thing to say about you. They believe in your integrity, and therefore, so do I."

Relief flooded her, along with a sliver of jealousy that Dr. Hawthorne's love story had a happy ending. "I...thank you, sir."

He stood and held out a hand. "Welcome aboard, Dr. Taylor."

Lauren went straight to the fourth floor and found Kiara and Emma waiting for her with bated breath.

"Well?" Emma asked.

Lauren made sure her face gave nothing away. "Well…"

"Oh, for fuck's sake, just tell us," Kiara cried.

Lauren laughed. "He offered me the job!"

Both women jumped up and hugged her, jostling her from one set of arms to the next. "It's such a relief." She put a hand on her head. "I can't believe I get to work with you guys every day forever and ever!"

"We need to sign a pact," Emma announced. "No one is allowed to quit unless we all vote on it."

Lauren laughed and Kiara nodded, turning to sit down and pull out a piece of paper. "I'm on it."

She wrote some ridiculous statement and made each of them sign it and posted it behind her computer for all to see. Lauren's heart swelled with happiness, but then her smile faded.

She wanted to tell Andrew. She dreaded telling her father, and the three people she knew would celebrate with her were Emma, Kiara, and the man she loved.

But she wouldn't.

Couldn't. She was miserable, and it would only make things worse if she called him now.

"Hey, you okay?" Kiara asked, poking her in the ribs.

Lauren pasted on a smile. "I'm great, sorry. Just spaced out for a second. So, who's up to go out tonight?"

Emma ducked her head and a blush spread across her cheeks. "Can't. I've got a date."

"Another one?" Kiara asked, appearing in disbelief. "Same guy?"

"Yep," Emma confirmed. "I think this one's a keeper."

"When do we get to meet him?" Lauren asked.

Emma arched a perfectly shaped eyebrow. "When I'm good and ready."

Lauren gave Kiara the side-eye. "Let's not hold our breath."

"Oh please. You kept Andrew a secret from us for months," Emma shot back.

Lauren's excitement deflated instantly. Noting her distress, Emma grimaced.

"Damn. I'm sorry, I wasn't thinking," Emma said gently. Though she hadn't gone into great detail, Lauren had told them both about the breakup, if that's what it even was. It felt weird...kind of like they were in limbo. They both wanted to be together, but each had reasons why they thought it best for the other if they weren't.

It was ridiculous, really, the more Lauren thought about it. But then she remembered the image of him in that hospital bed, and it strengthened her resolve.

"Don't worry about it," Lauren said with a wave of her hand. She glanced at the clock. Andrew was probably in the infusion center now, getting his treatment. "Just keep your promise that you'll take the best care of him, and I'm happy."

Well, not happy, exactly. Satisfied.

"You sure are putting the pressure on," Emma grumbled. "But I promise."

# Chapter Twenty

The past two weeks had sucked.

Bad.

After he and Lauren had ended things, Andrew threw himself into work, spending endless hours at the DA's office, helping with Isla's case and anything else they'd let him do. He also went to Children's Hospital last Sunday, when he knew Lauren wouldn't be there. He asked Jasmine to teach him how to paint, and brushing the colors onto the page had been surprisingly therapeutic.

He went out with Logan and Dan once, but drinking only made him feel worse, and he wasn't good company. Jeni came over twice and made him dinner, which he barely touched. Valerie threatened to drive down to stay with him, and as of last night, he and Rhonda weren't on speaking terms. He'd noticed she'd never been particularly friendly toward Lauren, but then again, she wasn't particularly friendly toward anyone. He hadn't thought much of it until the night before when she had called him.

"You never call me," had been his greeting.

"Jeni told Mom you and Lauren broke up, and that you're in some kind of mix between mania and depression."

He didn't quite know what to say to that.

"Are you okay?" she asked.

"Not really," he said honestly. She was the sister he spoke to the least, but strangely, he felt like he could be honest with her.

"It's better this way, you know."

"Is it? Doesn't feel that way. It feels like nothing could be worse than not being with her."

"She should never have allowed something to start in the first place."

*The hell?*

Andrew's hackles had raised immediately at the disapproving tone in her voice. "Excuse me?"

"You heard me. I thought it was a bad idea from the beginning. I saw the way you looked at her that first day in Dr. Patel's office. You were more focused on her than on what needed to be done for you to get better. At first, I really hoped she'd do the right thing and keep it strictly professional. But when she showed up for Thanksgiving, I knew it was going downhill. It was wrong of her to do that to you, Andrew. You're in a vulnerable position, and it wasn't fair that she took things beyond a working relationship."

Andrew had been so stunned that he'd sat in silence for a few seconds. It hadn't taken long, though, for anger to flood him, hot and fierce. "You don't know what you're talking about," he growled. "We fell in love, and it's no one's fault. She's the most honest, kind, and compassionate person I've ever met, and she's every inch the professional."

"You're not in love. You're in lust, and she took advantage of you, and now you're left with the consequences."

"What is wrong with you?" he'd yelled. "You don't know a thing about her, or us. What's your problem?"

"My problem is with someone putting your health at risk to get some—"

"Stop. Talking." His voice had been hard like ice. "We're done here."

He'd hung up on her, so pissed off he was shaking. And now, more than twelve hours later, he didn't feel any better.

Jeni noticed. They were sitting in the waiting room for his chemo appointment when she elbowed him in the ribs.

"Snap out of it," she said.

"Shut up."

"What are you, twelve?"

He scowled at her. "You told Mom about Lauren and me."

"I had to. You hadn't been answering her calls or texts, which is unlike you, and she was freaking out."

He sighed. He wasn't really angry about that. "Did you know Rhonda didn't like Lauren?"

Jeni shrugged, like it wasn't a big deal. "Rhonda doesn't like anybody."

Andrew guessed that was true, but he'd never really cared before. "Why not?"

"It's how she is." Jeni said it so matter-of-factly, and Andrew wondered if he should let it go. It was hard, though, not to take it personally. Funny how he hadn't cared when they talked crap about Caroline, but when it was Lauren… that was a different thing entirely.

"Andrew Bishop?" a voice called out, halting their conversation. They walked together to the desk, and an employee Andrew didn't recognize led them through the now familiar maze of chairs until they reached Mandi's section. He sat in silence while the assistant took his vitals, and soon Mandi was pushing her cart in his direction.

Her expression was worried. "How are you?"

Andrew tipped his head to the side. Was she asking about

him and Lauren?

"I read about the hospital admission in your chart," Mandi continued. *Oh, that.* "We're not giving you any more bleomycin. Just AVD now. But are you feeling okay?"

Andrew nodded. "I feel back to normal." His lungs did, anyway. The rest of his chest felt empty, probably because his heart was missing.

She looked relieved. "I'm so glad. I keep thinking about it, wondering if there's something I missed. I didn't notice a cough or labored breathing last time, but I don't think I specifically asked..."

"Stop it," Andrew interrupted. "You're the best nurse I could ask for. What is it with you people? Blaming yourselves for something like that? Don't you know these things happen, and it's no one's fault?"

Mandi looked between him and Jeni, her expression serious. "It comes with the job. Anytime something goes wrong, I'll always wonder if I could have done something differently."

Andrew wasn't sure he'd be able to carry that burden and thought it was a good thing he wasn't in health care. But then he considered his job, and how he knew he'd feel at fault when a case didn't go his way or if it didn't seem justice was served.

They all needed to realize that sometimes life wasn't fair, and there was nothing to be done about it.

"I'm perfectly fine, so don't think about it again, okay?" Andrew said.

Mandi nodded, unconvincingly in Andrew's opinion, but he wouldn't push it. Mandi accessed his port and started a saline drip, and disappeared to get his premedications. Andrew's gaze swept the surrounding area while he waited, hoping to see the person he thought about constantly.

They hadn't spoken once since that day on the phone. No texts, no phone calls, no cordial *Hello* at The Grind House.

Andrew had gone there nearly every morning for coffee, hoping to see her, but she hadn't been there.

Jeni pinched his arm and he flinched, moving away from her. "What was that for?"

She angled her head to the left, a meaningful look in her eye. Andrew followed the direction of her gesture, and that's when he saw her.

Lauren walked down the hallway, wearing a dark green dress underneath her long white coat, both hands tucked into the front pockets. Her hair was in a loose braid, curving over one shoulder, like the first time she'd visited him in the infusion center.

His heart surged to life, like it had been lying dormant and brought back by the beauty before him. He couldn't take his eyes off her.

She came around the corner, saw him, and stopped. A flush spread up her neck as her eyes drank him in, and he took a small measure of consolation that she seemed as affected as he was—to be in the same room, mere yards apart, though it may as well have been miles. Although he felt the connection deep in his core, he knew nothing would happen.

Not right now.

Their eyes met and held for a long moment. Hers reflected a deep sadness and yearning that made him ache. He didn't look away and didn't care if it was awkward or if anyone noticed. He never wanted to take his eyes from her again.

"For the love of Saint Mary," Jeni's voice reached his ear. "Get a room."

He replied to his sister, his attention on Lauren never wavering. "Believe me, I would."

"Gross," Jeni said. "You're my brother."

"You brought it up."

He watched Lauren's shoulders rise and fall with a deep breath, and she broke eye contact. She turned and walked up behind a nurse sitting at a computer and leaned over to speak to her, pointing at the screen.

Mandi returned, blocking his view as she hung the small bags of fluid on the IV pole. "Same premeds as usual," she said, pushing buttons on the pump. "You know the drill."

Andrew nodded, trying not to be too obvious as he leaned to the side.

"Looking for someone?" Mandi asked.

Andrew straightened. "No."

Mandi stood there for a moment with one eyebrow raised. They both knew he was lying.

"Have you talked to Lauren lately, Mandi?" Jeni asked. "How is she?"

Andrew shot his twin a glare that said, *Great job. That wasn't obvious at all.*

She shrugged and looked at Mandi expectantly.

"She's okay, I think. Hasn't seemed herself lately," Mandi's eyes met Andrew's briefly before she continued, "but she had an important meeting today about her job here. I think she's been worried about it."

"Oh, really? Do you know how it went?" Jeni asked.

"No, I don't. Do you guys need anything else right now?"

"Nope," Andrew replied. Nothing she could give him, anyway.

The minute Mandi left, he searched for Lauren, but she was nowhere to be found. He unlocked his phone and texted her.

Andrew: *I heard you had a meeting about your job today. I hope that's a good thing, but I can't help but worry. Was it about what happened between us? Will you tell me what happened?*

By the time his premeds finished she still hadn't responded.

Andrew: *Just tell me if it was good or bad. That's it, that's all I want to know. I won't tell you all the things I want to say, like how I can't stop thinking about you and how I miss you, and how much I love you. Because I still know what we're doing is best (at least, I hope it is. Because it sucks balls). So pretend I didn't say any of that. Your happiness means so much to me, and I have to know. Please give me one word: good or bad?*

Lauren: *Good.*
Lauren: *And I agree about the balls.*

Relief filled him. He wanted to keep talking to her and started another message several times but kept forcing himself to erase them. If she wanted to talk to him, she would, and he needed to give her space.

He sighed and aimlessly looked around the room. The patients surrounding him were of all colors, shapes, and sizes. He thought of Jasmine, and how cancer didn't discriminate against age, either. Cancer sure was an asshole.

His mind circled back to an idea he'd been mulling over, wanting to give Jasmine the normal day she so desperately desired. Away from the hospital, and like a normal teenager.

If the past few weeks had taught him anything, it was not to waste a single day. He returned his attention to his phone.

He had some calls to make.

• • •

The following week, Andrew received a call from Todd Griffin, asking him to stop by the office.

"Andrew." Todd stood and held out a hand. "Thanks for coming in."

Andrew shook the older man's hand and sat down across

the desk. "Sure. Is something happening with Isla's case? What can I help with?"

Todd shook his head. "Everything is moving along fine with that. I still expect our first court appearance in early April, like we'd planned."

"Oh, that's good." Andrew propped his ankle across the opposite knee, unsure why Todd had asked to meet with him today.

"Listen, Andrew. You're almost done with school, and I assume you're on the lookout for job opportunities."

"Yes, sir."

"You're the best intern I've ever had, and I'd love nothing more than to have you working alongside me on cases here in the Kansas City office. But unfortunately, we don't have any positions at the moment. That could change, but for now, we don't expect any openings anytime soon."

Andrew fought the urge to look down and accepted the news with a deep breath. "I understand. Regardless, I'm thankful for the opportunity to learn from you—"

"Hang on, I'm not done," Todd said with a grin. "I don't know how committed you are to staying in Kansas City, but I have a friend from law school who works for the DA office in St. Louis. He's retiring in May, and I told him I had an excellent intern, a real go-getter, who would be a perfect replacement. Barring any complications with graduation and passing the bar exam, they're very interested in you, Andrew. I'd be happy to set up a conversation between you and one of the lead attorneys, if you're interested."

Andrew leaned back and absorbed that information. He'd never seriously considered leaving Kansas City before. He loved the city, loved the area of town where he lived. He had good friends here, and Jeni had just moved here. He'd enjoyed some of the best years of his life in this town.

But...over the last six months, he'd also endured the

worst phase of his life.

A cancer diagnosis.

The worst heartbreak he'd ever experienced.

If he stayed, he would constantly be inundated with reminders of what he went through, and of Lauren.

The clothing store just down from his apartment building would always be the place he'd bought a handful of hats to cover his hairless head.

The parking lot next to the gym would be where he'd vomited after working out one day, and not because he'd pushed himself, but because of chemotherapy.

Betty Rae's would always bring memories of Lauren, and the time they sat there together, admitting for the first time that they wanted to be together.

Maybe leaving would be good for him…a place to start fresh.

Start over.

"Thank you," Andrew said, looking at the man who'd mentored him these last few months. "I would really appreciate that, sir."

# Chapter Twenty-One

A week and a half later, on a Saturday that was so beautiful she felt the weather was mocking her, Lauren stood at Andrew's door. She'd stayed strong and kept her distance. He had, too.

She had texted Jeni several times since his hospital stay, though, asking if he was okay and if his symptoms were improving. She'd begged Jeni not to tell him.

She'd kept a level head at work and at home, trying to return to the life she'd had before Andrew. The problem was, that prior life seemed black and white, and the time in between filled with color. She didn't know how to go back.

She hung out with her friends and watched documentaries. She went to Children's Hospital, careful to check the schedule and go when Andrew wouldn't be there. She studied for her board exam and worked on an educational lecture for the clinic nurses. She'd avoided the infusion suite yesterday, when she knew he'd be there receiving what would hopefully be his second-to-last chemo treatment.

Life sucked—especially after she'd moved to the thoracic oncology clinic and was two floors away from her friends—but she was making it. One slow step at a time, and she counted it a success that she hadn't crawled to Andrew's door in the middle of the night to say she'd been an idiot and ask him to reconsider. She'd thought about it more than once, but with some supernatural strength she didn't know she possessed, she'd stayed away.

But she'd received news today that he needed to know, and she refused to do it any other way than in person.

She closed her eyes and took several deep breaths, composing herself, and asking God to give him strength.

Not her. Him.

She raised her fist and knocked.

A few seconds later the door swung open, and Andrew's eyes widened in surprise before a smile spread across his face. It was short-lived, though, when he really looked at her face.

"What's wrong?" he asked immediately.

"Can I come in?"

He stepped aside, and she walked past, setting her purse on the table before she sat on the couch. Andrew closed the door and sat down next to her, concern etched into his features.

"Lauren, what's going on? Are you okay?"

She swallowed. "Andrew." She took his hand in hers. "Jasmine passed away today."

He blinked. Stared at her, as if he were solving a difficult math equation in his head.

Lauren brushed her thumb across the ridges on the back of his hand. "Did you hear me?"

His sharp intake of breath startled her, and he suddenly stood up. He jerked a hand up to the back of his head and opened his mouth like he was going to say something, but no sound came out. He stepped back, and his knees hit the coffee table with a thump.

"I...I don't..." he stuttered. "That makes no sense. I just

saw her—" His voice hitched, and he turned to walk into the kitchen.

Lauren stood up but stayed near the couch. "I'm so sorry, Andrew. I know she meant a lot to you." She gripped her hands in front of her.

He turned back around to face her. "How? What happened? She didn't seem sick…she wasn't getting worse. I don't understand."

"I don't know all the details, but she'd recently had chemo and her white count was very low. She went into septic shock, and then multisystem organ failure—"

"Stop." His voice was sharp. "Don't talk to me like I know that medical lingo. I have no fucking clue what you're saying." His volume was near yelling, but his voice wavered, and he swiped at his eyes. "What are you saying?"

Lauren wanted to touch him, the desire to hug him almost overwhelming, but she wasn't sure what he needed right now. His distress was clear and he'd walked away, and she'd dealt with more than one distraught family member. It was usually best to stay calm, collected, and to the point.

"She got an infection, and her body couldn't fight it."

Andrew bit his lip, squeezed his eyes shut, and turned his head away. "Dammit." He suddenly lurched to the side and slammed his palm against the wall. "Fuck!" His forehead hit the surface beside his hand, and his shoulders began to shake.

*Screw the breakup.* Lauren went to him, raising her arms to wrap around him, but before she could, he turned his tear-filled eyes on her. His eyes were cold and angry, and she stopped in her tracks.

"Is this how you'll be?" he spat. "If I die? Cool and collected, like I meant nothing to you?"

Lauren was speechless, and she took a step away from him, her mind whirring to process what he'd said. Shock, followed by indignation and disbelief, filled her.

"Well?" he demanded.

Her pulse pounded in her ears, hot blood rushing through her veins. Her thoughts were muddled, and time seemed to slow as she prepared to respond. He was in his own state of shock and was lashing out at her, but that didn't excuse a question like that.

"Do you remember what I told you about the three categories I put patients in when they die?"

He stared at her with dark eyes, his lashes wet with tears.

"If you died," she choked out, desperation and anguish building within her as she spoke, "I wouldn't even have a category, because it would destroy me. It wouldn't be that I couldn't talk about *you*, I wouldn't be able to speak *at all*. It wouldn't be that I couldn't think about you without crying, I wouldn't be able to do *anything* without crying. I try to keep my patients at work and separate them from the rest of me to save my sanity and be able to do this job. But you've infiltrated *every fucking inch* of my life. If you died, I don't even know how I'd exist."

Her own cheeks were wet, and she pressed the heels of her hands to her eyes. "I can't even think about that, Andrew. Don't ever ask me that again." Her vision blurred with tears and she snatched up her purse. "*Ever.*"

She walked out, slamming the door behind her. She began crying in earnest as she wobbled down the stairs and got inside her car. She put her head against the steering wheel, gripping the wrapped leather tightly in her hands. The passenger-side door opened, and the familiar scent of cedar and spearmint engulfed her. Andrew folded his large body into the car and sat beside her, his long legs bent at the knees, hands resting on his thighs. He leaned back and laid his head against the headrest, watching her for a moment before looking forward.

Lauren's tears slowed, and they sat in silence for several

minutes. She hadn't turned the car on, so the only sound was their breathing and the occasional car that drove behind them.

"You said fuck again," he said.

"I did."

"I'm starting to think I'm a bad influence on you."

"Or maybe you're bringing out the real me."

He shrugged one shoulder at that, and they fell silent again for a moment.

"I had a date planned," Andrew said, so quietly she strained to hear. He looked at her with a countenance completely devoid of emotion, but Lauren knew he was suffering inside. "A day date, for Jasmine. I'd set it up with her nurse and spoken to her parents and everything. We were going to take the city bus to one of my law school classes, where they're having a mock trial—everyone gets pretty riled up and it's incredibly entertaining. Then we were gonna find one of those cafeteria-style restaurants. You know, where you pick things that are lined up behind that big plexiglass window? Then I was going to take her to a high school soccer team practice, just to watch, and then we'd come back to the hospital and eat pizza and watch TV."

His head was still leaning back against the seat, and his eyes moved a little to the left. He looked out the window behind Lauren and blinked a few times. "It was the most ridiculous date I'd ever planned. But it was the day she wanted to have. Ride the bus. Sit in class. Eat in the cafeteria, go to soccer after school. Watch TV. Uninteresting and mundane to the rest of us, but in her mind, in her situation, something to be celebrated."

Andrew swiped at his eyes and put his forearm on the console, opening his palm, faceup, in invitation. Lauren didn't hesitate to place her hand in his, and their fingers entwined.

"You made her last few weeks on earth so much brighter.

You have to know that," Lauren said softly.

His chin trembled slightly, and he looked away. He took a few deep breaths. The first was shaky, but the last was steady.

"You don't have to hide from me." Lauren squeezed his hand. "When mourning someone who has lost their battle with cancer, I'm the last person you should be embarrassed to cry in front of."

His brown eyes met hers again, and though they were still sad, she found they were warm and gentle. "I know." He swallowed. "But for once, I'd like to be the strong one."

Lauren was taken aback. "You're the strongest man I know."

"It doesn't feel that way. I feel weak and pathetic."

"Showing emotion isn't weak or pathetic. If anything, it defines your strength of character. You have compassion and empathy, traits not all men have. Or at least, many don't show them. Knowing those things about you only makes me love you more." She attempted a small smile. "And I love big, strong men."

"Men? Plural?"

"I was speaking in general terms."

"Be more specific. But if the words Will Gearhart come out of your mouth, I'm leaving."

"You're definitely stronger than Will. In every sense of the word."

He appeared slightly mollified. "I'd kick his ass, that's for sure. And if I ever happen to run into him, that's exactly what I'll do. Actually, I'd start with his dick, then go for that ten-million-dollar right shoulder."

Lauren sighed and shook her head. "Anyway." She tugged at his hand, intending to get back on track. "Are you going to be okay? I thought it might be best if I told you. And I couldn't do it over the phone."

"It sucks, but I'll be okay." He dipped his chin a notch

lower. "I'm glad you came. Do you want to come back inside?"

She shook her head. "I don't think that's a good idea."

"You're probably right." He closed his eyes for a second. "I'm sorry. For what I said."

She didn't respond right away. She'd usually say something like, *That's okay*, or *Don't worry about it*. But she kind of thought he should be sorry. He needed to understand the gravity of what he'd asked, and of her response. She needed him to understand how deep her feelings ran, like a cavern in the ocean that had never been explored.

"I accept your apology, but I need you to understand something." The question she was about to pose put a lot of faith in his feelings toward her, and she hoped she wasn't overestimating them. "Think about how you'd feel if I asked *you* that question. What if I died? Today, on my drive home, I could die. What would that do to you?"

Andrew's face paled, and he yanked his hand out of her grasp to grab her face between his palms. His touch was gentle, but his expression was fierce. His eyes searched her features, as if he was making sure she was really here in front of him, breathing and alive. "I can't..." he rasped. "I can't even *think* about that." He crossed the threshold onto her side of the car and pressed his lips to hers so fast, she gasped into his mouth. "I can't," he repeated against her lips, brushing them over and over again with his own.

She should pull away. But he felt so good and tasted even better. She'd missed him so much, missed this. One of her hands went to the back of his head and the other grasped the front of his shirt, pulling him closer, her touch as desperate as his. She opened her mouth and his tongue entered with a groan that sounded ripped from his chest. She stroked his tongue with hers, leaning up and in to him as best she could, wanting to be closer. *Closer.* Beside him and inside of him, forever and always.

Even that might not be enough.

He pressed his forehead against hers. "What are we doing?"

"I have no idea," she breathed.

"Please, come upstairs. I can't do this anymore. We have to fix this. Figure it out."

Could they figure it out? She was willing to try, if he was. She nodded. "Okay."

The second they met near the hood of her car, he grabbed her by the wrist and pulled her against him. Thighs, hips, and chests pressed together, not an inch of space between them. He sighed, deep and heavy, like the breath leaving his lungs was something he'd been holding onto for weeks. He hugged her, his arms a vise around her, as if he was afraid to let go.

Lauren buried her face in his chest, inhaling deeply, taking in his scent. Her heart and stomach clenched simultaneously, love and desire for this man competing within her, each trying to prove themselves the victor. She traced the hard ridges of muscle in his back with her fingers, loving the murmur of satisfaction he breathed into her hair.

"We going upstairs?" she asked.

"*Mmm-hmm.*" He didn't budge, his chin resting on her head.

"Andrew?"

"Dammit woman, give me a minute."

She smiled, turning her face to the side and resting her cheek against his heart. The strong rhythm was soothing, and she let herself relax further in his embrace, content to stay as long as he wanted.

They finally vacated the sidewalk when an older man walked in their direction pulled by two large dogs on a leash. Andrew held tightly to her hand as they climbed the stairs, and soon they sat on opposite ends of the couch. She'd tried to sit closer, but he pointed to the other end and said he couldn't focus if she was that close.

"Fine." She crossed her arms and then uncrossed them. It wouldn't help to start this conversation on the defense.

"Where do we start?" he asked. "I can't remember a single reason why we've been apart that makes any sense."

Lauren could think of one. "You should know I got the job," she said, though as she'd mentioned before, she'd have given it up for him if it had come down to it.

Andrew's face lit up. "That's incredible news. You should know that even if you didn't, I wouldn't have let you go back to work for your dad. No matter what, you deserve a job you love, not one you feel obligated to."

He was right. She deserved to make her own way—forge her own path. "And I told Dr. Hawthorne about us."

His smile faded. "You did?"

She nodded. "When he offered me the position, I told him there was something I wanted him to know before I officially accepted. For some reason they think I have integrity and that I'm not going around having one-night stands with all my male patients." She winked at Andrew when he narrowed his eyes, apparently not finding that a bit humorous. "He seemed to understand it was serious and real, and agreed that sometimes these things are out of our control."

"I'm really happy for you. Have you told your dad?"

She groaned. "Not yet."

"That's fine. We can do it together, when I'm done with chemo and you take me down to introduce me as the boyfriend."

She raised an eyebrow.

He raised one back. "I have to say things like that, you know. I have to think about the future like it's an actuality for me. If I don't, I'll go back to where I was the day we broke up. To wanting to protect you from loving a man who might be dying, and who might leave you soon. Deep down, I know that's possible. But for now, until I hear the words terminal or incurable, I have to believe I'm going to be okay and that I'll be able to give you a long, happy life."

Lauren held up a hand. "That right there? I'm not doing that. I'm choosing you as you are, unknowns and all. I meant what I said, that I don't *need* you, Andrew. I don't need a man to provide for me. It's not your responsibility to give me a certain kind of life—I can do it on my own. I already am. I want you for no other reason than because I love you. Just being with you makes my life better. So please, let that go. I won't accept the thought that you'll try to push me away again—"

"I wasn't the only one pushing," he interrupted, but she shook her head and kept going.

"I'm in this because I love you, and we're great together. I want to be with you whether you're rich or poor, healthy or sick, happy or sad. You make me happier than I've ever been. I've never known you without cancer, do you realize that? That's part of the Andrew Bishop package I chose from the start, and I'd do it all over again. Every time."

A genuine smile had formed on his lips as she spoke, but at the end an ornery gleam entered his eye. "You still haven't seen the whole package, you know. You might change your mind…or be the happiest woman on the planet. You sure you want to take that risk?"

"*Andrew.* Be serious." Besides, she had some idea what she was dealing with, and she didn't think he'd disappoint.

He sobered. "I've never wanted anything as much as I want you." He broke his own rule and scooted closer to her, gently cupping a hand around the back of her neck. "But what I felt, just now? When you told me about Jasmine? It was terrible. And I know she's going in the backpack category for me, because she'll stay with me, in whatever small part, forever. And if the pain you'd be in, if I lose this battle, is like you say and will be so much worse than that? I..." He gripped her neck tighter. "I don't know if I can bear doing that to you."

She gazed at him sadly, tenderly. "Even if you walked away right now, and we never spoke again, I'd feel that way. It's too late, don't you see that? It's too late for me to ever think of you as anything other than the love of my life. We both have to let go of the things we can't control, and hold on to the things we can. Like being together right now. I'll choose these moments over any alternative, no matter how this ends."

Andrew pulled her close and kissed her. His lips were slow and determined, like he was communicating something he couldn't seem to put in words.

And she understood him perfectly.

...

A week later, Lauren and Jeni sat in a booth at Republic, having dinner after a day of shopping. Other than texting her to check on Andrew, Lauren had avoided Jeni during the breakup as well. She'd apologized for being so distant when they first met up that afternoon, and Jeni had waved her off with a smile and a hug.

"I'm just glad you're back together," Jeni had said. "He was driving me crazy. Don't ever do that to me again, okay?"

Lauren didn't plan on it.

They'd just finished eating, and as they waited for the server to bring the check, Jeni asked, "So, how do you feel about St. Louis?"

"The city? Nice arch, I guess."

Jeni laughed. "I meant Andrew's St. Louis thing."

Lauren frowned. "What St. Louis thing?"

Jeni returned her confused expression. "Andrew's

interview at the DA's office in St. Louis." She paused. "He didn't tell you?"

Lauren's pulse slowed way down. "No, he didn't mention it."

Though her face still appeared unsure, Jeni shrugged. "Oh...well, maybe something has changed. I'm sure he would have said something if he was still considering it."

Lauren rubbed her thumb along the seam of the leather booth. She thought about asking Jeni if she knew more, decided against it. "I'm sure you're right," she said. *He'd tell me.*

Wouldn't he? Surely, now that they were back together, and after all the things they'd talked about, he'd tell her he was considering a job in St. Louis.

But uncertainty continued to build throughout the evening, and by the time she and Jeni parted ways, insecurity coursed through her. What if he was just too afraid to say something?

Only one way to find out. She sent Andrew a single text.

Lauren: *We need to talk.*

# Chapter Twenty-Two

Andrew sat up straight, fear shooting down his spine. That was not a text message a man ever wanted to get from the woman he loved.

He tried to stay calm.

Andrew: *Okay, can I come over?*

Lauren: *I'll come there.*

Fifteen minutes later there was a light knock on his door. Lauren didn't touch him as she walked in and took a seat on his couch.

Apprehension churning in his gut, Andrew closed the door and sat down beside her, angling his torso to face her. He reached for her hand. "Is something wrong?"

"Are you considering a job in St. Louis?"

Andrew opened his mouth to speak, then stopped. That's what was bothering her? "How did you hear about that?"

"It's true?" Her lips dipped slightly at the corners. "Why didn't you tell me? That's almost four hours away."

He nodded. "I know. It's something Todd mentioned, because there weren't any expected openings here in Kansas City, and he knows a guy in St. Louis. I did a phone interview and they really liked me. It's a great opportunity—"

She pulled her hand away, and he stopped. "Did they offer you a job?"

"Yes."

"What did you say?"

"Keep in mind, this was when we were broken up," he started.

Lauren closed her eyes. "Just like that, you would leave?"

He scooted closer and put his hands on either side of her face, and she opened her eyes. He gazed into those green depths. "Would you ask me to stay?"

She just looked at him, her hesitation lasting a few seconds beyond comfort.

She wouldn't ask him to stay?

"Please stay." Her voice cracked.

Like a pressure valve being released, his insecurity dissipated, and he smiled widely.

"Okay," he said, and kissed her.

She returned the kiss for several seconds, then pulled back. "That's it? You're not going to take a great job offer, just because I selfishly asked you to stay?"

He kissed her again. "Yes and no. Yes, I would do that. But I already turned it down, and that's why I never said anything. The day you told me about Jasmine, and we got back together, I knew there was no way I wanted to live apart from you."

A wrinkle formed between her eyebrows. "You shouldn't have done that. We could have talked about it…"

"After all you went through for your job here? You're not leaving, and I'm not leaving without you."

"What will you do, then?"

"I'm not sure yet, but graduation is still months away. I've got time. I'll just find something else until a local DA position opens up, and hopefully they'll still want me."

Lauren processed that for a moment, then put her hand on his forearm. "And if they don't, or if you're unhappy with what you find, we'll talk about it, okay? Both of our careers are important."

He pulled her close against his chest. "Deal."

She relaxed into him.

"That wasn't nice, you know," he said into her hair. Damn she smelled good. "Sending me a text like that. You freaked me out."

"Sorry. I was a little blindsided by Jeni's comment about St. Louis."

"I shouldn't have said anything to her. She can't keep her mouth shut."

Lauren tilted her head up to look at him. "Women talk, you know. I'd have thought you knew that, having so many women in your family."

"Hopefully, someday I'll add another to it."

"You're not theoretically proposing again, are you?"

"No. But if I was, what would you say?" He loved this game.

"Maybe." She elbowed him in the ribs. "Speaking of your family...can I ask you something?"

"Sure."

"Do they...are they all, um, happy about this? Us? I haven't seen them since Thanksgiving, and we were just friends then. I'm a little worried what they think about it."

"They're thrilled. They love you, my mom especially. And Jeni, of course. Valerie couldn't care less, as long as I'm happy."

"What about Rhonda? I get the feeling she doesn't like me much."

Andrew shook his head. "Don't worry about Rhonda. She's the moodiest of the bunch, and the most protective. She's always looking at the negative side of things and expects the worst. She'll come around."

Her concerned expression didn't change.

Andrew kissed her once more. "I mean it," he said. "Don't let her get to you."

"You say it like it's easy."

"It is. But then again, I've had twenty-six years to get used to her…but I promise you—it's just her personality. Once she gets to know you, she'll love you as much as I do."

She raised an eyebrow at that.

He grinned. "Okay, not quite as much as I do. But close." He tightened his arms around her and brushed his cheek along her soft hair, loving the feel of her against his body. "I don't think anyone has ever loved anyone as much as I love you."

She slipped her arms around his torso. "I don't think anyone ever *will* love anyone as much as I love you."

"Don't try to one-up me."

"I'm competitive by nature. Get used to it."

He leaned her back against the cushions and sealed his mouth over hers, determined to prove her wrong.

• • •

Two days before his last chemo treatment, Andrew was alone at his apartment studying when a knock sounded at the door. He grinned and jumped up, hoping Lauren had decided to back out of her plans for a girl's night and come over instead.

He swung open the door and froze.

"Dad?"

His father stood on his welcome mat, wearing his signature Wranglers and a flannel button-up, hands buried deep in his pockets. His weathered skin looked darker than

Andrew remembered, and his previously brown hair was peppered with gray.

"Hi," his dad said. "Can I come in?"

Speechless, Andrew stepped back and held the door open wide. His dad took a few steps inside and stopped.

Andrew walked past him and pulled out a chair at the kitchen table. "What are you doing here?"

His dad rubbed a hand along the back of his neck. He stood in the middle of the living room and turned to face Andrew. "I came to see how you were doing."

Andrew just sat there, waiting for more. When none came, he simply said, "I'm fine. Last chemo is on Friday. At least, I hope it's the last one."

His dad swallowed. He stepped forward and sat at the table, directly across from Andrew. "You look good, son. I'm sorry I haven't come before now."

"You came at Thanksgiving."

"For a day. Didn't count."

Andrew hadn't thought so, either.

His dad gripped his hands together on the table. "I know we haven't seen eye-to-eye for several years now, and your mom keeps telling me I'm being a stubborn asshole. She's right. It was selfish of me to expect you to put your dreams aside to follow a plan I'd set out for you. It's not easy to get through college and law school, and I want you to know I'm proud of you and what you're doing."

A lump formed in Andrew's throat. Hearing his dad, the strongest, hardest-working man he'd ever met, say he was proud of him was something he'd wanted for a long, long time. "Thanks, Dad."

"I've thought about you every day since your mother told me about the lymphoma. I want you to know that. I'm not good with this kind of thing, and the thought of my only son with cancer was more than I could handle. I avoid things that upset me, and I don't talk about them. Thank God for your mother. You deserved at least one strong parent by your side through this. I'm sorry it wasn't me."

Those words shocked Andrew to his core. His dad was the rock of their family. A big, sturdy man who wrangled cattle and branded steers and threw bales of hay around like they weighed nothing. He worked from before dawn to dusk nearly every day, and treated his family well. He'd taught Andrew how to shoot a rifle, drive cars and tractors alike.

"You should see your face," his dad said with a humorless chuckle. "You think I'm the strong one? Your mother is. Every time we've almost lost the farm, she's been the one by my side to get me through it. I've done the hard labor to keep things going, sure. I'm not saying I don't work for what we've got. But it takes a hell of a lot more inner strength to do what she does for our family, and I'd say that makes her the strongest of all of us. And she makes it look easy, to boot."

Andrew had never thought about it like that.

"That's why I wanted to come here," his dad continued. "I've got that kind of grit inside me, too, and it's time I showed it. So here I am, to tell you that I miss my son, and I hate the way things have been these last few years. I wish you wanted to stay around and take over the farm so my old ass could retire, but it's not for you. I see that now. I respect and support your decision.

"I also don't want to set a bad example for my only son about what it means to be a man. I hear you and Lauren are getting serious, but that you're worrying too much about burdening her with your illness."

*Damn you, Jeni.* Andrew made a mental note to stop telling her things.

"I want you to listen to me, Andrew. If a woman loves you and wants to take care of you, hold on tight and don't let her go. You're an incredibly strong man to be going through this treatment. You've dealt with cancer and chemotherapy while staying in school and keeping a job, and you have to know how impressive that is. You *can* do this by yourself. You've got it in you. But don't do it on your own simply because you think that's what makes you strong, or that it's what makes you a man. A real man recognizes what he has in a partner, and what a blessing it is to have someone to share your burdens with. You'd do the same for her, wouldn't you?"

"Always."

"I don't know what I'd do without your mother, and I hope she'd say the same about me. We're a team, and we take turns bearing the different things that weigh us down in this life. If you've found someone like that, you're not a strong man if you let her slip through your fingers. You're a dammed stupid one."

Andrew laughed at that. His dad was absolutely right, and he'd had no idea how badly he needed to hear it.

"I'm glad you came, Dad."

"Me too. Now, where's the best barbecue joint in this town?"

• • •

Two days later, Andrew was once again cautiously optimistic. He'd just completed the final chemo treatment of his sixth cycle. Lauren had taken the day off and had come with him, sitting on one side while Jeni maintained her usual spot on the other. He'd noticed that dickhead Gavin was nowhere to be found, and he asked Lauren about it during his infusion.

"He got fired," Lauren had said, a hint of glee in her tone. "Apparently, he had a few sexual harassment complaints, and human resources finally put their foot down."

"That's better news than the fact that this is my last chemo," Andrew said, smiling widely. A tiny voice in the back of his brain reminded him that there wasn't a guarantee this was the last, but he shut it down.

Mandi finished applying the dressing to his port and looked at him. "Andrew, I can honestly say I hope I never see you here again."

He laughed as he stood and wrapped her in a hug. "This may be the first time I won't take offense to that statement."

"I'll be thinking about you next week," Mandi continued, and he assumed she referred to his PET scan.

He wished he knew what to say, to thank Mandi for all she'd done for him. Her confident and calm presence had been a comfort for him these last several months. He'd never worried he was being given the wrong drug, or that she didn't have an eye on him during his chemo. He'd had complete faith in her, and she'd made the entire experience a little less terrifying.

He swallowed, intending to find the right words, but Mandi just smiled at him, her chin trembling slightly. She shook her head and said, "Get out of here and don't come back, okay?"

He and Lauren walked through the infusion center hand in hand, and Jeni chattered away on his other side.

Andrew dropped Jeni off at her house before going back to Lauren's. He slowed just before turning into her driveway. "Want me to check the mailbox?"

"Are you making fun of me?" she said good-naturedly.

He grinned. "I would never."

She waved him forward. "We both know it's empty. Just go."

He complied and pulled into the driveway, leaving the car running. "I'll be back for you at six?"

Lauren leaned across the console and pecked him on the lips. "Yep. See you soon."

He grasped the back of her head and pulled her back.

"One more," he murmured. He pressed an open-mouthed kiss to her lips, and the sigh that escaped her seemed to breathe life into him. Every time he touched her, he felt more alive than the second before. He wasn't sure if it was the words his father had said, or the tentative joy he felt at this being his last day of chemo that brought him clarity. But whatever he felt in this moment—this warm, electric sensation of hope and amazement—it had everything to do with the girl in his arms.

When they finally released each other, Lauren's expression glowed with heat and awe, and he dared to hope she experienced the same overwhelming sense of wonder that he did. He'd do anything to make her as happy as she made him.

Andrew went home and spent an hour studying before he took a shower. He put on slacks and a dress shirt. It was times like this when he missed his hair the most. The hats he wore were casual and didn't work with dressier clothes, and he still wasn't confident in his ability to pull off the bald look. But Lauren didn't seem to mind, and that's all that mattered.

At six o'clock on the dot Andrew stood on Lauren's doorstep. He knocked and she opened the door immediately.

"Hi," she said, smiling wide. She had on the green dress she'd worn one day at the cancer center. He thought she had looked perfect that day and felt the same now.

"Hey, you." He slid one hand across her lower back and kissed her. "You're beautiful. Ready?"

She flushed at his compliment, which he loved. He always wanted her to feel pleasure at his words, always wanted that rush of happiness to fill her when she heard how much he wanted her.

"Ready." She joined him on the porch and locked the door behind her.

He opened the car door for her and went around to his side.

"Where are we going?" she asked after they settled in,

and he pulled onto the main road.

"Do you remember when we talked about New York?"

"Yes."

"Since we can't get there right now, I thought we could try our best to do some of the things we wanted to do there. I made reservations at the best upscale Asian fusion restaurant in town and got tickets for a show at the Performing Arts Center."

Lauren's wide smile told him he'd hit the mark. "That sounds incredible. You're wonderful, you know that?"

"I'm nothing compared to you," he said seriously.

She rolled her eyes, but the smile remained on her lips.

"Know what else?" he asked.

"What?"

"I heard this show is *Wicked*."

She shook her head. "Nope."

"No?" He frowned and tried again. "But it's o-*pun*-ing night."

She laughed. "That one was better."

"I thought of one for dinner, too."

She grinned. "Let's hear it."

They came to a stop sign, and he looked at her seriously. "I'm soy into you."

A twinkle entered her eye. "Are you pho real?"

"Udon even know."

"You make miso happy."

He couldn't hold it together any longer and busted up laughing. "This goes without saying. But I'm saying it anyway. I love you."

"Me too, handsome. Me, too."

After dinner and the show, Andrew once again pulled to a

stop in front of Lauren's mailbox. He rolled down his window.

"Let's check. Just in case." He pulled open the metal door.

Lauren gasped beside him. "Andrew! There's something in there! Get it!"

He chuckled at her excitement and grabbed the envelope. She nearly climbed on top of him to take it from him, but he leaned away.

"What are you doing? Give me my mail."

"Easy. Let's go inside first."

"Why?"

He let off the brake and pulled into the driveway, careful to keep the card out of reach. He shrugged. "It's too dark. Whatever it is, you probably won't be able to see it out here."

"Oh."

Once they were inside, he handed her the card, hoping she didn't notice how his hand shook.

She smiled as she took it from him, opening it as she walked to the living room. He came up behind her just as she slid the card out and began reading.

"Andrew? What is this?"

"What does it say?"

"It's from your family? It's blank inside except for everyone's signatures. Your mom, sisters, your dad...even Alva. But I don't get it—"

"Lauren." He dropped to one knee. "Turn around."

She did as he asked, and it took her a few seconds to look down and locate him. Her hand flew to her mouth, the card drifting to the floor.

He smiled. "What would you say if I asked you to marry me?"

She blinked, then slowly brought her hand down. "Is this another theoretical proposal?"

"No."

Her eyes turned glassy, and her chin trembled.

He couldn't stop looking at her. He thought he'd be nervous, but all he felt was excitement, anticipation. Like he had as a kid the night before Christmas, knowing the next day would be full of joy and wishes coming true.

He took one of her hands and reached into his pocket with the other. "I hope you'll overlook the fact that I don't have something from Tiffany's to complete our New York date. Later, when I'm a big-time attorney and have all my medical bills paid off, I'll get you that little blue box. I promise." He held up a simple gold band. "For now…this was my grandmother's. She died a long time ago, but you would have loved her. She and my grandpa were married for fifty years. I know she'd be happy for you to wear this, if you want it."

The hand he held trembled, and her other one pressed flat against her abdomen. She blinked several times. "Andrew…" she whispered.

He swallowed. Blood rushed in his ears, and his heart pumped furiously in his chest. He so desperately wanted her to understand what he felt for her, and he could only hope this gesture did that. "Lauren, there aren't words to describe what you mean to me. It defies explanation. You are the most beautiful, intelligent, funny woman I've ever met. You make me want to be a better person, and you've been a pillar of strength for me through the darkest time of my existence. I don't know how long my life will be, but I know I want to spend every second with you. Will you spend it with me, whether two years or fifty, and be my distraction forever?"

Tears streamed down her cheeks, and he hoped that was a good sign.

"Full disclosure," he added. "If you marry me, you're gaining a family. A big, loud, overbearing, get-all-up-in-your-business family. But also a loyal, protective, loving one. Every name in that card is someone who cares about you and wants you to be part of that. You'll never spend another holiday alone. You'll always have a home to come back to."

She sobbed once, the sound raw and unfiltered.

Now that he'd spoken his piece—stumbled through at least some version of what he wanted to say—he suddenly felt the claws of anxiety building inside his chest.

Still, he couldn't tear his gaze from her beautiful green eyes as she searched his face.

She lowered herself down to her knees, bringing her face almost level with his. A ghost of a smile formed on her lips, but her expression remained solemn. "In my entire life, I've never been so sure of anything. I want to be with you now and always, no matter what happens to you or to me. I have to know that you understand that. That I want this—I want *you*—however I can have you. As a cancer patient or a cancer survivor, it doesn't matter. I want all of it, with nothing held back. I want all of you for as long as I can have you."

He inched closer to her face and let go of her hand, sliding his fingers through her hair. "Is that a yes?"

Her lips brushed his as she nodded. "Yes."

He smiled then, and he thought this must be how superheroes feel. A surge of energy flowed through him, hot and magnetic, and he knew he could do anything. With that one promise from her lips, he could conquer the world.

Together, they could conquer anything.

...

It was almost a week later when Andrew received the call.

"Answer it."

Andrew didn't move, staring at the screen of his phone.

"If you don't, I will."

His heart pounded and his breath caught in his throat.

"Andrew!" Lauren tried to snatch the phone from his hand but he pulled away.

He swiped a shaky finger across the screen. "Hello?"

"Andrew? This is Dr. Patel, how are you?"

"I don't know, you tell me, doc."

He heard light laughter on the other end of the line. "I have great news. Your scan was completely clear, no evidence of lymphoma."

Lauren sat stiff as a board beside him, her eyes wide and locked on his face, searching for any sign of what was happening. He couldn't quite smile yet, processing what Dr. Patel said, but his eyes drifted closed and he slumped against the back of the couch. He felt Lauren's hands grip his arm. "Really?"

"Really." He could hear the smile in her voice. "We will need to perform surveillance labs and scans routinely over the next several years. But as of now, you're cancer-free. And the odds are in your favor that you'll stay that way."

"Thank you, Dr. Patel. Thank you so much." They spoke for a few more minutes before he ended the call.

He turned to Lauren, her expression pale and concerned.

"It's gone," he said.

"It is? You're sure?"

"That's what Dr. Patel said."

The most beautiful smile he'd ever seen lit up her face, and she launched herself at him. His back hit the arm of the couch but he didn't care, his arms clamping around her. She laughed, showering kisses all over his face. His heart felt like it could burst into a million pieces.

And for the first time since he'd met the love of his life, he allowed himself to really imagine his life with her.

Getting married and having children.

Growing gray hairs and traveling the world.

No matter what might fill their life, he'd be happy. Just as long as she was his.

Because whether in this life or the next, he would be hers. Always.

# Epilogue

*Three Months Later*

They got married in the outdoor courtyard of a church, surrounded by a small group of friends and family. Neither had wanted to wait long, and they saw no point in dragging it out just to plan a grand event.

Andrew's parents and sisters were there, as were Lauren's mom and dad. Her dad had been much more understanding about her decision to stay in Kansas City once he knew about Andrew. She'd have stayed either way but kept that to herself.

As they rode the elevator to the hotel suite they'd booked for the night, before leaving on a honeymoon to New York City the next day, Lauren relived the day in her mind. Everything had been flawless—from her dress, to the safe arrival of their family and friends, and the beautiful weather. Rhonda had even pulled her aside at the reception to welcome her to the family.

But above all, the most wonderful part had been the man who stood beside her, and who'd taken her hand and pledged to love her, protect her, and provide for her as long as they both lived. She peeked up at him now, still in his tuxedo, his thick brown hair swept back across his head. A light layer of facial hair covered his jaw, and her belly tightened. He'd asked if she wanted him to shave for the big day, but she'd said no. She loved that look on him, and it reminded her of the first day they'd met.

He must have felt her gaze, because he turned his head and looked down at her, his brown eyes soft. The elevator dinged and the doors opened, and he took her by the hand and led her down the hallway. It was near midnight and not a soul was around. In silence, they entered their room and the door clicked shut behind them.

They faced each other, and Andrew brushed a hand across her bare shoulder, sweeping her hair back. "This was the first thing I noticed about you," he said quietly. "I stood behind you and stared at it…and then you turned around and flashed those green eyes at me just for a second, and I was a goner."

She shivered at the look in his eyes and rose up on her toes to press a kiss to his jaw.

His large hands continued down her body. "This dress is beautiful," he rasped. "And you look incredible in it. But I want it off."

She smiled and turned her back to him. "If you'll unbutton the back, I'll change into something…else." She'd asked Emma to put a small bag in the bathroom when their stuff was brought to the room, and she couldn't wait to see Andrew's reaction.

His fingers worked quickly, and she felt the bodice loosen around her torso. She pressed her hands against her chest and stomach to keep it from sliding to the floor, and stepped into the bathroom, closing the door. She changed quickly, carefully hanging her dress on the padded hanger Emma had left.

When she reemerged, she found Andrew sitting on the edge of the bed. He'd removed his jacket and sat in his white shirt and black slacks, his bowtie undone and hanging around his neck. He leaned forward, his forearms resting on his knees, his head bent.

"Are you okay?" she asked.

He lifted his head, and a slow, seductive smile spread across his face as his gaze swept down her body. "You're wearing scrubs."

"Pink ones."

His eyes didn't leave her even for a second as she walked toward him. He was a little more subdued than normal, but in a way that was tender and focused.

"What were you thinking about, just now?" she asked.

His expression remained serious. "Lately, whenever I'm alone, I think about how lucky I am. I can hardly believe I'm here with you right now, as your husband. It seems too good to be true, and I want to do everything I can to show you how much I adore you."

Lauren's heart was so full, it almost hurt. She never could have imagined loving someone like this. She approached his legs and stopped between his thighs. Lifting her hands, she slid the bowtie from his collar with one hand and ran the fingers of her other through his soft hair.

"So show me," she said, kissing him softly. "And let me show you, in return."

He swallowed hard, and he tugged at the white string of her scrub pants. They fell loose immediately, drifting down her hips. His hands pushed them the rest of the way, and they pooled at her feet. She lifted her arms and he pulled the top off over her head, his hands searing her skin along the way.

In a single fluid motion he flipped her onto her back on the bed, hovering above her. His forearms and knees surrounded her, but his mouth was the only part that touched her. He kissed her slow and deep, then scooted back and stood at the foot of the bed. His eyes seemed to swallow her as he shrugged out of his shirt and then unbuckled his belt.

Her breath caught in her throat, and it felt as if the room had caught fire.

A moment later he rejoined her on the bed, and soon there was nothing between them, and they merged together, skin to skin. Eye to eye, gazing at each other, afraid to miss something. Soul to soul, coming together in a perfect dance that transcended words.

# Acknowledgments

This is surreal, to be sitting down to honor those who helped with my first published novel. I'm terrified I'll leave someone out, and if I do, I hope you'll forgive me.

Thank you to my sister Amber (I'll never forget the first time you said "I'm proud of you") and my friend, Fransen. You were the first people to tell me to keep writing. Author Darlene Graham, my mentor, who spent hours with me at coffee shops and in her living room, and without whom I'd never have made it this far.

My critique partners—Heather Gearhart, my first ever CP, and CPFL whether you like it or not, and the person I know is always in my corner and who helps me believe in myself. Denise Williams, who spends hours with me on Twitter talking through plot holes and character arcs and who challenges me to be a better writer—you make me laugh and you make me think, and you're a photoshop wizard. The world isn't ready for us.

I'm grateful to my agent, Andrea Cascardi, who took a chance on me, who makes my books better, and who was (and still is) always there to talk me through this crazy publishing process. To Entangled Publishing and Erin Molta, my editor, for believing this story was worth publishing and for every single suggestion that made this story what it is.

Thanks to my parents for always supporting me. Always. And my mother for painstakingly proofreading what I write before I send it to industry professionals.

To countless family and friends who read my early work and provided support along my writing journey, especially Jessica, Anne, Ashlie, Misty, Ashtin, Beth, Anna, Abby—I rely on your feedback and I'm indebted to you. To Mariah, for letting me steal several random things you said in clinic for this book. You're my favorite. The wonderful providers and nurses I work with every day who inspire me, and many of whom are found within these chapters. Mandi, I still miss you and I haven't quite forgiven you for moving. Thanks to Ashley Manning for making sure I didn't make any glaring mistakes regarding a person going through law school (and if I still did, the fault is mine), and Alison Slotterback for fact-checking Kansas City bits (also, your name is spelled wrong).

Thanks to Rachelle Gardner, Lauren Smith, Barb Crews, and Hayley Elliott for their advice and support. To Carmen Falcone and Christine Glover, the editors I hired after I wrote my first novel—thank you for not laughing at me and for being the first to give invaluable advice that I carried on to write this one. Amy Harmon, who is one of my favorite authors and a kind, kind person who took the time to give me advice on writing from the heart.

It may sound silly, but thank you Twitter, for pitch events like #PitMad and for the #writingcommunity where I've met thousands of other weirdos like me who write stories about their imaginary friends. You're my people. #TeamCarly, the #NaNoWriMo18 group who, more than a year later, still keep in touch and support one another—I'll always be thankful.

I couldn't have done this without my husband, who takes the kids so I can have time to write, and doesn't complain when I hide away in the dark, writing almost every (okay every) evening after the kids are in bed. You are in every hero I'll ever write. Finally, I'm forever thankful to God for the gifts of creativity and perseverance, both of which were required for this dream to become a reality. I hope He's pleased.

# About the Author

Allison Ashley is a music-loving, coffee-drinking mom of two who loves love stories. She's a clinical oncology pharmacist by day, and on the hard days her escape has always been books—specifically books about happiness, love, and laughter. She can think of nothing better than a world full of flirting, kisses, humor, and most of all, that coveted happy-ever-after.

*Discover more Amara titles...*

## GREAT AND PRECIOUS THINGS
### a novel by Rebecca Yarros

Six years ago, when Camden Daniels came back from war without his younger brother, his father wouldn't forgive him. Cam left, swearing never to return. Then a desperate message from his father brings it all back. The betrayal. The pain. And the need to go home. But home is where the one person he still loves is waiting. Willow. The one woman he can never have. Because some secrets are best left in the dark.

## COWBOY FOR HIRE
### a *Wishing River* novel by Victoria James

When Sarah Turner's parents pass away suddenly, she's left in charge of their ranch with little know-how. Determined to preserve her family legacy, she needs a hero—not to save her, but to show her how to save herself. When Cade Walker responds to the "Cowboy for Hire" ad, part of the job is unexpected—teaching his boss how to run her own ranch. To succeed, he finds they both have a lot to learn.

## THE AUSSIE NEXT DOOR
### a *Patterson's Bluff* novel by Stefanie London

It took American Angie Donovan two days to fall in love with Australia. With her visa clock ticking, surely she can fall in love with an Australian in two months. Especially if he's as hot and funny as her next-door neighbor... Jace Walters has never wanted much. Sure, his American neighbor is distractingly sexy, but she'll be gone in a few months... Except now she's determined to check out every eligible male in the town, and her choices are even more distracting. So why does it suddenly feel like he—and his obnoxious tight-knit family, and even these two wayward dogs—could be exactly what she needs?